The Village

The Village

NIKITA LALWANI

VIKING
an imprint of
PENGUIN BOOKS

VIKING

Published by the Penguin Group
Penguin Books Ltd, 80 Strand, London WC2R 0RL, England
Penguin Group (USA) Inc., 375 Hudson Street, New York, New York 10014, USA
Penguin Group (Canada), 90 Eglinton Avenue East, Suite 700, Toronto, Ontario, Canada M4P 2Y3
(a division of Pearson Penguin Canada Inc.)
Penguin Ireland, 25 St Stephen's Green, Dublin 2, Ireland (a division of Penguin Books Ltd)
Penguin Group (Australia), 250 Camberwell Road, Camberwell, Victoria 3124, Australia
(a division of Pearson Australia Group Pty Ltd)
Penguin Books India Pvt Ltd, 11 Community Centre, Panchsheel Park, New Delhi – 110 017, India
Penguin Group (NZ), 67 Apollo Drive, Rosedale, Auckland 0632, New Zealand
(a division of Pearson New Zealand Ltd)
Penguin Books (South Africa) (Pty) Ltd, Block D, Rosebank Office Park,
181 Jan Smuts Avenue, Parktown North, Gauteng 2193, South Africa

Penguin Books Ltd, Registered Offices: 80 Strand, London WC2R 0RL, England

www.penguin.com

First published 2012
001

Grateful acknowledgement is made to the following for permission to reproduce copyright material: The lyrics on pp. 183–4 from 'Pardesi Pardesi' by Nardeem Shravan (from the soundtrack of *Raja Hindustani*, dir. Dharmesh Darshan, 1996) © Tips Industries Ltd. The poem 'Self-Portrait' by A. K. Ramanujan on p. vii, from *The Striders: Poems* by A. K. Ramanujan (1966), by permission of Oxford University Press. The lyrics on p. 136 from 'Nights in White Satin' by Justin Hayward, © 1967 Tyler Music Ltd of Suite 2.07, Plaza 535, King's Road, London, SW10 0SZ. International Copyright Secured. All rights reserved. Used by permission.

Set in 13/15.75 pt Dante MT Std
Typeset by Jouve (UK), Milton Keynes
Printed in Great Britain by Clays Ltd, St Ives plc

A CIP catalogue record for this book is available from the British Library

ISBN: 978-0-670-91708-2

www.greenpenguin.co.uk

ALWAYS LEARNING   **PEARSON**

For Vik, my jaan, and Anoushka Tiger,
who have stained my heart with their gold

I resemble everyone
but myself, and sometimes see
in shop-windows,
     despite the well-known laws
     of optics,
the portrait of a stranger,
date unknown,
often signed in a corner
by my father.

'Self-Portrait' by A.K. Ramanujan

While open prisons do exist in various states across India, the people and places depicted in this novel are nevertheless purely fictional

I.

The security men are watching Ray. They regard her with a perfect indifference. There are three of them, of varying heights, their belted khaki safari suits finished cleanly with the bright gloss of winter sunlight. They loiter at the entry gate, two of them standing arm in arm, dwarfed by the high peepal trees behind them, the branches against the sky. The earth around them is pale and heavy, the colour of gram flour, interrupted rarely by weeds. They do not seem self-conscious. The third guard sits on the knee-high wall that forms the boundary of the hamlet, right against the road that connects the local farms to the main town. He is older than the other two. His hair seems paint-stained, the white unnaturally thick over the grey brush beneath. The badge on his cap glints in the sun. Ray can see the light flash as he turns, even at this distance. His posture is correct; a long neck lends him significance as he twitches abruptly to take in his surroundings, alert and urgent.

She sets about unpacking the equipment on the verandah, looking up and back at the three of them every minute or so, a reflex that she is unable to control. They are the people who met her upon arrival, just one hour ago, but they seem so different from the vantage point of the hut. She looks to see if they are still staring, hoping that they might now be bored of it. She remains in dialogue with them like this, brief flickers of acknowledgement, collisions of sight that are barely noticeable, until she can do it no longer. She takes the kit back into the hut.

★

The car had been sent to meet Ray at Delhi airport, a few minutes after midnight: a battered mini Maruti in baby blue, bobbled white towels smoothed over and tucked into the back seats to defend against passenger sweat. It was a five-hour road trip to their destination and she clutched at sleep as they hurtled through the dark cylinder of night sky. She was childlike in her fatigue, screwing her eyes up at the lights of oncoming trucks, hugging the camera bags to protect the equipment from shock turns, the violent bends in the road. Finally, as the engine began to slow, she passed through the gates of the Ashwer compound in a state of vague hallucination, her breathing muffled by the heat as she shook herself awake. The car was being followed by a string of kids. She could see them through the back windscreen in school tunics and shorts, fluttering together and apart like the ribboned tail of a kite.

The compound itself was a semicircular shape, the road forming the straight line, the huts nestled in the curve of the crescent. Beyond a small hillock a thin slick of a river was visible behind the settlement, the banks dotted with distant figures and scattered patches of brightly coloured material. Between this area and the road stretched a dry acre of desert soil, populated by little other than the trees and occasional farm animals – a handful of buffaloes were resting on their haunches beneath the shade of a central tree, a cluster of thin hunchbacked goats stood nearby, shaking their floppy ears, their skin camouflaged in patterns of brown and white.

The three security guards were there to receive her. Two of them set about dispersing the children, who were crowding around the car now it had stopped. The third opened the car door and summoned a tall teenaged boy, dressed in a white vest and cotton trousers, to unload the luggage. Ray lifted her own suitcase out of the boot, in spite of protests.

'Your colleague has taken breakfast,' said the guard who was dealing with the bags. He was a short young man with a trim moustache and round face, mahogany skin that was firm and clear, uninterrupted by facial expression. He spoke with a slightly nasal tone. Helping the boy balance the pieces of kit on his head, he said, 'This boy . . . he will take you to your quarters.'

Ray stared at the cushioned blue camera bags and radio-mic briefcase stacked on the boy's head, his long arms reaching up to stabilize them, the sweat beginning to streak down the back of his neck, just dissolving at the top of his vest.

The guard handed the boy a tiffin.

'No, no!' said Ray, moving forward. 'I can carry that, don't worry.' That he should be expected to carry her food in addition to everything, it was too much.

The guard dismissed her with a raised hand, closing his eyes in an expression of tolerance and shaking his head simultaneously. The boy released one hand expertly from the items on his head, bending his knees slightly to take the weight. He extended his left arm so that the guard could hook the top handle of the tiffin over and thread it through to his armpit. It hung from his shoulder, the layered steel column jutting out at an angle. The guard patted the boy on the back, as if to acknowledge that the job was not an easy one, and gestured at him to start walking.

'Lunch tiffin delivery is at twelve noon daily,' he said to Ray. 'Dinner delivered at seven p.m. Breakfast at seven a.m. As per arrangements of Thakur Sahib. Your tiffin is pure veg as per request. The others in your team are designated non-veg.'

Ray thanked him, and walked quickly after the boy, rolling her suitcase along the earth. The bags teetered on his head. She wanted to trust him, but anxiety propelled her forwards. The kit was so delicate; there was no way he could know what he was carrying. He was weaving his way quickly through the central expanse of the field, already under the shade of the first peepal, his bare feet slapping down in quick repetition so that he was walking in a style that was almost running, heaving his gangly form in a jerky motion to accommodate the weight on his head. She pulled her suitcase forcefully on the uneven ground. It was too heavy for her to carry, in spite of her remonstrations to the guards, and now she winced at the drone. Birds circling above squeaked tightly, innocently. As they approached the settlement she saw a white bullock rubbing itself against a small tree, horns flashing.

She was surprised by the harmony and calm of the scene before her, even if it did fulfil her expectations, adhering to the descriptions she'd fashioned for the programme pitch back in London. There were no pictures of Ashwer online; instead she had based her idea of the place on a couple of articles from the local press, blending these particular details with the images of rural India that had entered her subconscious from watching television over the years. She mistrusted the sense of familiarity, and yet it did feel how she'd imagined. She looked back across the dusty field at the guards. They were now bathed in the blush of morning light, tinted with the colour of pale peach flesh. It caressed them, this light, softened their forms as they sat on the wall, legs stretched out in poses of relaxation, a couple of them smoking.

She entered a matrix of short earthen paths, closer to the boy she was following. Around fifty dwellings faced each other in four huddled rows, separated by low fences roughly hewn from thick branches and stuffed with straw, leading to a tall iron water pump. Some homes were built of brick or stone, but many were not – their walls were made from the same corrugated sheet metal that formed the roof of other accommodation, long gaps visible at the joints. Others had thatched roofs in straw and wood. The front yards stored rolled-up plastic sheeting and thick bundles of spindly twigs in baskets or old wooden crates. A pylon at the back of the area lunged up towards the clouds.

She could hear sounds of people from behind closed doors, but there were only brief glimpses of the figures in the houses: a snatch of crimson sari through the hollow space of a doorway, a chunky man in chequered lungi and sweater drinking tea on a plastic chair, posters of Hindu gods and goddesses hanging from a clothes line against an interior wall. The noises were powerful. She heard the rattle of machinery, steel dishes, voices that she could decipher only by tone – jokes, commands, questions. Hens fluttered and dispersed with the same vocal forcefulness. She could smell fresh cow dung and baking parathas on the smoke in the breeze. A bony teenaged boy washed himself in the front yard of one home, standing in his briefs and pouring water from a bucket over his head with a jug, both utensils made of thick plastic with a marble-effect swirl of pink and white. A huddle of five rabbits chewed on sparse leaves in a pile of branches near him. He grinned with familiarity at Ray's rushing companion, the smile faltering when he saw Ray a few yards behind. She looked at the ground, unsure as to what the most respectful response should be, her cheeks flushing.

They reached a white stone hut at the end of the right-hand

row, the door fully open. Inside, the boy slowly lowered himself down to a squatting position, calves straining to prevent the equipment from falling.

'I . . . Can I help?' said Ray. '*Mein* . . . help . . . *karoon?*'

The boy dislodged all the luggage safely, unhooked the tiffin and stood up, taking a handkerchief from the back pocket of his trousers. He began wiping his neck in broad strokes. She could see his features properly for the first time: a sloppy fringe, defiant jawline; the preoccupied face of an adolescent perched precariously on an overgrown body.

'*Mein chala, madam?*' he said. I'll go, madam?

He squinted as a drop of sweat slid into one eye. She felt a sharp contraction of guilt.

'*Aap* . . . *pani lahenge?*' said Ray. Would you . . . like some water?

She looked round the room and saw a bottle of mineral water, half full. She pointed at it and turned round. He was already outside, back on the verandah.

'Um . . .' said Ray, worried that she had only large notes, recently changed at the airport, no appropriate tip. Surely it was insulting to tip him, anyway. You could not assume that someone wanted your small change. In his case, she had no idea if this was part of his job or if he was just part of the welcome committee. Maybe he had to go to school now? Or work?

He took his leave by flicking his head up with a questioning expression, to indicate that he was waiting for her consent.

'OK,' she said. 'Thank you for –'

He nodded and left before she could say any more.

There was a note from Serena on a small wooden cabinet.

Filming bits and pieces around the place – cutaways, GVs, just getting used to it. Team meeting tomorrow night once Nathan arrives? N.B. Governor walk and talk in the morning.

Serena had been here for twenty-four hours, and seemed to have made very little impact on the space. Her suitcases were under the bed she had occupied for sleep – there were two of them in the room, at opposite ends – wooden frames bound tightly with thick woven rope. A book lay on her pillow with some folded pyjamas. There was a metal cabinet next to her bed, and a small wooden desk supporting the shooting scripts, travel documents and a location schedule in which airport details had been highlighted with a luminous marker. Nathan, the final member of the team, would arrive tomorrow. Serena was due to coordinate his pickup.

Ray sat on the other bed and checked her mobile phone. There was no signal. She looked around. 'A one-room hut with outside latrine' was how it had been described to her on the phone during the planning phase. It was an accurate description, but nothing had prepared her for simple details: the lack of glass in the windows (a series of holes in circles and hexagons, the size of her palm), likewise the absence of a lock on the 'door' (a curved sheet of metal) that she pulled into place so that the gap at the joint was as narrow as possible, just two or three inches.

Wires sloped against the walls, seemingly at random, suspending a low bulb and trailing down to the ground. The walls were painted in turquoise; the floor seemed to be a treated version of the earth outside: a hardened texture, dusty, coloured like slate rather than sand. She rammed her heel against it a few times. Maybe it was mixed with concrete. The kitchen area was a couple of feet wide and ran the width of the hut to the right side. It was sectioned off from the rest of the room by a low stone divider that also functioned as a work surface, supporting a stove and a few dishes on one side. There was a tap in the wall with a bucket underneath. Washing powder had been left by the bucket in a string of small transparent sachets. It had a bluish-white tint, much like the external walls of the hut. She could see very little other furniture in the room. In the left corner there was a hanging of thin primrose-yellow muslin, drawn back to expose a bathing area: a tap in the wall near the ceiling, six feet from the floor, and a wide corner hole ready to drain water into the ground.

It gave her a little thrill, the sparsity of the environment, the uneven bristle of the rope underneath her thighs and hips as she unlaced her trainers and sat cross-legged on the charpoy. Their hut was just like the others. It promised sincerity, somehow; the chance of empathy with the people they would be filming.

Ray lay down on the empty bed. The heat was on her, a rash of disaffection that went against her best intentions, running all over her body, underneath her combat trousers, the long-sleeved jersey top. The air was dense, utterly devoid of movement. She craved nudity, the ability to remove all of her clothes and cool openly in the stillness. Even her thoughts felt soaked in sweat now that she was alone, able to relax. She stared at the ceiling, wondering at the sound that rain would make on the tin during monsoon. Torrential rain, running in rivulets through the grooves – hammering, battering on the metal, seeping in through the spaces and trickling down the walls. Again, there was a small charge, the recognizable curlicue of excitement in her chest. They would live like the locals; deal with these eventualities in the established ways.

She pushed herself up and took her top off, began to

unhook her bra. She looked down at her breasts, which felt suddenly huge, licked with sweat, the dark nipples like eyes on the hunt, ready for something erotic. Noise seemed to swell outside. It was the innocuous soundtrack of industry. People were cooking, working, tending to animals, washing dishes and clothes. Children were shouting out as they set off for school. She put the garments back on, confused by decorum, how to place her privacy, aware that she was very close to everything outside, possibly even visible if someone walked past, looked in for a moment through the gap in the door or one of the window holes.

She felt claustrophobic in her privilege, opening the tiffin and unslotting the three compartments in the steel tower. Food would be delivered to them every day while they were here, and they were to leave the empty tiffins for collection. Bottled water was to come with every meal. They were unlikely to use the kitchen area. She began to eat, ripping a chapatti and dipping it in green dal before using it to scoop up some fried okra. It tasted good, full of salt, and satisfyingly spiced.

Then she washed her body as quickly as possible. She pulled the muslin tightly across the shower corner of the room, concealing herself even though she was alone.

She emerged from the hut, a small camera in her hand, A4-sized rucksack on her back containing notes and a shooting script. She was likely to bump into Serena, and didn't want to have to return to the hut to get material.

There was a man stitching with a large sewing machine at a table in the front yard of the hut opposite Ray's. The machine rattled loudly. He wore a large turban of pale pink, a perfect coil of cloth. It dominated him, towering above his oval pockmarked face. His hut looked similar to her own, the white bricks emitting a fierce sheen in the sun. A plaited cane door, half open, revealed a woman sitting on the floor, working a needle into a mustard sheet of cloth, part of her sari pulled over her head to form a ghoonghat, hiding her face. They both looked up at Ray, stared in her direction for a few moments.

Ray pressed her hands together in greeting, projecting an enthusiastic mixture of hello and namaste. She gave a nod that was exaggerated enough to almost be a bow. The man nodded back, his gaze flickering away from sustained eye contact.

She made her way to the water pump, feeling the dust in the atmosphere, peppery in her nostrils, the heat presenting itself with a new candour. A girl was filling a huge earthenware pot. Her age was indeterminate, somewhere from mid-teens upwards, and she was using her entire body: jumping up and bearing down on the handle in a perfect rhythm, over and over, accompanied by a large wail from the machinery each time. Her long skirt, blouse and cardigan were all complementary in shape and hue – three different shades of purple – and her ponytail bobbed with crazy asymmetry against the sky. Ray lifted her camera and switched it on, using her other hand to adjust the focus.

'Aren't you supposed to ask her permission?'

Ray jumped, shuddering so that the shot was rendered useless. A woman was standing behind her, smiling.

'Sorry. I hope I didn't disturb you.' Her voice was as angular as her figure, the English spoken in a zigzag of local accent and quick rhythm. She wore a long, loose kameez in rough beige khadi cotton that reached her shins, wide salwar trousers underneath.

'Of course not,' said Ray. 'I'm so sorry. It's my mistake. I didn't want to bother her really, but yes –' She took a breath and addressed the girl at the pump in Hindi. The girl had stopped work and was now pouring some of the water from the overflowing earthenware mutka pot into a smaller tureen.

'*Aap ka filming kiya mein ne, bina puchhe. Aap ko . . .*' I filmed you without asking. You . . .

Ray searched for the Hindi word and then inserted an English word instead.

'*Aapne mind toh nahin kiya?*' You don't mind?

The girl smiled and shook her head. She lifted the larger pot and began to walk back to her home.

'Everyone's so polite here,' said Ray.

The woman laughed, cocking an eyebrow. 'Why do you think? It is hardly surprising.'

'You think they need to be on "good behaviour" for this place to work?' said Ray.

'It is not about this place working, it is about you being here. Do you see anyone stick around when you start walking towards them?'

She was in her late twenties, tall and precise in her movements, her matt-black hair brushed into a long ponytail, thin and sleek down her back.

Ray looked around. There were a couple of figures visible, but they were at a distance. 'Oh . . . You think it's us, that we are scaring everyone away? It's natural for people to be camera shy.'

The woman sniffed. It was a dismissive sound, mixed with a half-laugh. 'They think you work for the governor. Thakur Sahib, they call him. "Sir Lord". You're going to be filming them for him. You have total and open access, I hear?'

'Yes, but we don't want to offend anyone. I know it must feel like a great intrusion, one that you weren't party to deciding, people coming and living on your land . . . Sorry, I haven't even introduced myself – I'm Ray Bhullar, part of the BBC crew.'

'I'm Nandini.'

She took Ray's hand, responding to the shake with a perfunctory slide, mostly fingertips.

Ray smiled, attempted a friendly tone of voice.

'Do you work here or are you a –'

Something about Nandini's expression caught her off guard. She repeated herself, stumbling over the moment.

'Do you work here or are you an . . . a . . .'

'Convict?' Nandini smiled. 'Inmate? Prisoner? We have the same names here as other countries, you know. You're confused by the fact that I speak decent English?'

'No!' said Ray. 'No, of course not . . .'

'I'm both. I teach and offer counselling here. I'm also on a sentence, which has thirty-eight months remaining on it.'

'I see. So how long was the sentence?'

'Fifteen years. Life. Like the rest. Shortened for good behaviour. Everyone here is in for life. I thought you knew that?'

'Yes, I did . . . yes, of course. It is an extraordinary place.'

'Everyone here has killed someone.'

'Yes.'

Ray nodded. Nandini's eyes were constant, not even a momentary flicker away.

'That's why we are here,' said Ray, rushing the words. 'How do you find living at Ashwer?'

'Mine was self-defence.'

'I see.' Ray nodded again and met Nandini's gaze.

'I'm trained in primary counselling and have been offering that here for over four years. To the women. They might have killed a husband or lover. Or it could be dowry-related. The mothers-in-law who set fire to their sons' brides or the daughters-in-law who survive an attack but have killed a person as part of self-defence or retaliation.' She paused. 'Like myself. That was my situation. The latter, I mean.'

She waited for a response.

Ray held back the desire to ask more questions. It was too soon. She regarded the other woman. Like Ray herself, Nandini was of North Indian origin, of similar age, even height. Their colouring was close: Ray's was possibly a shade darker than Nandini's creamy-tea complexion. She had similar hair to Nandini – black, with a bruised-plum sheen in the sunlight. And yet, Ray thought, they must look very different standing next to each other. Nandini's figure was strongly delineated, fine-boned and disciplined, whereas Ray's was curvaceous, leaning to softness.

'There are plenty of straightforward killers here too, though,' said Nandini. 'In terms of your film. The three Ps, the governor is fond of saying. Crimes of passion, property and personal vengeance. They generally fall into one of these categories; he is right. We come from all over the place. Let me know if you need anything. I'm in unit sixteen.'

Ray watched her walk away, the white length of cloth that formed the chunni scarf hanging over her shoulders. Beneath her, the ground was solid – above her, the dense grey sky seemed to set her in place. She watched Nandini as she went further down the track, the long line of hair, lean back, the smooth progression forward, becoming distant enough to be part of the general movement of the peepal trees in the scene, a wild dog running alongside her as she reached the far horizon of huts. She raised the camera intuitively and filmed the scene, counting the necessary five seconds as she held the shot steady, registering the action as an afterthought, once she'd switched the camera off. She hadn't really known what else to do.

It was the first programme she had successfully won as a commission in her five years at the BBC and she wanted it to be ethical and empathetic: more like a documentary film than a formatted television programme. It was part of a series, filmed mostly in the UK but with occasional forays abroad, and as this was one of the foreign specials Ray had the chance to make it her own. The series aimed to present a 'non-judgemental slice of life inside the prison system' and there was an official agreement on the team to never broadcast details of the inmates' crimes, as protection for the families of the victims. Ray took the necessary rule of discretion a step further, by choosing to avoid knowledge of the details of inmates' crimes even off camera. Of course they knew each family in Ashwer included a person who had killed someone, but there was no need to learn the ins and outs of each crime; it could hamper the crew's ability to view the community without bias. She had suggested this as a house rule in the team meeting before leaving. But now, within hours of arrival, she had this knowledge, this information about Nandini's crime.

She walked to the river and sat under a tree with a notepad in her lap, away from a handful of men and women who were washing clothes in the stream. To her left, a man was shaving, crouching by the water with the swathes of cream thick on his face. Ahead she could see vast pylons slicing up the desert sky, the mesh of wires connecting the structures above the treetops like a line drawing, an old-fashioned sketch of the future in an old sci-fi novel. She imagined filming it all, boxing it away.

Serena was not at the hut when Ray returned. It didn't seem like she had gone far – her laptop was open on the desk, with a series of images paused from video. She had been loading material into the computer.

Ray clicked on one of the grainy squares.

It was the young girl in purple whom she had seen at the

water pump. She was chopping vegetables in a kitchen, sitting on the floor and being filmed from above. Serena must have been standing. The vegetables around the girl bulged with heightened colours: vibrant mauve onions and slender burgundy aubergines. She was talking to Serena as she peeled a mooli, a long overgrown white radish.

'*Aap ko meri bhasha samaj mein aati hai ke nahin?*' Do you understand my language or not?

She gave a wide smile; you could see her thinking as she awaited a response. She was getting ready to speak again. Serena's voice was apologetic, off camera.

'Sorry, I only speak English. Ray, my . . . Ray speaks Hindi. The Indian girl . . . with me? Ray Bhullar.'

Ray imagined Serena putting her free hand on her chest and shaking her head as she spoke.

The girl spoke over her answer.

'*Mere ko apne desh le chalo,*' she said. Take me to your country. She gave Serena a grin as she chopped the hairy white piece into small circles. '*Waapas apne saath, mutlab.*' I mean, back with you.

'Sorry,' said Serena, the frustration giving a crisp veneer to her voice. 'No Hindi. I bring Ray later. Hindi from Ray Bhullar.'

The girl picked up some thin green finger chillies and began to slit them in two. Her voice was placatory, as if to explain herself, her tone suggesting that she had noble motives, that she didn't want Serena to miss out: '*Apka aacha dhyaan rakhti, mein,*' she said. I would have looked after you well.

2.

Everything had been unpacked, the living quarters arranged accordingly, candles had been lit, and now it was midnight. Before lying down, Ray smeared repellent over the itchy red swellings on her feet and arms in an attempt to prevent the mosquito bites that had emerged after dark from multiplying. Instead of soothing her, the ointment exacerbated the pain, the stings erupting so vehemently that she had to go to the bathing area and wash her legs.

She draped a towel around her lower half and walked back, watching Serena, who sat in the centre of her charpoy, cross-legged, a book in her hands. She was reading in the spotlight of a torch that she had fixed with string to a nail in the wall above her head. She had the arms of a young boy, with a light hint of muscle. Her fingernails were serrated at the edge, unevenly bitten. Her face was like a fist in shadow, closed, taut.

Serena was in her late thirties, youthful-looking, although a decade older than Ray, and seemed to shoulder the additional experience more with resentment than with pride. It was almost as if she wanted Ray to release her somehow from the responsibility that it entailed. It was not clear to either of them whether she had been sent to partner Ray, or babysit her. Back in the office they had met mostly in team meetings. Their respective roles on this project were ill defined. Ray was the 'director', making her first full-length programme, and Serena was the 'producer', but these names did not offer much clarification of their relationship.

Ray thought about the office, the way in which she and Serena had stepped around each other under cover of politeness over the past few months, preserving the borderless cubicles of space that came with their seats in the open-plan set-up by keeping conversation to a minimum.

They seemed to be re-creating the same dynamic here in Ashwer and it was exasperating. They had spent the day working on the proposed shooting scripts, splitting up the initial filming between them. Serena was opinionated, at times dismissive.

'You've got the language,' she said, 'so you can start charming the villagers while I work with Nathan on pieces to camera.'

But Ray did not believe in the idea of 'charm' when it came to working in television. It was a word that had come up often during her five years at the BBC, and it affronted her. A medium like documentary posited itself as attempting to capture some kind of 'actuality': some kind of true experience. If anything, the desire to film in this way was about indulging a perverse curiosity, an inexplicable hunger to know and understand why people acted in a certain way: their motivations, needs, desires, the circumstances of their lives. It was a special kind of intrusion that was the opposite of charm, but that she hoped was in the service of some, as yet undefined, 'greater good'.

With Serena, similarly, she wanted to access something genuine. During the day she had found herself burrowing for the truth she believed lay beneath the topsoil of their conversation. She asked sudden, direct questions while they were unpacking or eating dinner – did Serena live alone, have any family? Did she like working in the Local Action Programmes Unit? Did she believe in their films? What kind of programmes did she want to make? The rebuttals were not rude – Serena mostly ignored Ray's questions or started talking about other things.

They lay down at a similar time. Serena seemed to fall asleep within minutes. Ray moved her body inside the sleeping bag, her cheek pressing against the zip train, and waited for sleep. She rolled and straightened herself, frustrated at the noise caused by her movements. Serena was breathing in her bed: a gentle in–out of air that offended only by its regularity. The sound itself was barely audible to Ray, but each draw tormented her, each exhalation preparing her for the repeat. It was their first night in the prison and Ray could not loosen the mantra from her mind: Weeks and weeks and weeks. Weeks of sleeping in the same room as Serena.

Scratch and tussle, her body continually moving, a robust and mobile strangulation inside the sleeping bag. The complete absence of light meant the darkness was throttling. It was so much more completely black than any dark room she had known since childhood. She lay still, then kicked her legs out over and over. To hit a wall. To kick it, feel it press up hard against her feet. These were her desires. She kept her mouth closed and made a small squeal of a sound at the back of her throat. It was a high-pitched grunt, almost a clearing of the throat. She made it to remind herself that she was here of her own volition.

The thing about sharing a room was that it felt awkward straight away, but not in the way she'd imagined. It was not the coming and going – the undressing, or sharing of storage space, even the arrangement of one's items and self within it. It was something to do with the ease and lack of inhibition that seemed to accompany the process of thinking in solitude.

She lifted her feet inside the sleeping bag, until her legs were stretched out above the charpoy. Then she let her feet thud down onto the mattress. There was an interruption in Serena's breathing, a sudden silencing of the in–out continuum. Oh God, thought Ray, I can't move, I can't do anything; how is this going to work?

From the other corner of the room, a sleepy voice manifested itself, topped and tailed with a yawn.

'You OK?'

Ray made a minute sound, a feather-light tweak in the air; again, it was only for herself to hear. She admired Serena's resilience, her seeming indifference to the situation. It implied an identity that was less volatile than her own. She cursed herself for being so reactive.

'Yes,' Ray said. 'I'm fine.'

She began to unzip her sleeping bag as quietly as she could. She was beginning to overheat.

They had been told the weather would be changeable at this time of year – veering between extremes of heat and cold from night to night. She lay still and waited.

Slowly, over time, her mind found its way to calmness, beginning to wean itself onto sleep in the early hours of the morning. She stared at the lining of light that emerged around the wooden shutter in the wall as the sun grew stronger. It throbbed against her retinas whenever she shut her eyes, a luminous wavering rectangle, like an empty frame in the progression of a television programme – a 'black hole' as it was called. She encouraged sleep like this, playing tricks with her vision in the darkness, absorbing the image then closing her eyes, letting it gleam all the more brightly, tiring herself out.

His eyes were friendly, and he was groomed – a side parting of thick hair, black aviator glasses with clear lenses, a luxuriant shine to his skin, the cheeks overly soft. There was a kind of 1970s bravado to his style, married with the conservatism expected of someone approaching fifty. He wore a patterned rust shirt in cotton sateen, a gold-buttoned navy blazer, tailored to soften his paunch, and he walked with a looseness, a generalized bonhomie that wafted behind him to the five uniformed men who formed his entourage. This honeyed mist of goodwill also blew forward on the wind to Ray and Serena, so that by the time he reached them, ready to shake their hands and enquire as to their comfort levels, they were already smiling.

He was Sujay Sanghvi, the governor of the prison, and he was due to do a 'walk and talk' with them, take them through the 'open camp' as he called it and help them understand 'the ethos of the place'.

'Be relaxed,' he said to them, nodding at the same time at a man who had appeared from somewhere with a tray of glasses. 'Consider this place your home. We are all about communal living.'

'Please don't trouble him,' said Ray. 'We can only drink bottled water.'

'Don't worry,' Sanghvi said, handing them a glass each. 'This is filtered. I myself don't have anything other than filtered water.'

'I hope you don't mind,' said Serena, smiling as she put up a hand in refusal. 'I'd better not.'

'Well, you will take one, surely,' he said to Ray. 'Being the Indian one of the team. You even speak Hindi, I hear. And you are vegetarian. Congratulations.'

Ray smiled and took a glass.

'Well . . . if you will throw down the gauntlet so soon . . .' she said. She drank it quickly, as though downing a shot of tequila in a bar for a bet, and placed the glass back on the tray. '*Bada maaza ayaa*,' she said, raising her eyebrows.

'Oho!' He tapped her gently on the back and laughed. A couple of the men around him murmured in amusement. 'Did you hear that?' he said to Serena. ' "*Bada maaza ayaa.*" A very colloquial expression of enjoyment. As in "I enjoyed it a lot!" '

They walked slowly. To the right, along the main road, Ray could see the constant transit of life outside – trucks, camels, bicycles, scooters – swelling in the midday rush. Between the prison and the road was the line drawn in small stones, a wall low enough for children to clamber across, into, or out of, the patchy grass of the prison grounds. They walked alongside this wall, Ray and Serena loitering as the governor walked further ahead. A scooter went past, puttering loudly, a whole family grouped on it – the young wife sitting side-saddle, holding a baby in her lap, her pale green sari skimming her toes, an older child standing in the front holding onto the handlebars with his father, whose hair was wild in the wind of their movement. The woman looked back at them over her shoulder, a compulsion in her gaze, before they disappeared out of her vision.

'Beautiful,' said Ray. 'Beautiful image. Nuclear family, the way they were slotted in together, that sari, the speed – gorgeous.'

'You're funny,' said Serena, smiling. 'Straight on the visual. Listen – I've got my eye on this wall. It's really interesting. It says it all: "the prison with no perimeter". It's a gift for pieces to camera.'

The governor turned round, looking for them. He raised an arm to call them over.

'By the way, where's your third leg, then?' he said. 'Your presenter? Let me think. Is it Nick . . . Nigel?'

'He arrives tonight,' said Serena. 'Nathan. He was on

another shoot. Filming in a British prison up north, near Newcastle.'

'Ah, I see. Flying him over separately on business class?'

'No, no, not at all,' she said. 'This is a very informal show, everything is going to be filmed on tiny cameras – we're extremely low budget, that's why we're living on site as your guests!'

'Of course, yes, I remember your documentation. He's an ex-prisoner, right? An armed robber? What an extraordinary title your series has. I thought so when I saw it. *Doing Time*, yes?'

Ray laughed. She was enjoying the gentle mockery, the irreverence. It felt good to hear it in the particular accent of the governor, a butterfat malai sound that was richly textured and grand all at once.

They stopped at a large tabular rock, near a man squatting on his haunches. He was spreading out a mixture of brightly coloured clothes to dry in the sun. To his right, Ray could see a bulging heap of sopping material, which he began beating out with a stone.

'See, everyone has a talent,' said Sanghvi. 'One person stitches clothes, another man runs a very successful quarrying business; some of the prisoners can play musical instruments and they have even made a wedding band together on the side. All prisoners are free to leave and work in whichever way they choose, wherever they like, so long as they are back in this camp between the hours of six thirty p.m. and six thirty a.m. OK? This guy collects laundry that needs doing from a shop in the marketplace in the main town. He brings it here and has it done by the end of the day. Then he leaves it to dry and takes it to another prisoner, who irons it and returns the load to the market within twenty-four hours. So you can see that with this business he has found a way to become an entrepreneur here. In reality we are functioning not so much as a prison but as a village, like the Gandhian idea of a village – that kind of sustainability and self-reliance.'

They watched the man hammer out a large-patterned sheet; he was methodical and persistent. The colours were utterly vibrant in the sunlight: an enchanted spread of turquoise flowers and foliage printed over lilac cotton. Ray wondered if she should find a way to speak to the prisoner – she was feeling a measure of discomfort at their discussion, talking about him in this way while he was working right in front of them – but she couldn't get eye contact with him.

'Gandhi,' said Serena. 'He was in prison, of course.'

'Sorry?' Sanghvi said.

'You were just mentioning Mahatma Gandhi's model for village life,' said Serena. 'He was in prison himself. Several different prisons, actually, is that right?'

Ray winced. Sanghvi was nodding vaguely and looking over at her.

'Yes,' he said. 'He was imprisoned four times.'

He must think we are idiots, thought Ray. Gandhi's activism – his repeated, defiant readiness for imprisonment – was hardly something to compare with the situation of these prisoners. She found herself stepping in, speaking over Serena.

'As a political prisoner, of course,' Ray said. 'Non-violent, that is . . . rather than . . .'

She had nowhere to go with the sentence. Serena looked at her expectantly, a half-smile masking her annoyance. Ray faltered. What was she going to say? She looked at the man with the sheet. He was reaching over the central map of colour, smoothing it gently with both hands.

'So unforgettable,' said Ray, trying her best to brighten up her voice, 'those hunger-strike shots, the definitive image of Gandhi in prison . . . aren't they?'

Sanghvi was back in conversation with the guards. Serena walked forward and crouched down to examine the man's process. He had begun work on another piece.

Not a great move, to contradict Serena in front of the governor, thought Ray. It wasn't going to help them in terms of teamwork. She looked at Serena's face, which was casually turned away, her fringe hiding her eyes in profile.

The two women retired to the hut for afternoon siesta. The hours coincided with their susceptibility to jet lag.

'We've got a nice good-cop, bad-cop thing going, don't you think?' said Ray. 'With the governor, I mean. We could make something of that.'

She was lying on the charpoy, on top of her sleeping bag. She had given up on sleeping. Her hand hovered over her stomach, underneath her T-shirt.

'Don't tell me you're sick already,' said Serena. She had hooked up a camera to the laptop and was testing it by filming different parts of the hut. She turned it on Ray.

'Ray is feeling the after-effects of drinking local water,' she said in the tone of a generic voice-over presenter.

Ray got up for the toilet. It was her fourth trip in the past hour. She had hoped, somehow, that Serena hadn't noticed.

'Spare me,' she said, smiling weakly and making her way to the door.

Serena followed her with the camera.

'Tell me you're going to stick to bottles now, like the rest of us,' she said. 'If you go down on the first day I'm not doing this film alone, mate; it was your big plan to come here!'

Outside, Ray crouched over the hole in the ground, grateful for small mercies. At least the toilet wasn't indoors, like the bathing tap. The waste hurtled out of her, became part of the general stench, drained her strength as it left her body. It came in several contractions, each one a false ending. *Loose motions*. That's what they called it here. She waited for the flow to cease, held the tissue paper ready in her hand. It was from the stash in her toiletries bag. Such a cliché, she thought. *Delhi belly right off the bat.*

She wondered if Serena had been affected by being in such close range with lifers today. It wasn't the kind of anxiety that either of them would admit to easily, and they certainly weren't on terms where they might share feelings. But should they have some kind of protection? Herself and Serena? Sleep with a weapon, or something like that?

She emerged from the toilet area, pulling down her T-shirt, and looked across the field in front of her. The children were back from school, playing near the central peepal. A few of the younger ones were flying kites, not visible in the sky at this distance, the shouts and upturned faces reflecting their excitement. Murder, homicide, victims, death – these words felt so vague here, a distant fog of white noise in her head. It was almost churlish to bring them up, a little vulgar in the face of such belief and serenity. She thought of the phrasing in the proposal she had written, which her boss, Nick Rabin, had used for the pitch to the channel commissioners.

Ashwer is a 'prison village' in India which houses inmates who have been convicted of murder. Every convict in the prison has killed someone. And everyone is free to come and go as they please. In twenty years, not a single inmate has reoffended and only one person has attempted to escape.

'Trust begets trust,' says Sujay Sanghvi, the governor responsible for the experiment. He is proud of the strong community that is Ashwer. It was a vision that began as just five huts on a piece of farmland in the mid-eighties. 'You trust them and they will return that trust.'

3.

She woke carrying the sensations of her dreams – heat, sex, isolation, hunger, need – an amorphous mess of urgent feeling that meant she was somehow aroused when she opened her eyes. Ray couldn't remember why this was the case, the exact details of the night's vivid journey eluding her as she lay drenched in perspiration. Her mind was numbed by the closeness, the sleek humidity that intruded everywhere, under her clothes, against her face, her hair, body, everything. She was alone. Serena's clothes lay folded on her bed, her suitcase was on the floor. A towel was hanging from the nail above her bed – a white cloth, as thin as a kitchen towel, with a navy and green check pattern on the border. Above it, black streaks were visible in the wall, webbed licks and cracks that seared their way down from the ceiling through the turquoise paint, revealing the grey stone beneath.

She washed freely, relishing the solitude.

Once dressed, she opened the door and collected the tiffin from the verandah. The turbanned man was not at his sewing machine this morning but she could see his wife sitting on a patch of cloth on the ground, leaning against a large metal cylinder of oil. Her right leg was extended, the bare foot lying on one end of a long tunic of straight-cut mustard cotton. Her foot pressed down to prevent the tunic from fluttering up in the breeze. She held the other end of the garment in her lap, working closely at the neck with a needle and thread. Ray smiled, putting her hands together. She could see only the woman's mouth; the rest of her face was covered by the ghoonghat of her scarf, wiry curls of dark hair visible through the thin georgette. She stared again at the leg of this mysterious woman: the firm muscle of the calf inside the cotton salwar, the exposed ankle encircled by a heavy bangle of dull silver. She wanted to film it, of course, but she berated herself for the thought, remembering the moment with Nandini. These were her neighbours.

The head in the chunni seemed to nod briefly in response to Ray's namaste, a barely distinguishable smile upturning the corners of the mouth. Ray grinned broadly, pleased with the connection. She backed into her own hut.

Her breakfast was a warm dish of steamed rice balls and soup. She ate luxuriously, dipping pieces of idli in the spicy sambhar and sucking the juice from each piece. Her stomach was stable now; it welcomed the food.

She left after half an hour, carrying her camera. She was due to follow Nandini today: shadow one of her counselling sessions while Serena began filming with Nathan, scripting and recording his first reactions to the prison. She was not supposed to film Nandini yet – she agreed with Serena that it would obstruct the building of intimacy at this stage – but she had brought the camera with her to pick up details and general views of the prison compound on the way.

The light was moving over the horizon, a quickening smear of colour that seemed very beautiful to Ray, the sky gaping over the trees of the village. She leaned tentatively against the border fence of the settlement, steadying herself, feeling the straw sagging against her weight. She switched the camera on. The image startled her by being visible straight away. She could film this right now – an eerily sentimental dawn, the promise of the landscape unfolding.

She saw a figure in the shot and realized it was Nathan. He was standing and smoking by the swing fashioned from rough rope on a solid branch of the central peepal tree. He had arrived, then. Serena must have gone to receive him sometime during the night.

Ray had met Nathan twice. The first encounter was brief – she'd been sent to operate second camera for another director, at an arts exhibition for prisoners. The second time was in the team meeting before leaving for India. He didn't look like an armed robber to her, with his boyish frame and fine features, but she was slowly realizing by this point, after two months on the series and a few prison visits, that most of her preconceptions about prisoners were based on prison-break flicks, or 'heavies' in soap operas. *Pretty boy*. That was the phrase that came into her head when she first saw him, how she imagined he'd been referred to inside. What had his role been in the group, in the robberies he'd done? He had been in and out of Borstal young offenders' institutes since he was a child, so they said in the office, his sentences totalling thirteen years.

He began walking in her direction. She started filming him, automatically.

He was in his mid-forties, wavy hair layered in a crop that curled around his temples, strong grey eyes, effeminate eye-lashes. In the office he had seemed mischievous, flirting with most of the women as if it was expected of him. He told anecdotes, laughed provocatively at his own jokes. Everyone laughed with him.

Now she couldn't be sure whether he could see her. He was still some distance away, coming towards her. Within seconds, his face was almost filling the frame, and then he was standing next to her, taking the camera out of her hand.

'This isn't a home-video set-up, you know,' he said.

'I know. I'm filming you for –'

'For posterity?' He smiled.

'No, just –'

'A presenter who doesn't speak?'

'No,' said Ray. 'More like an interstitial. A journeying shot. In between sequences?'

'Ah yes, the "mood piece". The presenter's inner journey. A musical interlude.'

'Something like that. Unless they whack voice-over all over it in the edit.'

He chuckled, and reached for a pack of filters in the back pocket of his jeans.

'Yes, you're one of them, aren't you? "Don't mess with my art." But filming an ex-con walking around a prison telling you how it works? Is it really the right step towards the Turner Prize?'

Ray laughed.

'Come on, man . . .' she said. She was uneasy, but pleased to be talking with him in this way. She wanted him to like her.

'Artists and video, though . . .' said Nathan. 'Went to the last Turner thing, Tate Britain, and there was this reel of a boy smoking a cigarette, about eleven. He puffs it out, it reverses so the smoke gets sucked back in. Out–in. Nice idea. In–out. Shocking image. It repeats over and over, back and forth, and you see the smoke, the kid's face . . . so young. I started smoking at that age, like most. But it looked nasty, the grain of it, ugh. Shaky, too, on purpose. What's that for, just to be clear that it's not for telly?'

'Yes!' said Ray. 'Yes, exactly – I always think this with video art. Does it have to be so visually ugly to be taken seriously? Do you keep up with the Turner, then?'

Nathan grinned, sucked loudly on his cigarette.

'Surprised, aren't you?' he said. 'Look at you, you can't believe it.'

'No, not at all. That's not true! Your painting – you mentioned it the other day – it's how Nick found you, isn't it?'

'So you know all that, then? Yes, that's how Nick found me. I won some competition inside, and got legit. BBC – they love that shit. Sorry – "you" love that shit. Pardon me.'

'You're BBC here, just like the rest of us. You love it, you slag,' said Ray, chuckling and punching his arm.

A moment passed, a lost couple of beats. Nathan looked at her, narrowing his eyes. He spoke quietly, as though he was commenting on a point of interest.

'Don't take well to being called things like that where I come from.'

He frowned. She could see perspiration on his upper lip. She didn't know how the word had come out of her mouth; she had misjudged it entirely.

'You're a bit sharp. Think you're funny. Like to be sarky, don't you?' he said. 'I've noticed that before. Like to take blokes down a peg or two? I know your type. Worst kind of prison officer. The need to humiliate. Woman prison officer, that is.'

Ray felt a sudden panic. The conversation was slipping through her grasp.

'I'm sorry,' she said. 'I didn't mean that at all . . . No, Nathan. I was joking – it just came out. I'm sorry . . .'

'Got you!' he said, putting his arm around her. His face was cheeky, boyish again, as he squeezed her shoulders.

'What?' She coughed slightly, almost a hiccup.

'It's fine!' he said. 'I was taking the piss. Relax, will you!'

He exhaled smoke through his nostrils, laughing, and started walking away.

She watched his back, feeling a twinge of dislike for the way in which he moved. He had played her very effectively – imagining, correctly, that she would see him as a cliché – and he enjoyed the power. 'Mischievous East End gangster with an artistic side, a soft heart.' Something like that. His manner was slow, somewhere between a swagger and a dawdle, but she could foresee him scurrying like a squirrel when he needed to, aggrieved and fussy if things weren't as he wanted. It was impossible to place him in the context of his background – violence, robbery, repeated break-ins, hold-ups . . . He was right. She struggled to conceive of his world, and it embarrassed her.

Up ahead she could see four children in school uniform, deep red tunics with pleated skirts, long shorts for the boys with short-sleeved white shirts and dark V-necked jumpers. They were stepping carefully through the small river on the border of the prison. Two of the boys, no older than seven or eight, had their arms linked and were chattering. It was a seductive shot. The morning light was weightless, angelic, a shaft of innocence upon their small forms. She lifted the camera and captured it as best she could, holding the machine against her chest to keep it still.

Nandini's hut was at the end of the walkway of houses, set apart from the main gully, close to the main road. The sheet-metal walls were covered in rough beige canvas, and gently sloped inwards, pushing in on themselves, giving the whole construction a slightly unbalanced feel. A couple of birds scattered and flapped in a short tree to the right of the house, the prickly branches pointing vertically, like the outstretched fingers of a raised hand. Ray stepped into the porch, an area in front of the door fashioned by four wooden posts with a printed sheet tied above for shade. The cloth was vermilion red, spotted with white flowers. It billowed slightly above her head.

She hesitated before knocking. They had arranged the visit by ringing the governor's office the previous afternoon, but there was no way of knowing whether Nandini would be amenable to the intrusion. Ray could hear voices inside.

Nandini opened the door before she could knock.

'Looking for the doorbell?' she said, gesturing to Ray to join her. Her manner was friendly; she spoke as though she was giving Ray a wink.

Ray brought her hands together in namaste. There was a woman sitting on the floor, knees against her chest, her feet on a striped rug knotted in rough khadi cotton. She was wearing a ghagra, a type of long skirt, and chunni, a scarf dyed in the rural style – a single colour without print – in bold primary yellow.

'We've been expecting you,' said Nandini. 'Please, do join us.'

The hut was dark. It had fewer window holes than the stone huts. Two bulbs hung from the opposite ends of the room, emitting a low-wattage light. There was a bowl of fennel seeds on the rug at the centre of their circle, a crumpled pale blue cloth underneath it, a steel teaspoon thrust inside.

'Have some,' said Nandini, noticing Ray's eyes on it. 'You have had this before?'

Ray nodded and leaned forward on her knees. She scooped her left hand into a bowl shape, quickly pulling down the back of her shirt, which was riding up over her trousers, with her other hand, before taking the spoon and pouring the rough green seeds into a heap in the middle of her palm. Stunning, she thought, looking at the still shot in the centre of her hand, fetishizing the creased lines of her own skin, the thorny, caramel grooves of palmistry running in and out of the cushion of flesh under the seeds, the lined mound below her thumb. She paused. Maybe one woman could pour the fennel into the other woman's hand when she returned to film them together. It would be a beautiful close-up, the shot working to show their closeness.

'Are you OK?' said Nandini. She had paused for too long.

'Yes,' said Ray, leaning to offer the bowl to the woman, who shook her head and smiled at Nandini, nervously pulling down the hem of her ghagra, a thin copper bangle sliding down her slender forearm towards the wrist.

'*Yeh Hindi bolti hai?*' she said to Nandini. Does she speak Hindi?

Ray was aware of the woman's nose-ring, the surprising brightness of her teeth. She could have been any age from thirty to fifty. Her skin had the worn quality that came from years of exposure to the sun; her hair was mostly black with a few strands of grey. Ray could imagine her carrying water in a large mutka on the top of her head, like the women she had seen on the side of the road during the journey to the compound. She felt a little ashamed of the image as soon as it came to her, the way in which her mind had automatically placed the woman in a background of dusty greenery, balancing an earthenware pot; it was straight out of some backpacker's guide to India.

'*Yes. You can speak to her directly,*' Nandini replied in Hindi.

The woman twisted her head from side to side, to indicate that she understood. She had an underhand beauty; it was there if you looked closely. Her cheeks were hollowed out, giving a piquant intensity to the shape of her face. The eyes were watchful: brown pigment ignited with flecks of amber.

'*Your name?*' said Ray. And then, in English, 'Please?' This came out for some reason as 'Plis?', shortened to give the word an Indian accent. She saw Nandini out of the corner of her eye; she seemed to be suppressing some amusement. Ray found her own mouth mirroring the smile.

'*They call me Ram Pyari.*'

Ray nodded. '*And you were born where?*'

Ram Pyari giggled, and pulled up the pallu of her sari to cover her mouth. She glanced at Nandini and shrugged.

Ray smiled. '*You find my Hindi . . . a little strange?*'

Ray looked at Nandini for help. The three women colluded for a moment in a sudden burst of shared laughter.

'It might be your accent,' said Nandini, in English. 'Let me help.'

They talked for a while with Nandini repeating Ray's questions when needed, or rebirthing them in a smoother, faster version of the dialect. Ray asked about Ram Pyari's background, her early life.

She was born in Mundro, she said, a village near Sonigarh. She lived on her family's farmland with four sisters and two brothers. They helped their parents daily, waking at five in the morning and all working together – someone would give the cows water, someone picked up the grass. Her job was to collect cow dung, which they used as fertilizer for the wheat; she did this till ten o'clock, when the milk came in from the cows. The milk was used to make butter, ghee, yoghurt. The remainder was mixed with sugar and eggs to make rubri, a sweet paste that they ate as soon as it was made, with dallia, the ground corn mixed with water left over from the yoghurt. After this, they took the goats out to feed until five or six in the evening. No, she didn't know how long ago it was; she didn't know her age right now.

Ray leaned forward and asked a whole series of questions at once, trying to get confident with her Hindi. '*Did you ever get tired? You did a lot of work. Did you have dreams? What did you want from life?*'

Ram Pyari laughed, her eyes darting with shyness. She pulled her pallu over her mouth again, stuttering behind the transparent shift so that it looked like she was coughing.

She spoke quietly, an amused aside to Nandini. *'What is she asking? What kind of question is it?'*

Then she responded to Ray.

No, they didn't get tired. It was their life. Dreams? They didn't know anything else. She was a child. At night they played gilli-danda, a game of wooden sticks, until ten o'clock, when they checked the goats before going to sleep themselves. They loved it, all the children, they were like wild kittens playing together, so mischievous.

Then, when she was fifteen years old, she had to go and live with her husband and his parents. She had been betrothed since the age of seven. That was how you did it then; her parents had arranged it. He lived in another village. She was scared to meet him.

Her eyes widened with portent as she told Ray the story. *'That day, I cried and cried. How I cried.'*

Her parents sent her to his home with just one outfit to wear – a lahenga choli. She took five utensils and one sleeping cot. She sat on a cart pulled by two cows and it took her away for ever.

When she arrived she ran to her mother-in-law in distress. He seemed so old, so unfamiliar.

Ram Pyari clutched suddenly at her own arm in a panicked fashion. *'I held on to her like this.'* Ray watched the copper bangle shake around her thin wrist. Her physicality, the sincerity of the reconstruction – it gave her an eerie thrill.

Her mother-in-law told her to behave herself. But Ram Pyari didn't speak to her husband for a long time. It was a year at least. She was too scared. At night he slept elsewhere.

'*Then slowly, slowly, he came to me.*' She grinned, her face reflecting the memory fondly. '*He brought sweets. And I let him stay with me.*'

She was given a job in the village nearby, washing bottles for the pickle factory. But life was difficult. There was not enough to go around the joint family.

'*Dreams? If we had food to eat, that was enough.*'

She had one outfit of clothes to cover her body. At night she would wash it, and hang it over the sticks so that it made a tent while it was drying. Then she would lie underneath it, for modesty, and sleep. In the morning she wore it again.

Ray interrupted, her voice betraying genuine shock. '*Just one set of clothes?*'

Ram Pyari nodded, looking Ray up and down before continuing, as though assessing Ray's own clothing.

Ray put her hands over her stomach. She searched for a word to encapsulate the feeling. '*So . . .*' But her vocabulary was too limited. What would she say if she could? So extraordinary? A horribly patronizing word. Instead, she let the sentence float, unfinished, gesturing at Ram Pyari to keep going. '*Then what happened?*'

Her life became full of stickiness then, like the home of a spider. Everything was confused. Her husband's father died and his brother took all the land. They went to the town, Ram Pyari and her husband, to try to live there. They had two children by then. All of them went together on his bicycle and lived on the road, in the jhopadpati, the shanty town. He worked on a building site and she started ironing clothes on the roadside for people who brought them. No, she didn't go home to her parents' village. She had left her home for the husband's side; you don't go back, it's shameful. Things were very hard. She didn't like to eat with her husband. She waited till he was asleep and then she could relax. They weren't one of those couples who share the same plate when they eat.

She examined Ray's face, as if to assess whether or not she was understanding the story. *'As it is, I can't eat food that has been touched. If I eat from another person's plate I get a rash on my face.'*

She stopped and stared at Nandini, as if waiting for confirmation of something. Nandini urged her to keep speaking.

'Truth is, I never liked him. He beat me and then he expected me to lie down with him straight after.'

She lingered for a moment, glancing from Nandini to Ray. Nandini gave her a direct nod.

'Speak on,' Nandini said, the tone of her voice full of assurance, as though she was referring to a contract between them that would not be broken.

Ram Pyari frowned.

'He had a friend. He would come over, drink with him.'

She touched her nose-ring, her eyes shifting away from Ray's gaze.

'He began to love me. I also loved him.'

Ray nodded, hoping her face reflected support.

'Didi has explained to me that it was not right, what happened.' She gestured at Nandini, for whom she was using the term 'didi', older sister, as a form of respect, even though Nandini was probably younger than her.

'What happened?' said Ray, before she could stop herself. She had to know the end of the story.

'We gave him poison. They sat and drank together the whole night, the two of them, then we put mouse poison in his last drink.'

Ram Pyari looked over at Nandini, then spoke again with renewed strength.

'But it didn't work. He was still moving. Then I found his knife – he used to keep a curved sword, his talwar.'

She looked at Ray, waiting for a reaction. Her eyes held an element of challenge in them. Can you take this? they seemed to say. Ray nodded. She was transfixed.

'I cut him up into pieces and buried him under the earth of our hut.'

She stared at Ray, her eyes wide open, moments of sunlight highlighting the amber flecks.

'I felt very calm when I had done it. Didi knows.'

Ray looked back, deep into Ram Pyari's eyes. She could feel the humidity in the hut, a feeling of suffocation in her breath. The thrill had gone; instead she felt a damp swathe of depression around her neck.

'Is he here, in the same prison?' Ray asked, breaking into English to address Nandini without realizing it. 'Her lover?'

Nandini shook her head.

'He is in another prison,' she said. 'They write to each other. They've been writing to each other for almost ten years now. "My rose, life without you is unbearable." That is the kind of thing Ram Pyari asks me to write to him. He writes back the same – he must be getting someone to read and decipher it for him too, and write back. She sometimes says she would do it again, if she was given the chance. But at least she acknowledges that it happened now. When she first came here she denied it, like many of them do. Only after many sessions did I convince her that I was not part of the police or the government, and that she could talk to me.'

'Would you tell her I am grateful that she shared her story with me?' said Ray, rising to stand. She needed air, had to think about what she had heard. Ram Pyari was hugging her knees to her chest, her skin glowing from the increased light that was coming through the large gaps in the tin walls. Ray picked up her camera bag and pressed her hands together.

'Really moved that she spoke of it in such detail.'

She bowed towards Ram Pyari.

'Thenk you' said Ray, again inexplicably saying the word in an Indian accent. 'I mean . . . *Shookriya.*'

Ram Pyari continued to stare at her.

Ray walked away quickly, seeking solitude, shade, some relief. The sun was vicious, heading towards peak midday heat, the fierce white howl right on her head. She lost her balance a couple of times as she walked. She had broken her own rule again, willingly this time, and not known how to proceed, ill-equipped to deal with the ramifications of her questions. The detail appeared in her head with ghoulish fervour: she saw a close-up of Ram Pyari's face, strained with the necessary force, as she dragged at the knife, cutting through the drugged man's limbs, right to the bone. She imagined a hut not dissimilar to Nandini's – wires on the wall, a naked bulb swaying above the bed. She saw a portly man with booze-swelled face, the deep cuts in his fatty flesh, the reality of his blood.

She retched twice without throwing up anything. She walked to a tree and steadied herself against the trunk. The stench of old dung was overpowering. A wild pig furrowed in a ditch nearby with two dogs for company. She retched again.

There were a couple of charpoys up ahead, placed out in the field. The security guards were sitting on them, talking and smoking with inmates. She could see the pink turban of her neighbour; it shone like a beacon in the glare of the sun. He had killed someone too. Property, passion, or personal vengeance. She could hear Serena's voice coming from the opposite direction, behind the tree.

'That's great, Nathan,' she was saying. 'Just give me a

second. I want this kid in the shot too. He's so adorable. Get him to sit next to you with his mate.'

Ray heard the giggles and whispers of two children rise on the breeze.

'OK, go again, Nath,' said Serena.

There was a pause. Nathan began to recite a piece to camera.

'I know from personal experience just how damaging prisons can be for people who live in them. They pay for your food, your bills; you don't have to care for your family. That's why I believe something like this is so unique for the prisoner – this is a unique experience for me to witness it and I believe in it . . . Nah, I'm talking bollocks.'

He laughed.

'Sorry, mate,' he said.

'No worries,' said Serena. 'Go again and we'll cut them together. Just say whatever you're thinking.'

There was a pause.

'I know from personal experience just how damaging prison can be. You don't have to worry about work or bills; the prison system does it for you . . . Nah, I have to think this one through. How about: That's why I think this place is so positive, because it undoes the damage that prison does . . . Traditional prison makes the transition back into society even harder . . .?'

'Yep,' said Serena. 'Sounds good.'

'Here, they have to care for their family. They have to put food back on the table. This place, I think, is a unique and special thing. Something like that? What you looking at? You got my balding patch?'

Serena laughed. There was a springy quality to her voice as she spoke. It made her sound younger, coy in her response.

'Don't worry, Nath, I'll be good to you. You can't see it.'

'It's a sad day when a man has to come to terms with losing his hair,' said Nathan.

'Listen,' said Serena. 'I'm thinking about these kids. Do you think it works? I think it's good to have them sit next to you in shot, but is it too cheesy? They're so cute, though. Look at them.'

'Nah,' said Nathan. 'Don't worry. They were here anyway, dicking around with their kites.'

He chuckled. Serena joined in.

'Come on,' she said, laughing. 'Let's go again.'

He began the piece to camera anew, clearing his throat and projecting the words with a new confidence.

Ray left the tree and began walking back to the hut. She did not want to join them, or be discovered by them. A feeling of sudden desolation came upon her, tears stinging her eyes. One of the guards called over as she walked past the charpoys. He addressed her as 'Madam', and pointed over the outer line of huts, in the direction of Nathan and Serena.

Ray nodded and pointed back to her own hut. She walked around the perimeter of the settlement so she would avoid contact with either group. She passed the animals, the man beating out the sheet on the large stone, a couple of women visible through the doors of their homes. The village was quiet at this time – most people were at school or work.

Ray was lying down when they returned to the hut. She was thinking about Ram Pyari and her armour – the single set of clothes that had covered her body in the early years of marriage. She pictured Ram washing and wringing the same pieces every day, hiding beneath the tiny tent to save her modesty at night as the faded material gradually dried itself, hardening until it was wearable at dawn. She wondered how many outfits Ram Pyari had now; she thought of her nose-ring, the way it sparkled quietly in the shadowed unease of the hut. A prized possession.

Their voices were loud as they approached the hut. They sounded jovial and united.

'You all right?' said Serena as they came in.

Ray sat up.

'Yes, just taking five. The workshop went well this morning. Met a new female inmate. Ram Pyari. Interesting character.'

Nathan entered the space after Serena. He grinned at Ray, then went to sit on Serena's charpoy.

'This place . . .' he said. 'I can't get over it.' He slouched forward on the bed, taking a pack of tobacco out of the front pocket of his denim jacket. 'Science fiction. That's what we used to call it inside. Imagine a prison village where you could live with your family, we would say. Where your son can grow up with you. We actually used to say that. And here we are! I'd like to find out where they got the idea for this place.'

He seemed entirely different from the man she had met in the morning – respectful, cheerfully subservient to Serena, acknowledging that she was the boss. Still playing with their expectations of him, though, thought Ray – the astonishment tweaking his voice nicely. She didn't trust him.

Serena was unpacking her camera. She wired it up to her laptop.

'Listen, I need more tobacco,' said Nathan. 'Am I going to have to go into town for that?'

Serena kept her eyes on the screen, moving her finger over the touchpad, scrolling forward through the footage. 'Ray can take you in after this. But first I need her to do something. Check this out,' she said to Ray, turning the computer so that Ray could see the screen. 'Tell me what they're saying here.'

She had filmed the guards smoking and talking with the inmates on the outdoor charpoys. It was the same group Ray had passed on her way back to the hut.

Ray pressed one of the keys of the computer to increase the volume. She was irritated by Serena's presumption in dominating her time, but she knew that one of them had to 'look after' Nathan and it fell to Ray as the one who could speak the language. However unconventional his role, Nathan was still the presenter of the programme, authorized to make requests of them at any time. She moved closer to the screen, trying to catch the dialogue.

One of the inmates was telling a story. The guards and two other inmates were listening to him. The speaker was a tall man in his forties, stately, with small round sunglasses, a large grey shawl wrapped round his torso over a long white kurta, gold hoops in his ears in the Rajput style. He leaned forward on one charpoy and made a series of pronouncements to all of the men – whether adjacent or facing him – with an insistence that demanded acknowledgement. His audience provided this assiduously, nodding in assent or murmuring to show that they understood him as he unrolled his story. He was a terrific presence on screen; as a viewer it was hard to look away.

She concentrated on what he was saying, sifting through the rippling force of his language to catch the back end of a sentence.

'It's something about being left somewhere,' she said. 'Something to do with . . . He's saying, "I was told to just wait here. Just wait. Look after him and don't move. We are going to get help. I thought they were going to get the doctor. And then who shows up? The police, of course. And

I'm just standing there. I'm standing with a dead body and I don't even know it. And that's how your life changes. It becomes a road that allows you to walk in only one direction."'

She watched the man talk. He spoke clearly, with purpose, had a gravitas that was helped by the attention of everyone in the scene, including the guards, who were as casual and relaxed as the inmates, differentiated only by their uniforms. The young guard who had helped Ray with her luggage was there; he turned and took a light for his cigarette from an inmate in a knitted brown gilet, a man with darker skin and wild eyebrows, sooty beard growth that patched his chin at random, giving him a slightly demented quality. The guard inhaled deeply before turning round, and then, in a surprise move that made Ray jump slightly, he addressed the camera directly. He shook his head, pointing at the cigarette in his hand.

'He's telling you not to show him smoking,' said Ray. 'He says, "Don't show my beedi. This beedi, it's not for showing on the TV. You're not to show it to Thakur Sahib, the governor."' She could hear Serena's voice off camera. 'Sorry – don't understand. Sorry – no Hindi.'

'Maybe we need to start going out together for stuff like this?' said Ray. 'That first guy seems to be talking about his crime. I think he was using the camera as a way to try to tell the story of his innocence. According to Nandini Gupta, the counsellor I was with today, they think we work for the governor, which would make sense. It kind of defuses the scene, if they're just putting on a show for us.'

Serena was abstracted. She blew through her lips as she fingered the touchpad, dismissing Ray's words.

'It's not a big deal,' she said. 'I was just getting background shots to have with voice-over. It's a more effective use of

the budget if we film separately and you do the interviews with villagers – we've only got a few weeks here. I'm
mostly doing Nathan's pieces to camera anyway. These are
just nice moments of actuality that I've been bagging as I
go along.'

'Still, Nandini could translate for you on site if you needed
it,' said Ray. 'She's pretty good at getting the gist across and
her English is great.'

'Right. We'd have to pay her, I suppose. Anyway, what
about this?' Serena pressed the touchpad so that the images
scrolled forward to another scene.

It was an older woman, showing Serena around her hut.
She looked to be in her mid-sixties or so, white hair tied back
into a bun, watchful eyes behind wire spectacles, a repeating
twitch in her nose. She was showing Serena a wall of pictures that had been given over to worship. The full-page
graphic illustrations of different Hindu incarnations of div-
inity were garlanded with necklaces made of thick metallic
threads and stuck in rows on the stone backdrop. There was
also a framed photograph of a man in his sixties; it was garlanded in keeping with the tradition of showing respect for
the deceased.

The white-haired lady was alternating between talking
and praying. She took a large fan, made of peacock feathers,
and waved it in the air near each picture. Then she closed
her eyes and pressed her palms together, muttering a tuneful mantra, opening one eye briefly during the process to
check if Serena was still filming her.

'She's saying . . . It's about freedom,' said Ray. '*Azaadi*.
Freedom . . . She says that she prays for freedom for everyone in their family in the next round of . . . not sure what
she means. Maybe it's a round of decisions regarding release?
She says they are god-fearing people. She is telling you:

"Understand that we are very, very devotional . . . Those who are devotional are the ones purifying their hearts . . . they have nothing to fear, they are only . . . at peace." Or maybe it is: "they are only cleansing their spirits"? It's tricky – some of her language is a bit difficult to understand.'

'Is your Hindi up to this?' said Serena. 'I thought you were fully bilingual.'

Ray flushed with annoyance. 'This is about local accent, a bit of regional vocabulary. Some words are tricky but I've got most of it. There's no problem. More importantly, we need to discuss how we're going to try to get a relationship going with any villagers we film so that we're not just getting them performing for the camera like this.'

'It doesn't matter!' said Serena. 'No one's going to hear her speak in this sequence. I just wanted to get her in her hut as part of a montage on village life – the fact that she's praying is pretty good too. There's nothing wrong with performing for the camera. This is hardly a major storyline, just good background village colour. Jesus!'

'All right, all right,' said Nathan. He stood up and put his hand on the curved metal of the door, pushing it so that a thick slice of sunlight entered the hut, causing Ray to squint as she watched him. 'It's like this: I need a chaperone – this tobacco is almost over and, honestly, you want to avoid seeing me go through withdrawal. So let's go now. Which one of you girls is up for it, then?'

They hailed an auto-rickshaw on the main road. The driver was a thin slip of a kid, hunched forward on his scooter as he waited for them to take their seats in the yellow and black shell behind him. Nathan shouted over the wind as they bundled through the traffic. He was almost inaudible.

'Sorry?' Ray said.

Nathan shouted again.

'HOUSE-PROUD. I said HOUSE-PROUD.'

He leaned over, his shoulder falling against her. He moved closer and gestured so that Ray offered her ear.

'This guy is quite house-proud, don't you think?'

Nathan pointed at the decorations that the driver had put up to customize his vehicle. Velvet had been sewn into the corners behind their heads, patched with plastic gemstones and ornamental glass pieces. On the dome of the ceiling there was a religious mural featuring Ganesh, the elephant god, and his followers. Right at the front, near the steering wheel, there was a small hanging deity. Ray hunched forward to work out which one it was.

'I think that's Laxmi,' she told Nathan.

He shook his head and laughed, putting a hand behind one ear.

'LAXMI,' she shouted, enjoying the air in her lungs as she belted out the word. 'GODDESS OF WEALTH. LAXMI! STOP WINDING ME UP!'

'OK, OK,' mouthed Nathan, spreading his arms with a grin. 'Forgive me, OK? Forgive me.' He put his right hand over his heart.

The bazaar was crowded. People were walking on the dusty road amongst vehicles and camels, beside a raised footpath presenting small grocery shops or jewellery and sari houses. Ray stepped out of the auto and waited for Nathan, her toes suddenly pressed against the sludge of a muddy enclave, her maroon-painted nails peeking out from her open-toed chappals.

'Is there any need for that?' he said, pointing at a huge mound of earth, hay and rubbish – plastic bags in green and blue, ragged bits of bright paper, vegetable peelings, plastic bottles. 'Why not clean it up?' he said, arching his back, uncurling from the journey.

A white bullock sat on the peak of the mound, stretched forward, resting its chin on the rubble, its eyes calm and unblinking.

She exhaled with annoyance, turning away. She was not attracted to this person, this creased man with his floppy greying hair and dirty expression that lurched between ages, and yet he had affected her. His teasing that morning had thrown her off balance. She searched herself, trying to understand it. His mockery angered her, but for some reason she was susceptible to his sudden patches of humour, the attention he gave her. She wanted him to rate her, in the straightforward way that she imagined he did with all women, sifting the wheat from the chaff.

The afternoon passed quickly. She sent Nathan to a paan stall to buy tobacco and cigarettes while she paid the driver. He befriended the owner and came away with stained lips, chewing betel, a satisfied look on his face. They checked emails in adjoining booths under the strip lighting of a dank cybercafe. She told him she had to buy something Indian to wear for a party with the governor, and any other official meetings that might come up. He offered to accompany her.

'Sounds fun,' he said, over a bottle of soda at a roadside grocery line-up. 'Get yourself a nice bright one. I've seen them drying in the sun back near the prison – stunning, they are . . . big-patterned prints, really sharp, biting . . . the colours they put together round here . . .'

In the clothes shop, they sat together on the low cushioned benches that adjoined the lengthy strip of mattress where the wares were displayed. By now they were starting to get used to being regarded as a curious couple, stared at by the people in the marketplace, and by the staff in the shop. A man sat opposite, cross-legged, and eyed them with lazy interest, a comfortable roundness filling out his kurta. He asked for information on their tastes – shades, textiles, the extent of embroidery or embellishments they preferred. He maintained a regular, non-committal smile, which gave him a lordly quality, interrupted only by the odd sideways bark, aimed at his staff.

'*Raju! Bring Sonu and Guddu from the store. Bring water, tea. Go quickly! What are you doing looking at me?*'

Ray mentioned possible colours as a starting point. Two boys brought them hot coffee to drink while saris and lahengas were taken from various shelves behind the man, and rolled out for their perusal.

'Ah, wouldn't she look beautiful in that?' said Nathan to a shop assistant, after he had unfurled a sheet of thin silk in peacock blue, printed over with a paisley pattern in pale green.

'Fucking beautiful,' he said to Ray quietly, almost whispering, causing her to nudge him. 'So fucking beautiful.' He spoke slowly and looked her in the eye, so that the swear word was lengthened and prominent, laughing as she looked away in embarrassment.

They made their way through various establishments, with most shop-owners welcoming them in as a married couple. She was drawn into the charade but it made her uneasy. Nathan played the chivalrous Western husband to a demanding young Indian wife, whispering things to her between the bantering exchanges with the shop-owners. She settled upon a purple ghagra choli, in the local style of embroidered cotton – a long skirt that brushed the floor, with short waist-length blouse tied with a shoelace rope at the back. She looked at Nathan for reassurance as she emerged from the curtained area at the rear of the shop that served as a changing room.

'It's fine,' he said in a low undertone, waving and smiling at the manager, who was showing his approval with a nod from a counter full of shawls and chunnis. 'But I'd rather see your legs.'

She changed back into her own clothes. As she stood in front of the mirror her own facial expression seemed disingenuous. She was not an idiot; she could hear him. It felt like he was still playing his designated role, but exaggerating it to humorous effect. Was it for her benefit, to make a point, set things back in their correct place? These interjections felt inappropriate, and yet they were some kind of compliment. There was no way to curtail them without it seeming stiff, misplaced, as though she had taken herself too seriously.

He bought a piece of material for himself, to hang on his wall back home. When the sun began to mute its colour and spread a pale, fading yellow over the horizon, Ray suggested they take a bus back to the prison instead of the auto. 'Nice to travel with locals, don't you think?' she said. 'Higher up, a better view.'

It was a straight route back to the prison. They found a bus stop for buses going in the right direction, and waited with two women in their twenties. A bus appeared within five minutes, rattling its long body through the traffic. It was painted in a series of blues, from dark to sky blue, the coordinating colours of an official's uniform. Inside, the light was fluorescent, giving a greenish tint to the dark interior; the double seats were filled with tired men on the way home from work, leaning against the horizontal iron window bars for air.

They talked about television on the way back. The BBC jungle, the department, Nick Rabin's empire in the Local Action Programmes Unit, and the series itself – the other prisons that Nathan had visited on camera.

'She's a bully, though, isn't she?' he said. 'Serena. She's trying to bully you. Put you down. I know her type. You want to stand up to her more when she gets like that or it'll get worse.'

Ray frowned. She didn't like the language. 'Bully' implied that she was at the mercy of Serena.

'I don't know what she's doing,' she said. 'I don't really know her.'

When he produced a small pouch of white powder from his pocket, dipping the tip of his index finger down to where it lay on his lap, out of vision, Ray did not flinch. Somehow it seemed the most natural thing in the world, to see him lick the stuff away, dip his little finger in next, and hold it out for her, near her mouth. There was no real reason for her to lick it off, but a brief flicker of her tongue, a snake's twitch, and it was gone, in her stomach, out of the way. She was certain this transaction was not some kind of sexual act. He did not seem to set it up that way, barely looking her in the eye as he offered the finger. It was more like some kind of bravado on her part. A way to disregard Nathan's wilful machismo, his scythe of provocation that she knew was supposed to nick her skin, upset her sensibilities, expose her lack of worldliness.

'What is it?' she asked, once the conversation started to flow from her mouth in a ceaseless, urgent fountain of word association.

'I think it's just a bit of speed. Don't worry,' he said.

'Got it from the paan guy, did you?'

He nodded and patted her shoulder.

And she didn't worry. Instead Ray told him why she wanted to make this film, how important it was that they found a way to represent these people as human beings rather than as ciphers or ideas. That she was Indian and that the British audience would see this film and understand what being Indian really means. How much beauty, honesty, trust, dignity and inspiration there was in this country. That it was more forward-thinking, this project, than anything you could find in the West. Inmates were living with their families and not choosing to reoffend. This was rehabilitation in its most humane and effective form. That the only point of understanding how to use film was to try to use it in a positive way, to spread light not darkness – to find hope in the human situation and communicate it. That the inequality killed her. She knew that this sounded trite, but she didn't know how else to say it. It was inequality after all, wasn't it? The words fell out of her, one after another. She didn't know how to approach inequality, she said, the economics of it, but could they not start somewhere, with the inequality of representation, of respect? Television – such a powerful tool, millions potentially watching – was the least elite tool, the most egalitarian. Could they not start by disembowelling the colonial legacy, the established hierarchies of East and West? The old idea of the rural 'noble savage', of 'foreign' natives living in a natural, village state that was ultimately less civilized than the West – could they not begin there and show just how ridiculous this idea was? Corrode the history, the legacy on which it traded, by superimposing the truth of the present?

Nathan listened to it all. He let her speak.

Outside, the sky shuddered along, disjointed and thunderous as it somersaulted to black, a film reel out of sync with the murmuring clatter of their conversation. On the coach the people who joined or left the double seats when the flickering neon came on to announce a new stop – the woman carrying a baby wrapped inside her sari, the slim young men carrying heavy bundles of cloth, the old man with his stick, yellowing lungi and fragile body, who nearly fell down onto her when the bus lurched as he walked past to the back of the bus – all of these people dissolved into the night as she spoke.

4.

The alarm woke Ray at dawn. It beeped only twice before her hand flicked the switch to silence it. She wondered if she had slept at all, but her head felt clear. The third night since arrival was over. She was relieved that it was time to wake up, get ready, act in some way. Serena was still asleep under a loose white sheet printed with purple clover and green leaves. She lay on her stomach, an arm hanging over the side of the bed, not even seeming to breathe. Ray picked her way past, to the bathing area, carrying a comprehensive bundle of clothes, towels and make-up in her hands. She had learned by now to do everything in one go – washing quickly under the tap, and using the small mirror which was tacked to the brickwork for everything else.

When she emerged, Ray could see Serena's face, now turned towards the shower muslin. She lay on her right cheek, her nostrils flaring slightly to suggest the movement of air. A strong nose, thought Ray. In a way it was too large for Serena's face, but was somehow insignificant when she spoke, her hard blue eyes dominating the view, demanding recognition. Watching it like this, rising out of the innocence of sleep, the nose seemed to represent some kind of sincerity that was absent when the face was animated.

Why was Serena here? What did she want from this place?

Serena probably had her own opinions about Ray. Maybe it was natural for them all to scan each other like this, like any other group of animals learning to live together. It was dark when they were in the hut, early morning or after sunset. They were like moles in their burrows. Only, instead of exaggerated hearing and smell in the shadowed space, Ray felt it was actually her vision that seemed to be intensifying.

Later, after eating from their breakfast tiffins, hair still wet from their showers, Serena and Ray prepared a list of questions that were deliberately non-invasive. For once, Serena was in agreement with Ray. It was the first round on camera and anything deemed too personal had the potential to upset their careful movement inside the perimeter of the lives around them.

'We have to get to know them first,' said Serena, 'and then once we have a relationship going we can film the things that matter to them. The real stuff comes later, the tension between what people want in life, and what they get instead. That's the stuff that makes you care about people, understand them, feel for them – if you see their battle actually happen on screen, of course. It's always there, though; it's just a matter of uncovering it, making the contributors feel like they can show it when we are around.'

They were to work together today, the three of them, filming with one of the families. First, they took another walk around the village for Nathan's benefit, escorted this time by two of the guards. Serena and Nathan smoked with the guards as they walked. Ray brought up the rear, checking the background elements in each hut – the schoolgirl sitting on a rug on the floor with a slate and chalk, working on maths; an older woman, maybe her grandmother, propped up on her charpoy by a fat cylindrical cushion, drinking from a steel tumbler. A wild pig that grunted and emerged from the bush with two young boys as they went round a corner.

She saw Serena inhale, her mouth around the filter of the

cigarette. It seemed so sexual, this open space, closing in on the shaft of a cigarette. Laughter was in the air, a shuffle of voices between them. The guards here, what would they think about a woman smoking with them so easily and effortlessly? She had a sudden flashing image of the mouth filmed through a lens: the long suck, the shine of brown lip gloss, Serena's thick lips forming the ring of 'O', the ridges and indentations of tiny lines in the pale white skin around her mouth, and then the release, the slow blow of smoke in an offhand exhale, almost post-coital, the smoke dissolved within seconds.

Getting in with the contributors. It was a standard television phrase. Serena was being attentive, smiling continually, responsive to anything the guards said in their broken English. Her manner was faultless.

Ray ducked into a hut to watch a woman silently stitch with a sewing machine, surrounded by mounds of material. The woman stopped and looked up, her face emerging from the pallu of her sari, which was draped over her head. She stared at Ray, waiting for her to do something. Ray deliberated, wondering how to address her, how to explain this pre-filming stage of straight observation.

She could hear Nathan outside.

'These rabbits,' he said. 'They're . . . how do you put it? Are they pets? Or for something else?'

Serena laughed.

'Nathan, you're such a joker,' she said. 'I'm not going to try asking them that.'

Nathan called out loudly, his voice carrying over the huts. 'Ray!' he shouted. And then, soon after, in a murmur: 'Where's she gone?'

Ray left the hut without speaking to the woman, hurriedly bowing, her hands in namaste.

'There you are,' he said. 'I just want to try something. Can you ask this man a question for me – directly, I mean, not through these guys?' He flicked his head over at the guards.

Ray nodded, and came up to stand with them. Nathan wanted to speak to a man with a wiry profusion of beard, a cloud of hair that puffed out widely and down to his chest. He could not be more than thirty. He was poised in an effort-ful way and seemed to be concentrating on standing very straight on the porch of his hut.

'Ask him what he did,' said Nathan. 'What got him here.'

Ray spoke to the man in Hindi. *'Which category of crime did you commit?'* she asked politely, as if she was asking which kind of food he liked best.

He turned to Nathan and spoke in English, loudly, as if Nathan was hard of hearing.

'Category two-nine-nine,' he said. 'Homicide.'

'Homicide,' said Nathan. 'Right.'

'Yes, sir. I killed a person!' said the man, slapping a palm against his own chest, eyes twinkling as though he was shar-ing a joke with Nathan.

Nathan nodded, with indulgence, like someone in dia-logue with a savant. They moved on in the tour.

'This is the thing,' he said to Ray and Serena, his voice lowered as a guard walked past. 'Is he proud of it, d'you think?'

His tone contained an element of mockery, enough to make Ray uncomfortable. She suddenly felt protective of the inmate, almost defensive.

'I think,' said Ray, 'that he was trying to show you how well he can speak English. Or maybe he found it amusing that you were asking a question to which you must know the answer, as everyone here is in for the same category of crime.'

Her comment was overshadowed by Serena, who had walked on and was shouting from the water tap, up ahead.

'What?' shouted Nathan in return, speeding up to get there himself.

'Hurry up, you guys,' yelled Serena. 'Just saw the time. We've got to set up for the shoot. We're late. Need to get this done while the light is good.'

The idea stayed in Ray's mind, swinging like a ball tied to a pole for a racquet game: was the man showing off, or was he putting the film crew in their place, gently mocking them? Either interpretation was possible.

She looked back at him. He was in conversation with one of the guards, the taller one whose hair was a mixture of grey and white. They stopped speaking and stared back at her, remaining silent until she had left the vicinity.

Through the viewfinder, the picture was suffused with a grainy wash. It caused Ray discomfort.

She checked the shot at intervals, trying to increase the exposure manually without degrading the quality of the image too much. She did this secretly, knowing that Serena would not approve, that they would have a difference of opinion. Serena would expect to use a bright hand-held light, which would blast all the layers of light and shadow out of the scene. It would make the image crisp, but vulgar – devoid of any detail.

Serena moved the charpoy so that it was in line with the daylight coming through the hut wall. The entry point was less subtle than in their own hut: a single square hole functioning as a window, instead of latticework. She shifted her attention to the small prayer table, the four sculpted deities upon it of different sizes, a garlanded photo in their midst. There was a lit candle on a bed of rose petals at the centre of the table, a stick of incense exhaling a thin curling sigh of smoke to complete the picture. She looked over at Ray, gesturing with her head and raising her eyebrows at the table. Ray responded with an attempt at swivelling the camera round to point it at the table, realizing, too late, that she had attached the camera too firmly to the tripod. Her movement destabilized the whole apparatus so that it toppled to one side.

Serena's response was urgent but pressed under her breath, an emphatic whisper.

'No! Not to film separately – it's to liven up the backdrop. Do you want to just move it there? I could put the whole thing behind the bed, and we could have it in the left-hand side of the shot?'

Without waiting for a response, she nodded at an undesignated place somewhere over Ray's shoulder. It was a gesture towards the woman whom Ray had seen sitting in her front yard stitching. She was in the kitchen, clattering pots and pans, sitting at ground level and hidden by a waist-high wall from the main room. Ray switched the camera off and walked around the wall.

The woman was warming water in a pan on the stove, crouched in the squat position, the pallu of her sari tied around her waist. Ray automatically searched out her feet, remembering the thick bangle she had seen circling the woman's ankle, but her lower half was completely covered. She was lining up small glasses for tea. Ray stood at the back of the kitchen space, wondering how to begin the conversation. It was not so easy without Nandini. She did not know the word for 'excuse me' in Hindi, and, as it was, it didn't feel right as a phrase here. She considered a name that would be appropriate to the woman's station, like 'Auntie-ji', or, given that the woman could be of similar age to Ray and addressed as a respected elder sister, 'Bhen-ji' or 'Didi'.

The woman stood up, turning round with a large ladle to scoop milk from a steel tureen balanced on the top of the fridge.

'Excuse me!' said Ray in English, panicking.

The woman jumped.

'Sorry,' said Ray. '*Mein* . . . I . . . *mein* . . . sorry . . . *hoon.*'

The woman gave Ray a polite smile, and continued with the ladling.

Ray watched her, ashamed at her own clumsiness. Again, she saw the image in front of her as if through the viewfinder of the camera: the ladling of milk, so natural, so seedy almost, this domesticity with the dirty yellow light bleating out from one corner of the ceiling. It could be an enigmatic portrait of the woman's private preparations, encased in near-silence; a close-up of the clean movement of the fluid as it slid into the vessel, shot through the blur of the glass itself, the green border of the woman's chunni at her neck. But the camera was screwed into the tripod on the other side of the wall, quietly rejecting any spontaneity, and when Ray looked at it she was immersed instead in Serena's gaze.

Clearly aggrieved, Serena made a noise of exasperation to indicate that she was tired of waiting. She put her hands on the table, picking it up and flicking her head at the scene set-up, before taking it over, the religious artefacts teetering as she walked.

'You mind?' she asked loudly in the woman's general direction, beaming. 'It's OK?' She placed it down, brandishing a bold double thumbs up, eyebrows raised.

The woman nodded, almost bowing, and retreated further into the kitchen.

'I was just asking her,' said Ray.

'What?' Serena was adjusting the piece, kneeling on the

floor. 'Can you just check how much you need of it in the frame, and I'll move it over.'

'I said, I was just doing it, I was just asking –'

'What? Come on, we're running out of time. This is supposed to be observational, as it happens – remember? No time for fussing. And the light is changing.'

'Why are you moving the table, then?'

'Eh?'

'Why did you move it? You changed the scene, put the charpoy at an angle. Why did you construct that set-up if we're supposed to be documenting it as it happens?'

She found it hard to hide her anger, did not care about the pedantry bleeding through her voice. Serena was approaching the shoot as though it was a travel programme, putting together an appealing backdrop, getting the lights just right.

'Jesus Christ, you're not serious, are you?' Serena came over to join her. 'I'll check it myself. This is taking for ever!'

She switched the camera on, waiting for it to power up. 'Sometimes you really sound like a –'

Her voice fell silent for a few moments.

'You've whacked up the exposure. What the fuck is this?'

Ray felt the heat rise to her cheeks. She burned momentarily with a kind of hatred for Serena.

'I just wanted to stay within natural light so there was some detail.'

'Oh my God. This is disgusting. What is this? Why didn't you get a light out? I assumed it was fine. It's like you have no concept of time. What have you been doing with the kit all this while – just pissing around?'

Serena walked quickly to the camera bag and began furrowing around inside it. Her nostrils were tense, a frown deepening in her forehead.

'I didn't pack any,' said Ray, collecting an umbrella to

shade her from the sun. She made her way out past Nathan and the husband, both quietly smoking on the porch, walking quickly to avoid questions. She crossed over the walkway and back into their own hut to look for the lights.

She emerged ten minutes later. The young girl she had filmed on the first day was at the water pump, applying pressure to the handle with her unique, jumping rhythm. Ray surveyed her from the verandah of her own hut, taken again by the wholehearted force of her movements. Today she was dressed in a salwar kameez in pale blue, the same purple cardigan fitting closely against her upper body. As Ray watched she saw an older woman appear, and remembered her as the woman whom Serena had filmed praying in her hut. She carried a small dog against her chest, and pressed its face away every now and then, teasing it. She reached the water pump and addressed the girl. Ray could not make out the words, but assumed she was urging her to hurry up, to let others in. Her tone was harsh around the edges, openly admonitory, tangled up with the dog's yelps. The girl matched the woman with a response that was equally sharp, her face sullen.

These were the moments in which Ray was interested: the unconstructed, unattended moments of revelation. Sometimes she wished that she could film every scene, every person secretly. There was something honest about it. The camera changed everything – it altered the situation you were filming, got people on their best behaviour.

When she first started in television, five years ago, she had been fascinated by a particular piece of kit: spectacles with cameras hidden in the lenses. A reporter had famously used them to go undercover at a battery farm in North Yorkshire. They were now in common usage, but for ethical reasons – privacy and contributor consent to filming – were reserved for investigative journalism. Ray had always dreamed of using the spectacles to film ordinary people going about their lives, to interview them unawares, as though she was just having a chat. This seemed to her to be perfect, the least intrusive way to record a situation authentically – to look at someone at eye level, through a camera which they couldn't see, to speak to someone in this way, free from the anxiety of being recorded, or to watch them, document the emotion in their facial expressions. It was different from the current fashion for 'reality TV', where contributors were placed in an environment of surveillance cameras, with their enthusiastic agreement. Her desire was for the complete opposite: to reach a kind of truth, a sincerity of experience, by filming people without their consent.

The interview was decent enough, once it got going. They filmed the husband and wife together in a double shot that moved to close-up on one or the other at different times. Serena operated the camera and Ray asked the questions. She took things slowly, beginning with the basics of daily living as usual – a catalogue of practical happenings including the family activities that one would not usually associate with a prison: cooking meals, walking the children to and from school, their current jobs (working for a tailor in the village market) and their financial situation. They were happy with the school, which mostly took children from the local town outside the prison; it meant their kids were mixing with them, getting a good education.

Then Ray ventured into talking about the reunion between husband and wife in the village. He had recently been released from the traditional prison further north in the state, after six years of good behaviour, and allowed to come to the open prison.

'In this place, there is this thing . . .' said Ray, feeling again the frustration at the seeming lack of variety at her disposal when it came to words in Hindi.

'A special thing . . . that you have to live here with your family?' Ray continued. 'It means it is seen to be part of your duty as a husband and father. How did it feel to meet again and live together after six years? Your first child was grown up? Had your wife changed after so much time apart? Now you're a family again, how is it?'

His response was entirely different from the nods and murmurings that she'd been receiving up until this point. She'd assumed, of course, that he'd just make some noises as to how it had been a positive, much-desired experience, a release from all of the hardship endured on both sides since the conviction.

'I don't like it,' he said. 'They don't like it. But we have to do it, so that I can be here. Otherwise I have to go back to that other place, that hell. It is the rule of entry here, that your family comes and lives with you.'

There was a pause, and then the woman spoke. It was difficult to place her tone, which dragged with monotony.

'The family becomes joined, and you eat together, you live together,' she said. 'You eat together, you live together. You can educate your children if you earn money. The state should give us something to help us start up again. But still, you eat together, you live together.'

Ray instinctively looked over at Serena at this point, more out of surprise than anything else. Serena winked at her briefly. Even though there was not a running translation in English, it seemed clear to her from the expression on Ray's face, the corresponding shutdown of the husband's expression, that there was an obstacle.

'*You don't like it because . . .*' Ray left the sentence open for him to complete. Nothing happened. She tried again.

'*Why don't you like it?*'

He looked at his wife next to him. Her eyes were looking away, with a middle-distance glaze, as though she couldn't hear the question.

'*Is it hard to make ends meet?*' said Ray. '*It must be difficult to make enough money?*'

'No,' he said. '*It isn't that. I just don't like it with them. I don't like it. What else is there to say?*'

It was his last answer.

They packed up the kit quickly, attempting to pull a drawstring around the silence.

'It's the governor's party tonight,' said Ray, as she condensed the tripod.

'You go,' said Serena. 'I've got footage to log. It doesn't need both of us to keep him sweet. Take Nathan. He'll appreciate getting a drink, being out and about, I'm sure.'

Back in the hut, Ray washed lightly under the tap, her back pressing awkwardly against the dividing sheath of yellow muslin. She left her hair dry to keep the experience brief, emerging wrapped in a towel after a few minutes, walking to the corner in flip-flops to keep her soles clean.

Serena sat on her charpoy. Her posture was determined – cross-legged, back straight, surrounded by sheets of paper, computer in her lap. She wore headphones with large earpieces, the thick black connecting band pressing down tightly on her skull so that elfin strands of blonde hair peeked out of the sides. She focused on the screen, two lines marking her forehead to indicate that she should not be disturbed.

Ray felt hampered as she dressed for the governor's party, restricting her movements so as to reduce her noise, a little embarrassed by the gaudiness of the ghagra choli she had purchased with Nathan, after days of filming in practical trousers. Serena looked over at her from time to time, in spite of herself, a blank quality to her eyes, as though she was just looking around whilst absorbing the sound in her headphones, then immediately tapping on the touchpad again to continue her notes. Still, Ray felt absurd in her presence, pulling the shoelace rope to tie the choli behind her back, looking down at the long cotton skirt, the detailed waterfall of embroidery stretching over the pleats. It was as though she was playing at dress-up, somehow. She picked up the chunni and draped it around her torso, covering herself up.

'Just going to the toilet,' she said.

Serena leaned in closer to the screen, as if to emphasize that she couldn't hear what Ray was saying.

Outside, Ray pushed the door, moving the concave sheet of corrugated tin in three stages so that it came to rest at the point now deemed by agreement to indicate that it was 'closed' – the empty slot of light between door and wall reduced to as thin a line as possible. She stood and looked out over the settlement. She was aimless, had no need for the toilet, but felt a strong need to escape Serena's company for the remaining hour before the party.

There was a slight chill in the air. She looked over at the pump. People were beginning to gather; the light was deepening; a few children in school uniforms were on their way to the central peepal with a kite, muddling around the animals, tossing exclamations back and forth. It was the onset of early evening. Ray could see two men settling into chairs in a front porch further up the walkway. They wore white vests and dhotis, thin sheets of cotton wrapped around their legs and knotted at the waist like towels. One of them opened a pack of cards, speaking in a low voice. The other lit a beedi, inhaling luxuriously and resting against the back of his chair, one leg crossed so that his foot rested on his other thigh. He nodded, acknowledging the words of his companion. Ray gradually placed his face, the lean, strong limbs, the deep matt-brown skin. He was the man from the rock, the washerman they'd seen on the governor's tour.

To her right she could see a distant figure, a woman carrying an orange bucket. Her height and directness gave her away: it was Nandini, her figure moving seamlessly in the direction of the pump, long plait swaying down by her hips. Ray waved, pulling her chunni around her shoulders self-consciously.

'Hello,' said Nandini as she diverted from the path to approach Ray's hut. 'Going desi for the evening?'

Ray smiled. 'Governor's party.'

'Looking nice,' said Nandini. 'This style of embroidery, it's called Pakka Bharat. Very sturdy and long-lasting. This thick chain design with the tiny mirrors is very popular here. I'm sure he'll approve.' Her eyes twinkled lightly as she looked at Ray, imbuing her last sentence with a moment of mischief, similar to the way in which she'd welcomed Ray to her hut for the workshop.

'Oh right,' said Ray with a smile. She warmed to Nandini's teasing. It was gentle, hinted at an intimacy between them. 'That's important, of course?'

'Quite unusual to see it in purple,' said Nandini. 'Normally you'd see red, green, yellow, a local design like this.'

'Listen,' said Ray, speaking quietly. 'Thanks for yesterday. Ram Pyari – that access, really, it was fantastic.'

'Were you OK? I thought you looked quite pale after-wards.'

Ray smiled again. She was really starting to like Nandini. There was something familial about her.

'Maybe,' she said. 'But I appreciate being able to get that close. It's invaluable, it really is.'

'Don't worry, you can stop being the BBC for just one moment,' said Nandini. 'Ram Pyari's story, it's quite com-monplace.'

Ray raised her eyebrows.

'Such violent crimes? I thought . . . I thought you had to be on good behaviour to get here? I suppose, yes, that means good behaviour during your time in prison.'

'Murder is a violent act,' said Nandini. 'What did you expect?'

'Yes. Of course. I'm being very tedious, I'm sure,' said Ray. 'Can I ask you something? Is it really true that no one reoffends here? I keep thinking about that aspect of Ashwer, am trying to understand what that means. I think it's the key to understanding this place.'

Nandini looked directly at Ray, pausing as though she was scrutinizing her for hidden intent. Ray held her gaze and waited. Eventually, after a few moments, Nandini spoke.

'No reoffending, yes,' she said. 'But it's interesting that you should mention this right now. Something happened last month, actually, to do with events from last year. One of the prisoners went missing – and I only know about it because . . . well, I can tell you, but I don't want you mentioning it to the governor.'

'Sure,' said Ray. The swiftness of her own response sur-prised her. This thought – of the promise she'd just given away so easily – scratched lightly, like an eyelash caught in her eye.

'Shall we take a short walk?' said Nandini. 'I can get this water later.'

They walked to the banks of the river, Ray lifting up her skirt to prevent it trailing in the muddy patches of the path, the mirrored patchwork in her clothes reflecting the sunlight. She could sense the stares of villagers as she passed them, but her awkwardness was dissipating. She felt girlish in her outfit, feminine, wrapping her chunni over one shoulder and round her waist like one of the women in the village as she negotiated her way over the uneven ground. She was enjoying the companionship of Nandini, who began her story as they walked.

'First, I can tell you this. I am released for one day each week, to attend a college in town, where I am working towards my magistrate's diploma. I have started offering advocacy to inmates here voluntarily, separate from my counselling job, and I am trying to finish my degree. I am used to studying; I have my M.Com. already, from before marriage. I grew up in a town some distance from here and my family believed in education. Anyway, there is a security guard in the college. And last year he disappeared.'

Ray nodded. Nandini continued, speaking with a mixture of speed and caution, like a person running along an uneven track.

'He had not told them, actually, that he was from here, the open prison. From Ashwer. Usually you declare it when you work outside. That is what all these inmates do who leave for the day to work in the local market or town. But he didn't. And so when this happened, and he disappeared, I revealed it . . . I assumed he had told them. The authorities began an investigation. They were worried, naturally; he was a murderer and he had gone missing.'

She raised her eyebrows and waited for Ray to agree with her. Ray mirrored the movement. She registered her own eagerness and tried to censor it.

'Gradually, slowly, the police found out everything. I knew him, Lukhi. He had come from a village not far from here. He used to work in the fields – gathering rice, that kind of thing. Seeds, planting, cutting. Something had happened with property in his family. His brother came and found him one night, with a gang. Lukhi himself had his own people and they all fought with lathis – these sharpened wooden sticks – which is what they do in these rural places.'

She paused for breath. They looked out over the river. It was empty at this time, a light breeze coming with the chill in the air. Together, they found a dry patch of earth and sat down. Nandini went on, the story tumbling out with urgency. At moments, she stopped, looked around to check that they were still alone.

'He had managed to kill two people in this dispute, and they were both his brothers. He was given twenty years. For good conduct after six years he transferred to this open prison. His in-laws had been looking after his wife and son; she then came here. He had a new baby with his wife, here, at Ashwer. There was a homeopathic doctor in the prison who did the delivery. He kept himself to himself, thought of himself as more educated than the other prisoners. He has left now, the doctor, his term expired.'

Ray nodded her head.

'Anyway, back to Lukhi . . . His youngest brother was left behind when he came to Ashwer. The older brothers were dead, of course. Just one left behind. He was brought up to study and to go to college in the city. This happens sometimes in the village; they make one of them – the youngest – go to school and all. So this is the thing – imagine

71

this, Ray. His brother grows up burning with the desire for revenge. It is a common feeling, no? He wants to revenge his older brothers. Chandru is his name. He is the only one left – Lukhi killed all of his siblings, destroyed his family. He finds out that his brother is in the open prison here. Anyway, this is what happened. Chandru came up to the main town and got together with a nurse there. He told her, his girl-friend, about Lukhi, and more to the point he offered her a deal: "You have to seduce him and entrap him in love, and if you manage it I'll give you fifty thousand rupees." She was a divorced woman with two children and she needed the money.'

Nandini paused, waiting for Ray to register the drama of the story. Ray nodded, urging Nandini to continue.

Two children appeared on the other side of the river, run-ning to throw some stones into the water, cheering at the noise. Nandini lifted her head and looked across at them, revealing the acute definition of her jawline, the purpose in her stare. There was such an unarguable quality to her, thought Ray. She seemed so definite. There was the sense that you could rely on her, on the veracity of the telling, the accuracy of her moral compass.

'The woman agreed. She needed the money. She came to my college when Lukhi was on duty and she visited him regularly. He would come out of the prison for his shifts every day and she would drop by towards sunset, before he had to leave. Slowly, slowly, she got to know him. Then she went back to her boyfriend, Chandru. She told him, "I have made him fall madly in love with me. He is ready to do any-thing I ask of him." And they hatched a plan.

'Then one night Lukhi told his wife, "I am going out of the open prison. I am going to get grain" or "I am going to see my family in the village", something like that he would have said. But to go out at night you need special permission and he didn't take permission. He was mad for her, the nurse. He went to Rishi Bazaar in town, to the Hava Hotel. They took a room there and she put five sleeping pills in his drink – Trica sleeping pills – and she danced for him. But he wouldn't fall asleep. And her boyfriend, Chandru, did not turn up. So in the end she took her chunni and strangled him while he was sleepy. It was four thirty in the morning and she left the hotel.

'Look, everyone who runs away gets found, that's why they don't run away from this place. One man has even been discovered after fifteen years. Anyway, the police found Lukhi's body and worked it out. She was convicted. Chandru managed to evade arrest because there was no proof he had hired her. But then something happened.

'She was in prison for only a month, then she was released on bail. Then she was back in prison and released after four or five months. You see, she had the fifty thousand rupees he had given her. If you have money, you don't stay in prison long.

'I didn't like it. I thought . . . well, she needs the money, she wasn't inside for long and she can do this kind of act again. What kind of signal does it send? And she is very beautiful and is so young, just twenty-three or twenty-four years old. I met her. She said to me, "I did it for the fifty thousand. I don't feel happy. But I needed the money." Anyway, Lukhi's family – his wife and kids – have gone back to the village so none of them are here now. This is all in the past.'

They walked back towards the huts, stopping at the pump for water.

Ray stood to the side of the apparatus, watching Nandini push the long handle. She thought of the nurse dancing in a hotel room while a man lay on the bed and watched her, drinking her sleeping pills on cue so that she could take the chunni from her neck and strangle him. This was not a story she could use in her own programme: it was in the past tense; none of the characters were left in the prison. But still, she wanted more.

Nandini increased her force on the pump handle. Ray checked her watch and said she had to go. She passed the men who were playing cards as she walked back. She felt less self-conscious in her outfit now, emboldened by her time with Nandini. She smiled as one of the men looked up, and put her hands together in namaste. It was the washerman, holding three cards in one hand, rubbing a thumb around the neck of a brown-glass bottle as the other man considered his next move. His eyes were not friendly. He made a noise to attract his partner's attention, somewhere between a whisper and an alert.

'Chhhh!'

His friend looked up. When he saw Ray, he made eye contact with his partner briefly. An understanding of some sort passed between them; she couldn't work it out, but she could definitely see distaste of some sort moulding his expression. Without warning, he spat to the side of the table, taking care to avoid the material of his white dhoti. He stared back at her, holding his cards down against the table, as if to suggest that he would not continue with his game until she had passed.

Ray brought her hands back down to her side and walked on quickly.

Serena was crouched with the camera in the forecourt of the hut across from them when Ray got back. Ray was surprised to see her filming and slowed her steps to watch the scene as she returned down the walkway.

There was a rare feeling in the air; it was soaked with hilarity: everyone was laughing. The neighbour whom they had interviewed earlier, the one with the thick silver bangle at her ankle, was sitting in the yard at a table with a sewing machine, while her younger son, aged around three, was leaning back against her knees and 'stitching'. Her husband was nowhere to be seen. The little boy pressed his foot against the rubber pad on the ground and the needle thrust itself repeatedly, the machine chugging loudly. He pulled a piece of material through, so that a random, nonsensical stitch ran all over the cloth. He shrieked with joy, looking up at his mother for validation, turning to his teenage brother, who was standing behind him to the left, and increased the pressure of his foot, pumping it again and again, pulling the material in different directions so that the stitch careered all over the cotton.

Ray squinted at the camera. The red light was on, so Serena was definitely filming this, it wasn't a dummy shoot, even though the footage was not something they could really use at all.

The boys' mother convulsed with laughter, looking up at Serena with large, merry eyes, her body hunching repeatedly with the giggles, chandelier earrings wobbling at her ears. Serena laughed too, seemingly genuinely; it was a light, gasping noise, as if she was trying to control herself enough to film the scene. The two women were connected by this shared amusement: Serena shook with the same mirth as the mother as she steadied the camera against her chest. Even the teenage boy had a smile on his face, one hand drawn across his body to hold his arm loosely at the elbow. Occasionally he guffawed, abruptly, a kind of pride on his face as he registered his brother's bursts of enthusiasm.

The little boy beamed. He was dressed smartly, a little

shirt tucked into his shorts, his thick, muscular black hair combed to the side and oiled, his small face incandescent, glowing in the early evening light as he shouted out in glee, doubling, tripling his efforts. His joy was infectious. You wanted to scoop him up and kiss him on the cheek, be part of it, touch it somehow, thought Ray.

Still, she was surprised at Serena, leaving her log to invest time in this when she could be working, using the tape stock on something that would ultimately be thrown away. She usually seemed so obsessed with results, with the project on camera. To see her like this confused Ray.

'Cute kid,' said Ray, when they were both back in the hut.

Serena nodded, taking the tape out of the camera.

'Adorable,' she said, smiling at Ray. 'Just too adorable. All the kids in this camp, they've got something magic about them, don't you think? I'm always filming them. Tragic, I know!'

Her manner was lighter now, frivolous, almost comradely. She seemed refreshed by the experience.

'Well, it looked like the whole family was loving it,' said Ray.

Serena sank onto her charpoy and lay her head back against the pillow. Her blonde crop was damp against her head, the sweat causing her hair to clump slightly, revealing the pale underlay of her skull. Her cheeks were pink with the effort, her forehead a little shiny. She looked at her watch.

'I wonder what's in the tiffin this evening,' she said. 'Always seem to be starving a good hour before it comes. I'm glad you're taking Nathan out for a proper feed at the governor's. It can't be easy for him, living like this – just eating at set times, the heat and mozzies – in spite of his hard-nut schtick.'

She laughed, taking a swig from a bottle of mineral water

at the side of the bed, shaking it so that the remnants swilled around at the bottom.

'Warm water. No cold beer at the end of the day, or glass of wine. I suppose there're fags to break things up, and apparently Nathan's got a stash of rum if we need it. Don't get me wrong. I'm fine with it myself. I think it's good for us. Character-building stuff. But I'm just saying . . . it's not easy, eh?'

Ray murmured in agreement, relieved to be sharing some solidarity with Serena.

'You're doing better than me,' she said, straightening her ghagra and transferring some make-up into a small handbag, to take with her. 'I'm the one who's running to the loo all the time.'

5.

The governor has sent a car for them. It comes with a driver called Zafar. He is a short, neat man in his early twenties, quietly alert at the wheel, managing the texts on his mobile phone with his left hand as he drives Ray and Nathan from Ashwer to Sanghvi's place for the garden party.

The car is muggy with silence and fatigue. The sun is on its way down and a rivulet of traffic comes towards them out of the wild sheen of golden light that blots out any road signs or adverts on the way. The cars come at them with unwieldy vehemence on the relatively narrow road, pumping their horns, large trucks jutting right up against them, face to face, before going past. Zafar swerves and dances their car through like the rest, dodging bullock carts and motorbikes with ease. That is how they all work here, thinks Ray – understanding the flow, unconstricted by conventional traffic rules. Still, there are a lot of accidents on these roads, and it is important to remember to do longer journeys for filming while it is still light, so that Zafar is not left to do these acrobatics in the dark with only bleary headlights for guidance.

Nathan is quiet, introspective, leaning against his passenger window and looking through the glass. She does not interrupt his thoughts.

They pass through a small village, lessening in speed over potholes, moving past low walls plastered in film posters, paan and cigarette stalls, men sitting near their scooters. Everywhere there is the mixture of language: all the signs, the scrawls, the painted adverts on the walls adorned with Hindi–English in block fonts and curls. They form a contrast to the billboards on the highway, where towering fonts form English words to advertise everything from communications to Raymond shirts, using pale-skinned models.

'M. R. Traders' is written in large, statuesque white capitals against a scarlet headboard that crowns a stall crammed with jars of sweets, numpkin and hanging supari strips. They stop to buy mineral water. Zafar nips out of the car with some cash from Ray so that she doesn't have to do it. She thinks how he will attract less attention than her. She winds down the window on her side and watches him run across the road, dodging scooters and pedestrians, overtaking a woman whose hair is tied tightly in a bun of white and charcoal grey, her sari printed in red, black and yellow, minimal gold jewellery at her ears, wrists and neck. She is clutching a blue plastic bag in which Ray can see some long white vegetables – maybe mooli again. She wonders if it grows locally.

Ray unbuttons the small case in her lap and brings up the camera, simultaneously switching it on with her finger and thumb. She is interested in the woman's expression. The woman is frowning at the effort of negotiating the mud on the side of the road whilst carrying her groceries, hitching up her sari to reveal thin chappals, the leather thongs binding her feet like parcel string as she steps over an uneven, scarred patch of ground. Her gait consists of a lumpy staccato movement instead of a smooth walk. She takes her time to come closer, eventually looking in at them with the same frown as she passes the car, lingering momentarily in the frame as if to understand Ray's need for surveillance. She looks directly into the lens, then at the two of them sitting together in the back.

Ray moves the camera immediately so that it points

instead at Zafar, who has reached his destination. She finds herself blinking with embarrassment. The woman walks on. At the stall Zafar brushes up against an older man who is buying tobacco, dressed in a white turban and tent-like white material that reaches the ground. She can see Zafar making his apologies by pressing his hands together and smiling, his body and face much looser, more relaxed than she has ever seen them during their brief interactions in the car. He runs back over the road in a couple of seconds, the figure losing and regaining focus in the shot as he gets closer, hugging the huge bottles against his chest. Ray watches his face for signs, parts of his personality that might be left over in the crinkle of his eyes, or even a smile. But, instead, there it is: the zipped, polite clarity as he hands over the bottles, wipes down the windscreen and starts the car again.

She leans forward, to speak to Zafar. They converse in Hindi, Ray finding an overtly deferential tone creeping into her voice. She is aware that she is trying to create the kind of banter cushioned in equal terms that is expected in London, but senses that it may be seen as a little odd here, considering most people speak without adornment to the drivers who are routinely hired along with cars. Words like 'please' and 'thank you' remain in English as she talks, constantly appearing and festooning their dialogue, twirling around her sentences as though she is presenting her Hindi like some kind of gift for the recipient – one that, of course, has not been requested. Most awkward is the gaping hole of the word 'aap' in her mouth, used instead of the more intimate 'tum' or 'tu'.

'*How long have you been driving?*' she asks.

'*Seven years,*' he says.

'*How old were you when you began?*' she continues, trying to catch his eye in the mirror.

He indicates to turn left and uses the loud confusion of new traffic as a chance to ignore her.

Sanghvi had been given a house and field as part of his appointment, an isolated patch of land off the motorway twenty minutes' drive from the prison. Ray and Nathan arrived at about eight o'clock that night. Zafar parked the car among the jumble of vehicles at the side of the house and Nathan gave him a wink as they left, saluting him with his right hand.

The governor's garden was almost full to capacity. There were about thirty people, the men in kurtas of white or beige, the women forming a spectrum of darker colours in their saris, salwar kameez, pyjama kurtas. Above, against the sky, no buildings distinguished the skyline, no clouds imposed on the space.

Nathan began talking as they made their way to the back of the garden. Ray watched him, surprised by the gentle quality of his movements. He seemed to have already softened in the minutes since leaving Serena.

'Look at that sky,' he said. 'It's fucking amazing!'

She looked up. The colour was indigo, utterly clear.

He began to describe the light and shading of the moors and river near Newcastle, back home in England. He mostly did portraits when he was inside, he said, but this one landscape had got to him. The sculpture of the earth, its troughs, bushes; how things changed in such tiny ways as the day went on, slight changes; how vicious it was to do the sky, how difficult. He described the thumping grey of the water that washed over the stones without let-up, polishing them hard.

'It felt like it was pounding on my thoughts,' he said. 'Bashing away like that.'

'You went there to film?' Ray said.

'It was the first time,' said Nathan. 'First time I was with the people who had the key, if you like, walking round with the officers, on that side of the door. We filmed their whole routine, from dawn till nine at night – meals, exercise, art, everything – then it was lock-up time, and I left.'

He had an almost sheepish smile. Ray nodded.

'I left the place loads of times before that, though, really. Came out onto the moor and just stood there, looked out, smoked. Did it all day, whenever it started getting to me. Which was probably every hour. Long filming day: fifteen hours. I'm a chainer, like you've seen. Up to two packs a day. No one noticed.'

A light pattern of music beat its way towards them. An expansive raag, the low vocal elongated over one note, unadorned by tabla or sarangi. It was humid. Ray felt the dampness at the base of her neck, the hot sheen on her forehead. There were crickets in the grass. The first people at the buffet table turned away with full plates, allowing the line to move forwards. She thought of their driver.

'Shit, I need to give Zafar some money for dinner,' Ray said, touching Nathan's arm. 'Give me five minutes. Don't go anywhere.'

She passed the buffet table, then stopped, as an afterthought. At the front of the queue she asked one of the serving men to make a plate of food that she could take out.

'For the driver,' she said to the couple whose place she had usurped, flicking her head in the direction of the cars. They looked perturbed – either at her audacity, or at the idea itself – although she was not sure if they had heard her. She chose cashew pilaf, brinjal and onions, muddy black urad dal in a steel bowl on the side of the plate, some mango pickle. To work out what he might like, this felt oddly intimate.

'Here you are,' said Sanghvi, as she turned around. He used his arm to bring her into a circle of four people.

'This is Ms Ray Bhullar from the BBC.'

Smiles and mutters of acknowledgement.

'She has come all the way from London to make an example of us, our policy here. They are filming with us for a while.'

He smiled, the lower round of his chin skimming a cravat-style folding of paisley silk at his throat. His eyes were friendly, and he was groomed for the night – a side parting to his thick hair, the casual shine of oil or pomade.

Ray stayed long enough to meet everyone in his group. She was introduced to one civil servant and three prison officials, the latter including a curvaceous woman dressed in a khaki uniform, her wavy black hair falling forward onto her chest. Ray could see Nathan through the throng, leaning against the white wall that supported a row of potted plants, and she was anxious that it might seem as though she had dispensed with him before mingling with the governor and his guests.

'Ashwer is just . . . more and more intriguing,' she said, speaking to the group, but heard only by the governor. 'Such a gamble, as an experiment in self-reliance. But it seems to work. As an ecosystem, I mean.'

Sanghvi nodded. 'You have settled in OK, then? Been meeting and greeting? What, *yaar*, I heard you got ill. So quickly?' He winked at her, a momentary crinkle of warmth in his face.

'How did you know that?' said Ray. 'Wow.'

She was genuinely impressed. Then she realized it was absurd to assume that only she was observing and report-ing, when she was obviously under constant surveillance herself. Had it come from the security guards? She had a quick flashback to her daily trips to the toilet next to the hut, crouched over the cloistered hole in the earth as the waste tumbled out of her, the quiet moans. Had someone heard her?

'I'll get you a doctor, don't worry,' said Sanghvi. 'He's a good guy, speaks English – if any of the others need him too. Anyway, aren't you supposed to be hardy, you BBC journalist types, out climbing mountains with your kit and conquering native communities all over the place?'

'Conquering!' said Ray, spluttering out a laugh. *'Kya baat hai!'* What a thing! 'But we're hand in glove with you. We're your guests. What's to conquer? We are here because we admire you. The ambition. The nerve, in a way. You know that? Seriously, though, I was thinking about this last night. Regarding the recidivist level alone, you've got virtually no one reoffending in over twenty-five years. That is one hell of a statistic.'

'Kya baat hai!' said the governor, repeating her words with approval. 'Foucault – *Discipline and Punish*. Have you read it?' He began using a more serious, commanding voice, so that the rest of the group stopped their individual conversations and turned to listen, even though he was facing and addressing Ray.

'Foucault talks about how prison is always going to produce delinquents. It's the nature of the system. It isolates inmates in their cells, even though man is a social being; it gives them useless tasks to do, for which they will never find employment outside. And prison also creates delinquents, indirectly, because it makes their families destitute.'

Ray looked back through the garden, suddenly remembering Nathan again. He raised his glass at her, high up so that it was visible above the heads between them. She pointed at the plate she'd made up, explaining to Sanghvi that she had to leave.

'For the driver?' he said, turning so that his expression was visible to the rest of the group, a patina of mild amusement that he wore lightly, with ease. 'He will have been fed by the kitchen along with the other drivers, so you don't have to worry about that.'

Ray covered her embarrassment.

'OK,' she said, 'I'll take this over to Nathan.' She pointed across the garden.

'You are veg, yes?' said the governor, looking at the plate. 'I forgot.'

She quickly surveyed the plates of the others in the circle. They all seemed to have chosen vegetarian food. She had noticed the key distinction in the governor's voice, and was not surprised by it: veg/non-veg signified a lot more than just food in this country. It was a kind of shorthand for the kind of person you might be. She looked at the governor's hands, wondering if he was non-veg. He was not holding a plate, just a glass of red wine, which was half full.

Vegetarian meant that you were probably Hindu, one of the dominant majority, spiritually active or aspirational, unlikely to drink alcohol or smoke cigarettes, 'pure' in sexual practice (none outside marriage, relatively demure within marriage, heterosexual, naturally). Non-veg stood for an attitude that could only be termed licentious. The phrasing had always fascinated Ray. For a start it put veg at the centre, establishing it as the right way to go about things; and the addition of 'non' always felt to her like it signalled perversion of some kind. Meat, poultry, fish – all these things were also expensive, high up the food chain, indicating luxury, indulgence, higher earnings. To opt for something that was not plant matter was to choose a different way to line your stomach: eating food that was dense, bloody.

Nathan was rolling a cigarette when she got back. He

didn't want the vegetarian things she had chosen so Ray began to eat them instead, avoiding eye contact and the attendant need to speak. She did not know how to re-enter the intimacy of their earlier conversation.

Around them, people talked in their groups. A tumble of voices, an odd stab of excitement, a piquant laugh or exaggerated groan within the solemnity – these displaced parts rose through the air. Behind Ray someone said quietly, 'You can't take these things for granted. Whenever a system is questioned, it is forced to defend its vulnerability. I mean it. It is like Engels says: anything genuine will be proved in the fire, the rest will be forgotten.'

'That guy,' said Nathan. 'I wonder what his deal is?' He was referring to the governor, now standing with a couple near a table dedicated to mineral water, nodding and dabbing his mouth with a napkin.

'He's supposed to be an extremely liberal force for change,' Ray said, swallowing a mouthful of brinjal. 'Provocative. Gets into trouble for proposing the kinds of things he does. As regards penal reform, at least. He's what they call an "IAS Officer", elite branch of the civil service. This gang he's collected here, some of them must be up from bigger cities like Delhi – maybe there's a conference on at that big fort hotel we passed on the way, or something. Anyway, we've got a sit-down interview planned with him. I'll know more after that but I'm just going on the cuttings from the research in London. We've met him a couple of times now; we're still getting to know him.'

'But I mean what's his score, personally? Does he live alone, what matters to him, why does he do it?'

'I'm not sure,' said Ray. 'I haven't seen his set-up at home. Hard to know, isn't it? Anyway, what matters to you?' She felt regret before she had even finished the sentence. Do not assume you can be relaxed with this person, she thought. Too intimate. Learn from your mistakes. But she genuinely wanted to know, that was the problem – and now the words were out there, part of the suspension of dust, warmth and cigarette smoke in the air. 'Did you leave someone behind?'

Nathan took a swig of his beer. He didn't seem to mind the question; there was something confessional about him tonight. He was urgent, energetic: his speech ran so quickly, fell over itself in the attempt to get ahead. She wondered if he had taken some more of the speed while she was away. It was very likely. Such a drug was easy to take discreetly in these surroundings; he'd just have to dip a finger into a pouch in his front pocket, lick it off quietly.

'Mariella,' he said. 'I still remember the first moment I saw her. She walked in, this white dress right up high . . .' He sliced the side of his hand halfway up his thigh, forcefully, so that it hit his faded jeans with a thump. 'She knew there was a light on her wherever she went that night. A spotlight, like a dancer on stage. At the bar, or on the floor. I tried to paint it, but it just turned out cheesy. Kept coming out as a halo, a full-body halo, and she was no angel.'

Ray nodded. She suppressed the desire to ask more, kept her mouth closed. She was held by his eyes. They shone under his long eyelashes, as if his pupils were filmed over with tears, but there was no sense of melancholy.

'So we had the kid, Michael. But I went in for the big job. Eight years it got me, and over the first year she stopped coming down to the prison. Naturally. And he's grown up, doesn't really know me, the boy. She's got her latest bloke. There you are. Mariella.'

Ray frowned in sympathy. Behind Nathan, five or six figures were sitting on the steps leading to the house, drinking and talking. A mild wind rustled the plants now, carrying traces of scent from the blossom on the fence. Ray looked at Nathan intently, urging him to continue, without speaking. She didn't trust her words or intonation; the tiniest of punctures would be enough to deflate the fullness of this moment.

He talked about being one of them, the community they had inside. The lost years. The years speed up after twenty-five anyway, Ray would find that out soon enough, but when you're inside they slip away like sand through an egg timer – you wake up and someone tells you it's your birthday, again. He came out when he was over forty. Not satisfied – that was something positive. This was the other side of contentment. The loss of hunger, thirst, ambition. Something never ventured. Except for the weeks filming on this series, during the three years since coming out he had slept late in the day, smoked through the night, looked out at the sky in the early hours from his flat in Bayswater, high up, a tower block. With his head through the window he was the only listener, receiver of all these sounds – an open ocean of noise. The hugeness of it threw him, how it went on for ever, the London sky like that, with everything hidden inside it – the fear, the different needs, the shock and harm it contained, the lack of control people had over their lives. Sulphed up, all that powder in him, alone, no sleep, speeding his tits off, willing himself through the night.

They made their farewells to the governor. He called over a waiter, speaking to him in Hindi.

'He's asking him to pack dessert for us,' Ray whispered to Nathan.

They carried the box, a white cube of cardboard, over to the car. Ray sat in the back with Nathan and opened it, revealing eight gulab jamuns, semolina balls drenched in honey syrup. They seemed debauched to her, somehow: the density, the rich texture . . . She could smell the hovering sweetness.

Nathan dismissed them with a flick of his hand.

'Not for me,' he said, winding down his window as the car took off.

She left the box with Zafar when it was time to get out. He shrugged and took it as though this was part of his duty, putting it on the passenger seat and looking out through the windscreen, awaiting further instructions. Ray felt a sudden seediness in the exchange, this assumption that he would want their dessert.

'*I mean,*' she said in Hindi, '*only if you like it? You can check it, if you like?*'

Zafar frowned.

'*Madam, do you want me to take it somewhere?*'

'*No,*' she said. '*No.*'

The hut was humid, the smell of mosquito repellent dominating the room, along with the sandalwood flush of shampoo. Serena was watching rushes on the computer, her hair still wet.

'Did you use that Mysore soap?' said Ray, throwing herself down on her bed so that her feet were hanging off the end. 'Smells nice.'

'Mmm-hmm,' Serena murmured. She paused a scene on the screen, then shuffled through a moment in which Nathan was grimacing, so that each frame stuttered out a different phase of creasing, frowning, even a cough, until his face lost all force and came to rest in blankness for a period before he spoke. She paused again, scrolled back even more slowly, until the beat before his piece to camera began, then she typed the time-code of minutes and seconds marking the shot, which appeared in the bottom corner of the frame, into a spreadsheet on the computer and wrote notes beside it.

Her face seemed drawn in hard lines. Ray admired the way that Serena did not need to look over even momentarily, did not succumb to even a cursory glance.

'So, we talked to Sanghvi,' Ray said. 'He's a strange fish, isn't he?'

Serena nodded.

'Wants to have dinner with me, talk. He told Nathan he didn't need to come. Quite funny. I do like him, though. He's interesting.'

'Why is it funny?' Serena said. 'You're supposed to be the director, aren't you?'

That night Ray heard branches tap the corrugated tin above them, the door rattling loosely in its frame. She lay in her sleeping bag and thought of the animals on this land. She could hear sounds out there but had no way of identifying which animals might be making them. It was colder now; the wind brought a bite that would need to be dealt with. How did they stay warm at night here? She thought of the stories hidden in each hut in the village; how many stories to each hut? All forty-eight sets of people in this social experiment had their tin roofs shaking in the wind together. She thought of Nathan and his confessions, which had opened an unexpected space in the midst of those people. She imagined him now, wearing his solitude in his bed, a thick fleece of protection against the cold, sleeping alone in his hut as a matter of survival. There was something contained about him, perhaps after all those years of sleeping alone. Ray couldn't imagine him sharing a room or even a bed as he slept.

6.

Rana Pratap was gesticulating as he spoke, the stream of language swelling and increasing in speed until he reached an abrupt, confident climax, adjusting his sunglasses on the ridge of his nose and pulling forth his waistcoat, breathing in deeply, the Nehru collar slotting into place around his neck. It was conceivable that he would turn and ask for water, thought Ray, swallow it and begin again in the manner of a professional speaker behind a lectern. He glinted like a Mafia man, the small golden hoops vibrating in his ears as he spoke. He was the man on the charpoy in the footage Ray had watched with Serena, the man who had been telling his story to the guards and other inmates as they smoked.

Behind him, the ridged orange sandstone of the quarry rose and intercepted the heated blue of the sky, the intense colour daubed with cloud. Ray felt dizzy, almost drunk with the heat, and yet emboldened by the scene. To Pratap's left, four labourers worked in relay: one hammering, two collecting the stones in bowls above their heads and dispatching them to the fourth, who was shouting instructions from the steering wheel of a large truck. The air had density, peppered with the sepia haze of rock debris suspended in the light. It was thrilling, combustible, like gunpowder.

'He says he's going to stay here now, in the village,' said Ray to Nathan, who was waiting for her translation. 'He's bought a plot of land and he's marrying his daughter to a local businessman, so when his time is up at the prison, he's going to settle here rather than return to the northern part of the state, where they are from. He says he's been here for five years now and he's built up this whole quarrying business from scratch, that a man can really be something if he doesn't fear the future. A man studies for twenty years and then makes his field – his area of expertise is what he means, I think. He says he did that when he was back in his old neighbourhood, from the age of twenty until he was thirty-eight, then he came to the prison. Now he has a new field – this quarrying business – he's started again and built it over the last five years and it's paying off.'

'Hm,' said Nathan, grunting and nodding to show reception of each sentence.

On the way to the pit the three of them – Nathan, Serena and Ray – had travelled together in Pratap's truck. It had been an attractive opener for the quarry sequence, their subject hoisting his tall form confidently up the narrow steps of the truck, then reaching down with a smile to help Nathan up. Pratap had stopped the truck at a flower stall to buy a long string of marigolds, which he had arranged on his windscreen for good luck, winding part of the long strand around a small statuette in the centre. It was a visually intoxicating moment, saturated with saffron petals, incense smoke and market hubbub. Ray filmed steadily through the side of the stationary truck. The radio mic on Pratap captured his assertive bark at the seller to not cheat him. It was a different voice from the one he used to communicate with the crew – more aggressive, less smooth, an interesting suggestion of the way in which he might act when he thought the cameras were not on him.

The sounds of labour rose behind Pratap as he waited for his next question. He opened his mouth as though he was about to issue orders to one of his workers.

'Ask him if he found it difficult to start work after coming from a traditional prison to the open prison,' Nathan said, maintaining eye contact with Pratap.

Ray began the question in translation. Serena interrupted within seconds.

'This isn't working,' she said, pulling down the camera. 'I don't know what you're doing with eye lines. He's looking at you, Ray, but he needs to be looking at Nathan as though he's speaking to him, doesn't he? Or the viewer's going to be confused. Yes?'

'Yes, I'll tell him, but the main thing is that he's very lucid. It's good stuff,' said Ray. 'I need some eye contact with him, at least while I'm asking the question. He's not going to trust me otherwise.'

'Sorry, Serena,' said Nathan. 'What can I do to help?'

Ray asked Rana Pratap to continue, stopping the response after seconds to explain that he should look directly at Nathan, not at her.

'Sorry,' she said. 'That's how we film it.'

Rana went on with his sentence whilst looking at Nathan. Ray interrupted again.

'Would you start again?' she said. 'From the beginning of your sentence. Or it won't make sense. My questions are going to be cut out, you see, when we edit and . . .'

Serena stopped the camera and rolled her eyes at Nathan. He shrugged in response.

'Look, this is not –' said Ray. She caught herself. She was speaking over Pratap once more.

Serena's comments during filming were beginning to affect her. They were tiny, sharp, biting moments of pedantry, but gathering weight – a small mountain of proposed evidence like iron filings on a magnet. Added to this, Nathan was immeasurably different when Serena was around, as though any warmth or agreement with Ray was out of the question. It was a childish triangle, and Ray was tiring of it. They only had each other to reflect the story, the three of them, and increasingly this shared story was being distorted.

'I'm sweating my fucking nuts off, standing here and repeating things over and over,' said Nathan, directing his frustration at Ray. 'Not to mention this guy. Fuck knows what he's thinking.' He glared at her, his nose reddish in the heat. 'And I don't suppose you've got any sun lotion, as usual. More to the point, when are we going to eat? I'm tired of waiting for those fucking tiffins day in, day out. Can't we get lunch somewhere proper for once?' He lifted a bottle of water and groaned, rubbing the sweat from his forehead with the cuff of his denim jacket. 'Can't you organize some cold water too, while we're at it? I don't know about you, but I'm about ready to throw up on this shit we get delivered; it's always bloody warm. Surely one of these guys can get us something as simple as fucking cold water?' He gestured at the men who were standing around them, watching.

Ray waited for him to calm down, forcing herself to stay professional.

'Look, we're nearly done,' she said. 'I'm sorry, I know it's hard. I'll get one of Pratap's workers on the case with the water. Let's just finish.'

They had started work early, at just six a.m. It had been a calm morning, raw and fresh on the tongue. The sun had felt new, unripened, not yet high enough in the sky to melt or sicken the spirit. For Ray it was full of optimism, this pale citrus air that scuffed her cheeks as she adjusted the viewfinder, waiting for the daily roll call of prisoners, enlivened by the welcome abrasion of early morning wind. Somewhere she heard a boy singing and keeping time with his hand against a surface, maybe his satchel, as he left for school. His voice mixed with the distant clatter of utensils in a kitchen, the hammering out of metal near the road boundary, the quiet creak and roll of a wheelbarrow containing empty earthenware pots, pushed by a woman who passed the three of them and their small camera on her way to the water pump. As she came closer, the woman revealed herself to be Mayawati, another of the sewing wives.

Ray tried to work out if she knew the song that the boy was singing. She wanted to film everything, record all of it at once. At this time of the day, the prison was a rural idyll. Every time she pointed the camera somewhere she would hear or see something out of the corner of her eye that was more suggestive of poignancy, something that hinted at being more revealing or atmospheric. She could hear the hysteric flush of the water pump, calling her with the pleading sound of a trumpeting animal, curtailed after several pushes only to be started again. She could imagine the scene: Mayawati sweating to fill the pots with enough water for the day, using the weight of her whole body to pummel the creaky pump, the navy-blue border of her cream sari forming a line that twisted tightly around her form and held it in, any spare material efficiently tucked into the fold of cotton around her waist so that she was quick, fit, free of encroachment.

Now, at the pit, in the swelter of late afternoon, this optimism had leaked away, leaving in its wake the damp, claustrophobic panic of need – the scramble to get all of the constituent elements so that the quarry-pit experience could be a usable sequence and not just a vanity piece.

Pratap finished speaking again, taking a handkerchief from his pocket and wiping a trickle of sweat from the side of his nose.

'He says no one resents him being a prisoner,' said Ray.

'Everyone knows he is a prisoner and they still respect him. It took some time in the early days to find horses, vehicles, tools, but he used his natural intelligence to set things up. He went to the bank and he gave the prison as his address, and he still got the loan with which to start the business. I asked him if that was true even of these people who work for him. They aren't prisoners, how can they work for him happily? Surely some must resent their boss?'

'Well, maybe not,' said Nathan. 'Tell him I'm like him. I was in prison.'

'He knows that,' said Ray. 'But it's a good idea to get it on camera, yes.'

'Just tell him, will ya?' said Nathan.

Ray frowned and looked away. He was withholding basic courtesy as though it might damage the filming process.

'I think we're done, actually,' she said, taking the camera from Serena and forcing a smile. 'I'm going to film his team. I'll be ten minutes. Leave your mics on in case he says anything interesting while you're chatting.'

As she walked away, without registering their response but aware of them behind her, she adjusted the two receptors for the radio mics in the back pockets of her combat trousers.

The ground was hard and dry. Ray walked to her left, curving round behind the truck, towards the south-facing part of the pit. In her ears, the chat became background noise, a scratchy rubble of voices and activity. The dirty orange colouring transfixed her, the way the uneven stone emanated a kind of powder into the air, was part of the heat, the atmosphere. Two labourers worked in a carefully honed rhythm, beating the rock face, collecting the stone in their bowls. Then they balanced the bowls on their heads and disappeared round the corner, where she heard them throwing the rocks into a truck. Even the casual punctuations seemed to be wired into the rhythm: a moment to unwind a bandana and wipe away sweat, or a loud cry to accompany the lift of a heavy bowl. She began to film the sequence, squatting down low to capture the establishing shot – an expanse of foreground between her and the workers, their muscled forms in constant movement. She tilted up the camera so that a strip of blue sky crowned the scene, before slowly counting to ten.

There was a crackle in her ear and she heard Nathan talking, his feet crunching against the gravel.

'Round here,' he said, his voice lowered but loud in Ray's radio receptor. Serena's voice was intermittently audible, but less clear, bouncing off Nathan's mic.

'Rollies,' she said. 'They're better with a filter, aren't they? Fewer chemicals and the rest. So much cheaper. Should really get into them again.'

Ray stiffened. She felt a twinge of anxiety that was not entirely unpleasant. Some part of her wanted to hear what they might say when off duty, alone. She walked closer to the labourers and began filming a mid-shot.

'This is good,' said Nathan, yawning and shuffling in her ear. His voice felt overloaded with Britishness in comparison with the scene before her, his accent oddly lopsided with its sloping vowels. She heard him inhale, and a loud rustle on the mic, as though he was adjusting his collar.

'Bloody hell,' said Serena. 'This heat is fucking killing me.'
Nathan laughed.

'You're hilarious, girl,' he said.

They laughed together. It was a kind of relief. Ray felt a smile on her face. She zoomed in and steadied the shot, waiting for the haphazard shapes of stone to fall in and out of the frame, the smoky fissure of rock dust to move up through the air.

She listened to them talk. It was standard stuff. Serena was in a lively mood, her laugh intercepting the dialogue with a boyish honk when Nathan joked about his toilet habits.

'I can feel it coming, hours before its time,' he said. 'It's bubbling up inside me now, as it happens, a little promise for later.'

They discussed the office, back in the UK. The labourers began emptying their pans into the truck, creating an avalanche of noise so that she could only just discern their voices.

'Thing about Lucy,' said Nathan, mentioning another of the directors from the series, 'is that she's early thirties, wants a kid. And I'm not into that, so I didn't go there when we were up in Newcastle. Could've, though, if I'm being entirely honest with you. She gave enough signs.'

Ray put her finger on the zoom button and began to film the bumpy surface of the rock wall in close-up. She felt a vague anger: Nathan's arrogance, the casual sexism, his presumption that Lucy would be interested in him, that she was his to reject. They began talking about the shoot, the prison set-up. Their words were more distinct now.

'I just want something to happen,' said Serena. 'Otherwise we're going to have to make it happen. TV doesn't just turn up on screen like that, does it? We need to put ourselves right in there and start getting things going. Maybe I should stir up the sewing wives. They've got to be hiding something. How long has Ray been on the villagers, anyway? I'm going to start hearing it from Nick if we don't have something soon. There're only so many picturesque sequences or friendly interviews that he's going to take.'

'Don't worry, I've got something I'm working on,' said Nathan.

'What?' said Serena. 'Tell me, tell me.'

'Nah!' said Nathan. 'Give me some time. I've gotta sweeten up my lead.'

Serena laughed.

'What is it? Someone tell you the governor's got his hand in the till or something, and you actually believed them?'

'You can take the piss, if you like,' said Nathan, exhaling loudly. 'But you're going to be all over this when it comes out.' He laughed.

'How are you "sweetening your lead", anyway?' said Serena. 'Sounds dodgy.'

They carried on for a few seconds until, inevitably, the conversation turned to Ray. She didn't flinch but she heard it was happening, and concentrated on their words to try to get a proper sense of what they might be saying.

'She gives it all innocent,' said Serena. 'Little old Indian princess, butter wouldn't melt . . . But she knows what she's doing.'

'D'ya think?' said Nathan.

'Yeah, man. Why does she unbutton her shirt like that? It's to show her chest. Why the fuck else? What's with the tight trousers? They're even tight down here. I mean, down in her crotch. For fuck's sake!' Serena laughed again, releasing a stuttering honk into Ray's ears. 'It's embarrassing. What's the point? Getting men to look at you here is like shooting fish in a barrel.'

Ray flushed and took the headphones off. Some perverse part of her wished she could continue to listen, find out what happened next, as though she'd be able to absorb it as an outside observer, like a radio soap opera. She sat down on the ground and put the headphones in her lap. She imagined

Serena's thick lips downturned, pressed into a crescent as she laughed, shuddering, recoiling at her own words.

'*Bhen-ji?*'

It was one of the labourers, the shorter one in a blue vest. He was balancing a bowl on his head, and jerked his neck briefly to indicate that he was about to walk round the corner, squinting at her with one hand shading his eyes. Ray nodded and forced a smile to show that she'd follow him with the camera and record his journey, surprised by his active involvement in the filming process. Maybe Pratap had told his workers to cooperate with the crew. Keeping the distance between them constant so that the shot could run uninterrupted, and winding along the track to stay on the smoother parts of the ground, she followed his back. In the final stage, she moved the camera slowly in a pan up close against his vest, over an exposed shoulder and right down his arms at the moment when he tipped the bowl up and heaved the stones out into the truck. It was a pleasing climax to a fluid, journeying shot, over which she'd retained enough control to achieve her intention. And yet she felt unable to be in the moment.

Later, when they were dismantling the kit to pack away for the return journey, she took the radio mic back from Nathan and thought about whether she should tell him she'd been listening. Did he know, anyway?

Zafar had come to pick them up. They drove for ten minutes, and Nathan began to snore, his head bumping against the window. Ray tried to film out of the side of the car to capture the clouds which pressed down, suffused with the now familiar pink and peach shading, onto the dry, cracked landscape. She didn't want to start directing Zafar to drive at a certain speed – they needed to get home and she imagined the other two were unlikely to take kindly to delays – but occasionally, by chance, the car moved slowly enough to make the shot work. Then, unexpectedly, through Nathan's window, she saw a long ravine on the right, a wide dark artery through the ground, that was full of dust and labourers.

'What's that?' said Serena, pushing up instantly and leaning over to get a better look. Nathan continued to snore, shifting slightly against Serena's weight. Ray leaned over too. It was an astonishing perspective – the gash in the earth full of human activity, and washed through with gold, the final harvest of that day's sun before it disappeared.

'Zafar, stop!' said Ray, getting the camera ready as the car pulled over on the opposite side of the road.

'What're you doing?' said Serena.

'It won't take a minute,' said Ray.

'But it's already –'

'Just a sec,' said Ray. She slammed the door to make sure that it shut properly, and the sound seemed to reverberate in the air. She pulled her shirt down over her trousers, then buttoned up the front to the collar so that her vest was not visible. It was suddenly very quiet, no traffic, just the same, pared, rhyming sounds of rural life: the toned whirr and click of insects or unknown animals that she heard every night in the hut, the odd winnowing cackle through the air of a bird overhead. Amongst this, she was aware of the distant hacking and crushing of rock. She crossed the road and climbed up the small incline which overlooked the pit. She moved carefully, without rush, almost inserting a deliberate delay between steps, as though this hesitation, the fact of enforced slow motion, would make her invisible to the labourers once she appeared over the horizon.

There were about twenty men, dispersed along the line that stretched out in front of her. As soon as she started filming, they stopped working. Within seconds they were all staring at her, right into the lens, some of them leaning against each other or against the wall. One or two sat down on their haunches. There were a few sniffs, a couple of coughs. Rather than observing them at work, they were observing her like an oddity, and if she was capturing anything then it was the mockery and bewilderment contained in their stares. She knew this was the moment when she should have stopped filming – she would never be able to use this footage – and yet she could not stop filming so quickly because of the humiliation. She had to go through with it now, show that she knew what she was doing.

She should have asked their permission, she knew that; it was the basic rule of ethical documentary practice, and she had already been called on this by Nandini, on the first day in the prison. She should have asked them if she could film them. Of course. It was beyond question. And yet she hadn't. She had been too nervous to go over and try to explain in her hesitant Hindi, had found it too daunting to be an Indian woman alone, confronting a valley of men. She'd been too anxious and self-regarding, that was the truth of it, and so she hadn't even asked. Fear was not a good enough reason. She had treated them like animals in the ground for some natural history film. Her cheeks burned as she counted to herself. Thirty seconds and I'll stop, she thought, putting her weight over onto one leg as she continued to film. I have to keep going. They stared back at her, stared right into the lens.

One of the men laughed, muttered something she couldn't hear. There were more laughs.

'*Hijra!*' shouted one of them uncertainly, with a high-pitched voice, and as the laughter scurried around the group a couple of them began to work again, whacking their axes into the rock and yet still continuing to turn and stare up at her.

She brought the camera down and walked quickly out of vision.

'What does that mean?' said Serena as she got back in the car.

'What was he shouting?' said Nathan. 'Hijar? Heejar?'

Ray caught Zafar's eye in the mirror, feeling the shame heat her face.

'*Hijra,*' said Ray, speaking with a determined clarity. 'A man who looks like a woman. They are considered eunuchs here. They can be transgender or transvestite, and they make money dancing at weddings, or end up as prostitutes.'

She forced a laugh, to get it in before them. She heard herself and winced.

'Bloody hell!' said Nathan as Zafar started the car. 'Mate, that is rough!'

He looked over at Serena, who rolled her eyes to signify embarrassment, coughing out a giggle.

'Eunuch, eh?' he said. 'That's what they were shouting?'

'Yes,' said Ray quietly.

She rested her elbow on the curve of glass of the half-rolled-down window, welcoming the breeze on her face as the car began to accelerate.

7.

The email came the next day, right on cue. Ray wondered, momentarily, if it was a coincidence, hoping that Serena had not been responsible.

Ray,

Can you mail me some of your proposed storylines, character breakdowns, etc., and book in for a phone call with me asap? You've been there a week now, and I'm concerned – do we have something tangible to follow in terms of present-tense narratives? Conflict, jeopardy, etc., usual stuff. What do the characters want? Why aren't they getting it? Will they triumph over adversity? Are they compelling enough? What kind of revealing actuality will we see on screen? The more conflict we see with our own eyes, the better, but you know that, of course. That's the stuff you need to focus on. Don't make me regret going out on a limb for you!

Book in as soon as you can after your Sunday reprieve.

Nick

The language was too didactic for it to be a coincidence. The brusque cheerfulness, reminders of television staples, clear list of necessary ingredients – all of these things strongly hinted at the idea that Serena had contacted Nick that morning with her worries. It was noon now, and Ray sat in the cybercafe looking at the words on the screen, oppressed by the dampness in the air; it limited her, staggered her breathing, as if through a mask. She toyed with the mouse, clicking it in idle repetition. The sweat on her body was perforating the whole of her existence. Everything was blurred.

She leaned against the booth divider and took a swig of lukewarm water from the plastic litre bottle that she now carried with her daily. She was especially embarrassed at the 'advice' in the email – the way it reminded her of her responsibility, the need to justify the budget and commission for this programme. It had been her idea.

This was her first programme as a director, and she had been supposed to reveal herself as an original voice presenting a true, affecting portrait of these people and their lives. *Heartbreakingly beautiful.* Even as she heard her own thoughts, she cringed at the vanity in them, the uneasy boundary between the honourable and dishonourable reasons for coming here.

She slumped back in the plastic chair. It squeaked forcefully against the floor, causing the person in the booth next to her to jump at the noise. He was one of the men who had quickly minimized the image on his screen when she had walked into the place, switching to a game of solitaire as she made her way past him to a booth in the corner, on the proprietor's instructions. She knew they were all likely to be watching porn, these men bending over the keyboards in their thin slack trousers and creased shirts tucked into the waistbands, their cautious eyes bumping against her for seconds, noting the intrusion before turning back to their screens. She didn't care. She was wearing one of two cotton kameez tops bought that morning: loose, long-sleeved, high-necked shifts in local prints. She had singled out these items in extra-large sizes so that there was no chance that they would do anything but cover her effectively.

Ray coughed quietly from behind the camera. Nandini nodded her head. It was a tiny movement, just visible enough. It was part of the code that had developed between the two of them over the hours of the shoot, a game of tiny snorts and sighs used with care to punctuate the background of filming, indiscernible to the subject. Ray had offered Nandini a fixer's fee for the day, to try working with her. It was an attempt to forge an intimacy with the inmates, bypassing the formality of structured filming. They had begun with Jyoti, the woman opposite Ray's hut.

Nandini continued to talk to Jyoti for a few more minutes, waiting for a natural break in the conversation. She was seated with her on the floor, shelling peas while Jyoti stitched. Ray could hear them talking through her headphones. They were discussing the production line of the garments. Commission, stitching, collection and sale. The image through the lens adhered to a loose idea of authenticity. Jyoti's red sari, printed with repeating squares and diamonds, small shapes in yellow and white, was loud against the backdrop of whitewashed stone walls; the pallu of loose material draped around the back of her neck was tucked into her waist as she focused on stretching the cloth in her hands under the jabbing needle, stopping at intervals to bite the thread.

The sewing machine droned intermittently. The sound functioned as some kind of release, cutting through the weak fuzz in Ray's mind. *Conflict, conflict, conflict.* She used the familiar hardness of the word as something to react against, to keep her awake. She drank some lukewarm water from the fetid bottle that never left her side, and waited. *All art is born of conflict. Jeopardy.* Another sharp, too-obvious word. She loosened the central lock on the tripod and found a place to start a pan across the back of the hut.

After several dry runs without recording, she decided to begin with the head of their charpoy. It was neatly made up for daytime sitting, pillows hidden under a chequered, tasselled bedspread. The shot would end with the two pairs of children's flip-flops, positioned on the dusty floor below it. This would be a vertical pan from top to bottom, reflecting the order within the house, and the priorities of Jyoti. She was a wife and mother, and she ran a household like any other, in spite of being in prison – in spite of having to earn her keep by stitching clothes for her husband to sell.

Halfway through the shot, Nandini tapped her on the shoulder. Ray ignored it, continuing against her better judgement, even though the pan had a jerk in it now, which rendered it useless.

'She is going to start preparing the evening meal soon,' said Nandini, brushing dust from the back of her kameez and adjusting her chunni. 'Have you been getting our conversation down OK?'

Ray nodded.

'It's been a bit difficult with the sound of the machine,' she said. 'And it is material we've got down before. But she's more relaxed with you. It's good to have it in this situation, while she's active, doing something.'

Jyoti brushed past them, nodding deferentially towards Ray, and spoke to Nandini.

'*I need to put the chicken in,*' she said. '*It's a festival so he'll be home early today.*'

'*Of course,*' replied Nandini, courteous and ready. '*Today there'll be a lot of celebrations all round, good fun for the children.*'

'*Got it fresh this morning. It's a big one, not one of our own; he dropped it off from the market,'* said Jyoti, pulling the skinned, headless bird out from a large steel tureen and placing it on the work surface.

'*If there's chicken, it's a special occasion, eh, Didi?'* said Nandini with a smile.

'*Well, chicken costs money. And for him to dig in his pockets for this is not common,'* said Jyoti. She was cheery, emphatic. '*So much to save for, with two children. You understand what I'm saying? You might be eating chicken every week, but for us it's something we really have to think about. How often do you think we have it?'*

'*You tell me, Didi,'* said Nandini. She made a tiny movement, a flicker in which she raised her eyebrows at Ray, suggesting that she start filming again.

Jyoti began to cut open the chicken, removing the giblets and placing them in the pan.

'*You guess, Bhen-ji,'* she said. '*If you don't guess then it's no fun!'*

Ray detached the camera from the tripod and took it up to her eye-level.

'*Just a handful of times, Didi?'* said Nandini. '*Not more than a few?'*

'*Four times a year,'* said Jyoti, turning and holding up four greasy fingers. She smiled and invited a reaction from Nandini.

'*That is rare enough,'* said Nandini.

'*Rare enough? When we were in the village we had it at least once a month. I mean that was the minimum. Often it was twice, maybe more. How often do you have it?'*

'*Actually, I don't eat non-veg,'* said Nandini.

'*Very good!'* laughed Jyoti, pouring water over two limbs that she had detached from the bird, before putting them in a saucepan. '*What about her?'* She nodded over at Ray, still looking at Nandini.

Nandini turned to Ray.

'She is asking how often you . . .'

'I know what she's asking,' said Ray, irked at being referred to tangentially.

Attempting a jocular tone, she explained to Jyoti that she was vegetarian. Without thinking, she said the word vegetarian in English, a long multi-syllabled word that she attempted to swallow back as it left her mouth.

'*What did she say?*' said Jyoti to Nandini. She gave the same dismissive flick of her head over in Ray's direction. '*She seems quite . . .*' The word she used was 'hatti-ghatti', a word Ray didn't understand. Jyoti made an accompanying gesture in which she tightened her two fists and held her arms out in front of her to imply weight, strength, a particular solidity. She laughed, and Nandini joined in.

'You . . . like?' said Jyoti to Ray in English, speaking very slowly and pointing at the chicken, as though Ray was hard of hearing.

'*You like this?*' she asked again, now speaking in Hindi, sniffing as she began to chop a small onion. She winked at Nandini.

'*I don't eat meat,*' Ray said. '*I don't eat it. I am . . .*'

'Veg?' said Nandini, looking over approvingly at Ray. '*I didn't know this fact but she doesn't eat non-veg, it seems, Didi. That is a surprise.*'

Jyoti threw the chopped onion into some heated oil.

'*What's that?*' she said. She seemed to have lost interest.

'*Didi, I wanted to ask . . .*' said Ray, bluntly inserting the words into the sizzle of the kitchen.

Jyoti looked over at Nandini, shaking her right hand and clicking her tongue. It signified that she didn't understand what Ray was saying.

'*Do you ever think about the future? You've made your home*

here. But *do you mind that this is a prison, after all? For the children?'* said Ray, loudly now, over the sounds of cooking.

'What's she saying?' asked Jyoti of Nandini, nodding over
at Ray conspiratorially. She chuckled. *'She's getting angry!
What does she want?'* She began to chop some green
chillies. *'Don't make her angry,'* she giggled. *'Who knows what
she'll do? Do you want to stay for dinner, by the way?'*

'No,' said Nandini. *'Don't worry, Didi, we'll be going soon.'*

*'No, I'm just asking because the children will be coming back
very soon and I have to make sure they get everything ready for this
evening. Like I said, he'll be early . . .'*

'Of course,' said Nandini.

Ray began fiddling with the camera while the two women
spoke. Her annoyance was building. She detached a battery,
then re-inserted it, starting the camera up again from scratch
and running through the checklist of white balance, focus
and audio levels.

'She can stay if she has to,' said Jyoti. *'She just has to get someone to tell him when he comes home. Someone from her group – the
man can do it, or a prison officer.'*

'No, no, Didi, we'll leave you to celebrate,' said Nandini.

*'But if the governor wants it then we'll do it, of course. She can
stay, if he asks. And you can stay in either case. I'm making a very
nice bhindi saag you can taste. The children will be happy to see
you – that much, of course, you know yourself. Sonu was asking
for you just yesterday.'*

'No, Didi, I have to go,' said Nandini. *'I'll come back tomorrow
and we'll talk some more. Maybe we can talk about things that are
on your mind – if there is anything you want to talk about in
particular.'*

Jyoti frowned, dabbing the corner of her eye with a cloth.

*'But where will you spend this evening? It's a festival day. You
don't have a family, so think of us as your family. I've said it a*

thousand times. What will you do otherwise? Go and eat bread-butter with her?' She laughed. 'Dry, dry, bread-butter. Who knows what these white people eat?'

Ray could feel her breathing quicken. Her hands began to shake as she raised the camera up to put the viewfinder against her eye, simultaneously pressing record.

'*She is not a white, though, Didi,*' said Nandini, smiling. '*Anyone can see that.*'

'*Not a white but she lives with whites, doesn't she, Bhen-ji? When you're around it long enough, then colour sticks, doesn't it? Tell me if I'm wrong.*'

Ray stopped recording and held the camera in her right hand. She held out her left arm.

'*Actually, I'm quite dark-skinned for a girl from North India, Didi, isn't it true to say?*' She attempted to insert humour into her voice, directing her words at Jyoti as she gestured at her arm.

Nandini opened her mouth to intervene, but Ray raised her hand to quieten her. A flicker of a palm up for a second, then back at her side.

'*Didi, talk to me!*' said Ray, a forced lightness at odds with the request in her voice. '*What do you think?*' There was a silence for a few beats. '*Didi?*'

'*Talk?*' said Jyoti, turning from her worktop. '*Who says I'm not talking? Say what you want.*'

'*I'm quite dark-skinned, wouldn't you say?*' said Ray, unable to stop herself from trying again.

Jyoti raised her eyebrows and looked at Nandini, then back at Ray. She shrugged her shoulders.

'*It means no one can call me white,*' said Ray, smiling through her anger and presenting her arm again.

Jyoti looked at Nandini for guidance. '*What does she want me to say?*' she said, wiping her hands with a cloth.

'*I'm just saying that I'm Indian,*' continued Ray. She exhaled with frustration. This was not going well. Nandini was staring at her with unconcealed anxiety. It's a car crash in slow motion. The tacky style of phrasing from the internal narrator, who was now back in her head, was more than slightly unnerving her. She took a deep breath and closed her eyes.

'*She's a funny girl,*' said Jyoti to Nandini. '*Calling herself dark like that with such ceremony, like it's something to be proud of. "Look at how blackie black I am." They're a strange lot, aren't they!*'

She turned back to the saucepan, stirred the mixture and turned up the fire.

Neither of the women was willing to break the silence as they walked back through the compound. Nandini stopped at the water pump to drink; Ray stood back, waiting for her.

Ray checked her watch when they reached Nandini's door. It was seven o'clock, time for dinner back at base. But she had no desire to join the others.

'When did you become vegetarian?' asked Nandini suddenly.

Ray was surprised. She had not expected Nandini to speak.

'About . . . well, it's sixteen years now. I was eleven.'

'It's strange, no? For someone living over there?'

'Not really. Many people are vegetarian, in the Indian community and also outside that, whatever their racial origin. It's very common.'

'Why did you choose it? Isn't it difficult to find things to eat there? Are you very religious?'

Ray laughed, in spite of herself.

'Oh many reasons. It's a long story. I was eleven, after all. It was a serious decision!'

'Did something happen to you?'

'No, it's more straightforward than that, actually. Just decided one day that there was no need to eat animals, that there was no benefit to it for anyone. Not really religion. More common sense.'

Nandini nodded. They stood for a moment under her porch, lingering under the shade of the tented material.

'OK,' said Ray after a few moments.

She felt she should refer to her momentary loss of control with Jyoti, her irascible, slightly childish response. But Nandini's face was impassive; it had returned to the smooth, unmarked terrain of polite exchange. There didn't seem to be a way in.

'Thanks so much for your help today,' said Ray. 'Speak soon, then.'

8.

They laugh, the three of them, at a joke from Nathan. He is laughing most loudly, a boyish tone combined with a bronchial wheeze now and then. It is Sunday, their first weekly day off, built into the schedule as a matter of legality under health and safety rules. Serena, Nathan and Ray are travelling to the fort together. Zafar has picked them up from their various wanderings in the market and is speaking to Ray, in an uncharacteristic, albeit mild, display of enthusiasm. He looks at Nathan in the mirror, at intervals, a smile opening up his face.

'What's going on?' asks Nathan, rolling up some tobacco.

'He's asking if you're famous,' Ray says.

Serena sits up and takes some tobacco from Nathan's packet, starts to fashion her own cigarette.

'He says you're like an actor called Jackie Shroff,' Ray says with a laugh. 'It's a brilliant parallel. Shroff is a guy from the eighties who now advertises black label whiskey: weedy moustache, thinning hair, stacked body, that kind of thing.'

Before getting in the car she has taken a few puffs of weed, handed to her mid-conversation by Nathan outside a paan stall, whilst waiting for Serena to turn up. The touch of Nathan's hand against hers is like a whisper in that moment, an unspoken assurance of solidarity, the rollie slotting between her fingers as he peers at her, eyelashes flickering, in a quiet gully off the main road, enforcing the moment with intimacy. The weed has loosened Ray's tongue, unwound the spring of formality around her speech, anaesthetized the bleak feeling that has been upon her since reading the email. It is their day off, after all, she thinks. Fuck it. Fuck them all. She leans her head out of the window, letting the sun caress her face.

'A Bollywood legend? What's he called? Jackie?' Serena says, smiling. 'Brilliant. Thinning hair, though . . . that's harsh, Nath. True maybe, but harsh.'

Nathan yelps in response, nods at the driver, urges Ray to translate.

'Can you tell him I'm fighting for my life here, with these two BBC bitches ready to cut my balls off?'

She jumps at the unexpected turn of phrase, and then finds herself laughing with Serena.

'Oh how he is emasculated,' says Ray, in the tone of a sports commentator who has been presented with a dramatic injury on the pitch.

'Oh yes – how he falls,' says Serena, winking at Ray.

'Oh how will he play his mind games now, without those wonderful balls?' continues Ray.

'Dem beautiful balls,' says Serena with a sigh. 'It's a tragedy. Where will he go from here?'

'What are his options?' says Ray. 'A man needs his balls. But here he is, on a dirt track to nowhere with two bitches at his heels. It's a lonely ride.'

'Listen!' says Nathan. 'You little . . . Can I get some bloody help here? What's his name?' He gestures at the driver.

'Zafar,' says Ray.

'Zaaf?' Nathan calls out, overlapping her. Zafar smiles into the rear-view mirror, flicking his head up with raised eyebrows, a movement that asks Nathan to continue. 'These two,' says Nathan, gesturing at the girls either side of him. He pretends to pull his hair out with both hands. 'These two?' Then he winds his finger round on the side of his head.

'Loopy, eh? Fruit loops. Drive me loopy?' He laughs, a guttural, dirty sound.

'Easy,' says Ray, suddenly on alert. 'We don't want him to get the wrong idea.'

'He's going to need some refiring,' says Serena, still in the same commentator's tone as before. 'Some fuel for his tired little engine.' She picks up the camera, nods at Nathan before pressing record. The red light comes on, blinking to fullness.

'Now, Nathan. How would you describe your time since you got here?' Serena says.

'Yes, Nathan,' says Ray. 'What about your feelings and emotions?'

'Well,' says Nathan, turning to deliver his speech directly to the camera. 'It's . . .' He pauses and smiles, looking down at the seat. Then he takes a breath and looks up abruptly. His voice is clipped, shiny. He is in presenter mode. 'It's day seven and I'm about to collapse because I haven't had the love of a good woman for many, many hours. As you can imagine, this is very trying for a red-blooded man like me. I'm like a bear with a sore . . . a sore . . .'

'Oh the pain,' says Ray, laughing from behind him, returning to the same tone of faux tragedy. She shakes her head, tutting. 'It kills me to think of it. How he lies awake at night with his sore wotcha . . . Oh how he bears the weight of his own machismo.'

'As I was saying . . .' says Nathan. 'Instead I'm being tormented by these BBC bitches, who have made it their mission to torture me and –'

'How are you finding India, Nathan?' Serena interrupts sharply, moving her right hand to press the zoom button.

'Ah yes, India,' says Nathan almost instantly. 'I'm enjoying the varied sights and sounds that make up the tapestry of life in India. Happy?'

Serena pans from Nathan to the window and films a cycle rickshaw moving past with two large women sitting in the seats, shopping bags at their feet. The women both turn to look at her, remaining steady as the cycle stalls in traffic. One of the women looks over at Ray and back at Serena and Nathan. Ray can see her trying to work out the dynamic between the three of them.

A camel moves past, filling the view with sandy fur.

'I love it when they walk past like this,' says Serena. 'The colours are fucking phenomenal.'

Ray looks at the huge eyes of the camel, its direct stare, the astounding curve of lengthy eyelashes. She is reminded of Nathan and turns round to look at him. He is rolling another spliff, crumbling the small block and sprinkling it through tobacco.

They leave the town square and move through a large gate to a more open road outside. Ray sees the image of the gate in the pull-out viewfinder of the camera.

'That's some nice framing,' Ray says to Serena.

'I'm always good at framing,' comes the response, somewhere between querulous and dismissive. Serena seems more childish now than when they are alone in the hut. It is as though she wants to impress Nathan in some way. Her voice becomes more formal and projected. 'We are leaving the city. Going through the gate.'

Ray chuckles.

'Is that supposed to be voice-over?' she says.

'Escape from Ashwer,' says Nathan.

'In which Nathan finds his true identity,' says Ray.

'Chapter Two,' says Nathan. 'In which the BBC bitches rob Nathan of his true identity.'

'What's that?' says Serena, pointing at a ruined building in the centre of a reservoir of water on their left.

'Palace of the whispering bitches?' says Nathan. 'Actually, that's where I live. I go out on the town, and I invite you both back for coffee. We take the boat over – you're behind me, and she's in front and –'

Ray pushes Nathan on his shoulder, laughing.

'What is this?' she says. 'What's with the bizarre lothario act? How is that kind of stuff allowed, man?'

'Oi,' says Nathan. 'Don't get overfamiliar, now.'

He sees Serena's finger on the zoom button.

'What're you up to?' he says to her. 'Staring into my soul? The lens is so cruel. I know I've been exposed. Darkness is mine. A whole load of darkness.'

'You can't get enough darkness. Give me some darkness, Nathan,' says Serena.

He narrows his eyes and peers at her.

'More darkness,' says Serena. 'I want more darkness.'

'Chapter Thirty-eight,' says Nathan, his thin lips moving into a smile. 'Darkness is smiling. It's a later chapter, naturally.'

They arrive at the local fort, as planned. Ray leans back and shades her eyes. She stares up the slope to see the medieval ruin imprint itself high in the sky, already a postcard against the vivid blue. The layered terraces and imposing archways are scooped out of heavy, beige stone. Monkeys flurry surreptitiously through the alcoves and walkways. She thinks, momentarily, of the pointlessness of the trip they are about to make, the photographs that they will no doubt take of this place that has probably been documented on tourist films thousands of times.

Serena asks Ray to accompany her on an elephant for the journey up the hill. Nathan decides to walk instead. They mock his fear as they are settled into the saddle by guides.

He claims that it is a speed-related decision: he'll beat them to the top as the elephant looks so slow.

Serena starts filming as soon as the elephant rises up from the ground with them on its back, and they wobble in the saddle as they ascend. They begin the journey with slow, lumbering steps. After five minutes they turn a corner and see Nathan standing and smoking a cigarette.

'Hey!' shouts Serena. 'Nathan!'

He looks up and smiles at them, into the camera.

'Nimble Nathan,' says Serena, almost muttering it to herself.

'Yes, I know,' says Ray, thinking to recapture the spirit of mischief in the car. 'Bet he loves it that you're filming this as a top shot. The thin patch.'

Serena doesn't reply and they have little to say to each other as the elephant sways and heaves itself onwards, each step bringing an unsteady element to the rhythm of their movement. Only when the driver in the saddle starts hitting the elephant with a stick, urging him to turn away from the edge of the hilly path, does the silence end.

'What!' shouts Serena. 'What's he doing?'

Ray, who has been roused from a reverie, shrugs.

'I don't know,' she says.

'Well, ask him!' says Serena. 'For fuck's sake!'

'What?' Ray is confused by the violence of her response.

Serena leans forward.

'Why?' she says to the man, swiping the air to re-create his movement. 'Why hitting? You . . . hit . . . him?'

The driver laughs and speaks in Hindi to Ray.

'*What's she saying?*' he says. '*She likes it? That I hit him?*'

'*No,*' says Ray. '*She wants to know why you did it. What's the reason?*'

'*Hm?*' says the driver. '*Why? He's going the wrong way.*' He laughs.

'Yes, but do you need to hit him that hard?' says Ray. 'Doesn't it hurt him? That's what she means.'

'OK, OK . . .' says the driver. He leans forward and strokes the elephant's head, making a squeaky kissing sound with his mouth.

'Hear that, Frooti? The whitey is worried about you.'

He pats the top of the elephant's head gently and laughs.

'My sweet son, Frooti Frooto. Ha! This woman has fallen for you, and why shouldn't she?'

The elephant slows and stops on a corner. There is a carpet seller down below who shouts up at them.

'Madam?' he says, gesturing half-heartedly at the spread of different-sized rugs around him.

Ray shakes her head at the carpet seller. Serena is now otherwise occupied. She is leaning round and attempting to film the elephant's droppings behind her.

'Don't bang against me,' she says to Ray. 'I need to be steady.'

A few moments of quiet pass, punctuated only by the steady plop of the faeces. When the process ends, Serena stays focused on the elephant's behind.

'Now I just need him to exit frame,' she says.

'God, Serena, that's going to be slow,' says Ray. Her tone is amused; she is still attempting to regain some of the bonhomie of the car.

'It's not a problem. I've got almost ten minutes of batts left,' comes the reply.

The lumbering movement begins again and Ray looks down over the vista of the town. Without Nathan, their dynamic seems to have returned to the brusque norms of the hut, even though they are paying deference to the idea that they are on holiday today. Ray is reminded of the politics between them, Serena's email to Nick, her own lack of stature or dignity in the proceedings. The memory makes itself known through the thinning fog of marijuana in her mind. The driver suddenly begins to berate the elephant.

'*Abhay chaal mere baap!*' he shouts, launching into a tirade.

'He's saying, "I give you all this love and what for?"' Ray says to Serena. '"Come on. You tell me where to go? Thanks a lot." The literal translation is "Come on, my father", a bit like "Come on, my son", but it's a more annoyed version –'

Serena yells with excitement.

'Look!' she says. 'It's the little man in denim!'

Nathan is much closer this time. He has turned a corner on the steep path so that he is walking on the same level as the elephant.

'You happy walking there, mate?' shouts Serena, laughing.

He nods back, the smile a bit more strained this time.

'It's nice up here,' says Serena, bellowing out the words with a big smile. 'Don't we look relaxed?'

Nathan mutters something that is audible only to Serena, as she is on that side of the elephant. She chuckles.

'Nah,' says Serena. 'A very gentle ambling motion.'

She hands the camera over to Ray.

'Film something, if you want. He says we look scared.'

They climb higher and are suddenly amongst monkeys – maybe fifty or more – hanging from the ramparts with large hooped tails, furry beige haloes of hair surrounding their faces.

'Look at those monkeys. They know they rule the roost,' says Serena.

Ray films a wide panorama of a royal court of monkeys in clusters of various sizes, mostly stationary in the ruins, dignified, observant, unaffected by the odd momentary scurry or dash of stray relatives.

Nathan is already waiting when they reach their destination. The final steps take them lurching slowly through the main arch of the fort. Serena requests a photograph before they descend, and Ray arranges it. They attract a new band of followers: four men who welcome them with gusto and offer them a sixty-minute Sony DV tape, as recommended by the elephant driver.

'*How much?*' asks Ray. Serena has entreated her to find out while she takes some final shots of the start of sunset before descending.

'*This is a really up-to-date, special, imported model of a tape . . .*' begins the driver.

Ray is impatient. The heat is getting to her.

'*Bhaiya, you know that some of us are "imported" as well,*' she says, nodding over at Nathan and Serena. '*And that's why you're trying to sell it to us. So don't worry about all the preamble. Just, please, tell me the price.*'

He waits for a few seconds, glancing at her surreptitiously as if to assess how far he can take it. Then he places the answer in the mix, impulsively, like a ball into a roulette wheel.

'*Forty dollars.*'

Ray stutters out a laugh.

'Forty dollars!' she yells up to Serena, frowning. 'For something that's worth less than five quid.'

Serena is busy switching the camera off. Ray can't tell if she is ignoring her or can't hear.

'*Madam, you are getting angry?*' says the driver in surprise.

'Yes,' says Ray. '*I am getting angry. OK, I have to go now.*'

'*But, madam, there is still —*'

'*No, really, I don't want it.*'

'*Madam — just listen —*'

'*Look, I've said it — and you won't respect it?*'

'But, madam, I am only –'

'This is tiring for me, you know?' Ray says earnestly. 'Having to argue with all of you, and sort everything out for them, doing all the negotiating . . .'

She points at Serena and Nathan, and continues, rubbing the sweat from her forehead.

'You should help me by listening to me when I say that I don't want this tape.'

'No, madam, it isn't that, it's just that –'

'Why won't you just help me out?' says Ray. 'Why do you make it more difficult?' She makes her voice placatory, requesting a kind of comradeship. 'Do you see my point of view? Do you agree with what I am trying to say? It's hard, isn't it?'

'Yes, but madam, it isn't that – it's something else.'

'OK, then. What is it? If it isn't that, then what is it? Tell me.'

'You haven't paid me.'

'Oh . . .'

'It's one hundred rupees plus twenty-five rupees for the special photography from the saddle.'

The amount is paltry, less than two pounds. The man's voice is edged with insecurity. He is visibly worried that she might not pay now, because of her anger. It is clear that, in spite of his bravado and swagger, he is at the whim of the rich tourists he serves. Ray is instantly embarrassed, the shame blushing through her face with a violence that causes her to feel increased fatigue. She wipes a droplet of sweat that is trickling down her neck from behind her ear, then finds a hundred-rupee note for a tip. She hands the note back to him, weary, when he returns it. He thinks she has made a mistake. His expression is twitchy now. Giving a tip of one hundred per cent is clearly signalling wealth and class difference in an even more overt way than they have already shown with their camera and clothing. She can see the looks being exchanged between him and the rest of the group.

'*Thank you*,' he says, moving away once he realizes that the process is complete and nothing more is expected of him.

Ray walks to a soft-drinks stall a few yards away and buys three one-litre bottles of mineral water. She wonders if he will get lynched now, for receiving this extravagance single-handedly. She should have given him a bunch of twenties: easier to share. Maybe he will join forces with the rest of the guides and mob the three of them – Ray, Serena and Nathan – on the way back, now that they all know how freely the money flows in this particular group. Rifling through her pocket for change, she tells herself she is be-yond caring. She is forced in the end to ask the stall-holders if they can 'break' a five-hundred-rupee note.

They are sitting in one of the balcony chambers, smoking together on a raised stone ledge. Their bodies are in silhou-ette, foregrounding a scrubbed, cloudless sky visible through the rectangular space. Nathan has his legs stretched out, his back resting against the narrow stone wall of the opening. Serena sits near his feet, bent over and holding her stomach, laughing uncontrollably, the camera shaking in her right hand. In the background, the view is framed by the walls like a large blue-screen film projection, the reddish layers of the fort receding behind them, the disordered maze of the town below. Ray steadies her breathing as she walks over to them, hugging the litre bottles to her chest so that the thin turquoise bag in which they are housed does not split. Her heart is racing from the slog up the hill, the unexpectedly steep final minutes. There is moisture on her face.

'I'm serious!' says Nathan. 'I'm going to do it.'

'I'm going with you, Nath mate,' says Serena. 'Fuck me, that's funny. I'm going all the way, if this is what you've decided.'

Ray hands them both a bottle of water and sits on the ground below them, crossing her legs and wiping the sweat from her forehead with her right kurta sleeve.

Nathan hands her the spliff and she takes it, inhaling the smoke lightly. She feels dizzy, as if they are at altitude. Serena raises her eyebrows. It is the first time they are doing this together, smoking, and she seems surprised to see Ray partaking.

'What's going on?' says Ray.

'I'm talking about saving your virtue,' says Nathan. 'The guards in the prison. They think I'm up to something. Corrupting the flower of the youth of India.'

'What?'

'Yeah, I didn't hear this part,' said Serena. 'I just thought you wanted to go to a brothel. What's this bit?'

She swings the camera over and starts filming Nathan.

'Give me the backstory,' she says.

'This is the story so far,' says Nathan, leaning into the camera. 'Unbeknownst to Ray, I'm under scrutiny in the village. These guards, the other inmates, they're all very worried, trying to work out my relations with her since I came back late the other night.'

Ray laughs, wide-eyed. She is a little confused, excited, trying to get up to speed with the game, but the dope has made her slow. 'What! What are you on, man?'

Serena swings the camera over and focuses on her. Ray creates an expression of fake shock for the camera, extends the length of time it is on her face.

'I'm serious,' says Nathan. 'You think I'm joking? Think

again.' He speaks directly at the lens, urging it back onto his face.

'They've got their eyes on me, the guards, the boy who brings the water – what's his name? Raju? They're all suspicious of me since the other night, when I came back on the bus with her from the cybercafe and was a little the worse for wear, a little wobbly walking back to my hut.'

'This is ridiculous,' laughs Ray, lying back and putting her head on the ground.

'They want to check that I'm not defiling the flower of India. Their beloved Ray of sunlight. And so, I've come up with a plan. It's pretty good of me, if I say so myself, pretty thoughtful.'

Serena laughs loudly, the sound stabbing his words like the repeating beeps of trucks on the highway.

'I've got to hear this,' she says, moving closer to film him. 'This is genius!'

Nathan begins speaking, stopping for a series of screeches from the monkeys. After a few moments he begins again, as if he is some kind of family counsellor offering a strategic solution that might help them all as a group.

'The only answer is for me to go out to a brothel late at night, come home maybe four, maybe five in the morning, then they'll know I haven't been able to express myself with their beloved Ray. This way, it will be clear that I'm going elsewhere.'

'What the hell is this?' says Ray, sitting up. 'Their beloved what? Where do you get this stuff from?'

'I'm serious. They think that you're in the claws of a . . . of some white beast!'

Serena laughs again, the loud hiccups sending an echo around the chamber that repeats itself quietly. Ray joins in, giggling in spite of herself, closing her eyes, embarrassed. It is, somehow, very funny – Nathan's fake sincerity, the way in which he is urging them to listen, believe him, have faith that he can solve the problem.

'So I'm going to ask them to sort me out with a brothel tonight, and – just to be clear – I'm willing to go through this for you, Ray, even though I've never done it before, lie in the arms of . . . of someone I don't even know! Just to save your –'

'And I'm going with you, remember, Nathan?' says Serena.

'And Serena's coming with me,' says Nathan, 'for the ride. For the adventure, the experience. She won't bring her camera, though. She'll be off duty.'

'It'll be like *The Story of O*,' says Serena.

'What?' says Ray. She is overcome with a feeling of petulance, a hot blush throughout her body. 'You're not serious? You're really going to do this?'

'Of course we're going to do it,' says Serena from behind the camera. 'What's your problem?'

'It's just I . . .' Ray looks at Nathan. She can feel an imploring expression shaping her face, her voice beginning to falter. The weed was making everything stand out so harshly, reveal itself in slow motion, even her own expressions. 'I thought you wanted . . . to all hang out tonight.'

He grins.

'Oh, there there. If you don't want me to go, I understand. I know it's hard for you.'

'I thought we were friends,' says Ray, smiling at him. 'I thought we were going to hang out this evening.'

'You don't want me to go, do you?' says Nathan.

'Bloody hell, you are SO annoying!' says Serena. 'Why do you have to ruin everything?' She exhales loudly, glaring at Ray.

Ray hesitates. She is taken aback by Serena's reaction,

the forthright quality of the attack. She keeps her voice light, the smile fixed on her face. The camera is on her again.

'Why are you giving me a hard time, Serena?' she says.

Serena's response is one of exasperation.

'I'm just saying I like people to be honest.' She addresses Nathan, keeping the camera on Ray. 'She feigns ignorance, like she doesn't know what she's doing – her clothes, for example. I hate people who pretend.'

'My clothes?' says Ray, steeling a rush of anger. 'Sorry? My clothes?' She pulls at her kurta top, lifting it out to demonstrate its looseness.

'She doesn't get it, does she?' says Serena.

'Nah, she does get it,' says Nathan, taking a lengthy drag on the spliff. 'Like when she went round the prison in a miniskirt.'

Serena laughs appreciatively.

'What the hell is this?' says Ray, her voice rising, all trace of humour gone, her speech bruised with outrage. 'I've never done such a thing! I'm always in trousers. I didn't even pack a miniskirt to bring here.'

'Are you sure?' says Nathan. He grins. 'Maybe you're right. See how easy it is to fabricate things on camera? Maybe it was someone else.'

'Well, it wasn't me,' says Serena. 'What was she wearing when we went round to film the sewing couple opposite? Can you remember? What was it?'

'Why the fuck am I justifying myself here?' says Ray. 'What is this? FOR FUCK'S SAKE!'

Nathan's voice softens instantly, infantilizing her, an authoritative manner in his voice as if he is soothing someone in the midst of a violent panic attack. 'Calm down. OK . . . Calm down. We're only having you on. It's OK. As if you'd go round a prison in India in a miniskirt.'

Serena laughs. 'Might as well have been,' she says, stopping the camera and sniffing in disgust. 'For India. In Indian terms, that is.'

'Don't worry,' says Nathan. 'I won't go to the brothel if our Indian princess doesn't want me to. Not tonight, anyway.'

Somehow, they disbanded upon returning to Ashwer. It was exhausting, the three of them being together, thought Ray, as she watched Serena walk ahead to their hut, the irritation she felt sharpening her posture as Nathan turned in the opposite direction to get to his own place. He yawned dramatically as he turned, making a declaration up to the skies.

'I am ravaged by hunger!' he said. 'Bloody hell, I need food.'

It was late; their dinner tiffins would have been dropped off a couple of hours ago. Ray picked up her own meal from the doorstep of their place and walked on to the river, feeling the neurasthenic slide of the drug. She didn't want to be around Serena.

The compound was dark, odd pockets of yellow light distributed amongst the dwellings. It was very atmospheric. She peered into the forecourt of a low hut crowned with straw, situated on the other side of the water pump. She could see a woman seated on the floor inside her home, watching a television that was balanced on a cloth-covered box. Ray strained to see what was on the screen, moving in closer so that she entered the front yard. It looked like a family saga, a soap opera, from the melodramatic close-ups. The woman looked like Ram Pyari, although Ray could see only her lean back, the greenish yellow of her clothing.

Two guards walked round the corner and she jumped, guilty at her indiscretion. They gazed directly at her, looking away within seconds, out of decorum. She thought of how they must regard her, skulking around at this time of night, just after nine o'clock, a time when the darkness came down so completely over the village, enclosing the place with finality, a black hood. The day was over and yet here she was, huddled in front of someone else's house, with her dinner in her hand.

'*Namaste,*' said Ray, putting her hands together so that the tiffin came up near her face, the hooped handle between her palms.

She recognized the tall, rigid man on the right; it was the older guard with the thick layer of white hair. They nodded back and walked on quietly, comfortable in the shadows. The other guard turned back to look at her as they walked away. He was chewing paan; his right cheek was swollen with the stored betel, his jaw moving slowly, his mouth slightly open so that she could see his tongue, the red viscous saliva. She shivered, thinking back to Nathan's words. Maybe they did indeed think of her as 'loose' here. She tried to dismiss the feeling. Paranoia. They had smoked a lot of dope today; the nausea was still in her stomach. But he turned again, when they were further up the path, causing her to recoil inwardly. There was a contradiction in the two, his reaction the opposite of the cool indifference of his colleague. A kind of leer. *I know your sort.* That type of thing. *Is this what you want?*

By the time she reached the river the place was too dark for comfort, the crickets sounding out madly, as if they were on heat. She ate standing up, hypnotized by the black satin reflection of the water, wondering if she was still stoned.

He made no attempt to mask his surprise.

'Well, well,' said Nathan, ushering Ray into his hut.

'A booty call? I'm honoured. But surely you could have made more of an effort, love?'

Sinking back onto his charpoy he gestured at her jeans, the loose kurta, her chappals.

'No,' said Ray. 'Listen, I wanted to ask you something, actually. It's work.'

His hut felt damp, full of the smell of marijuana. The scent was so strong that it seemed to register on her tongue as a melancholy aftertaste. The staleness in the air was exacerbated by his clothes, which were in piles everywhere – on the charpoy where he slept, thrown onto the pillows, across the floor, even heaped upon the spare charpoy at the other end of the room. He cleared his bed, swiping at some jeans and a denim jacket so that they fell onto the floor behind, and invited her to sit down as he rolled a spliff.

'What you looking for?' he said.

Ray stared at the cigarette packets lying by the side of his bed, the half-empty bottle of rum, keys and ashtray. Her eyes kept darting about the room. He had not put any photographs up on the walls, which were painted a dark green, giving them a heavier tone than the colour in her hut. There were no books visible, just the shooting scripts, which they all updated regularly, in and amongst the general mess. What was she looking for? She smiled, apologetically.

'Nothing. Of course, nothing.'

He shrugged.

'Nothing to hide. More's the pity.'

She sat next to him. She looked him over, watching him wrinkle his nose as he went about the business of rolling. He smoothed the papers so that the thin cylinder widened out to form a perfect cone. It was a moment from university days: the cocooned intimacy of a room strewn with the debris of general bedroom living, the way in which they were sitting parallel on a bed. It almost felt as if her legs could dangle playfully from the height of the charpoy, like a child's.

He lit it and puffed a couple of times, brief and methodical, before passing it over. His face was pretty in the candlelight, boyish and attentive. Ray released her sandals to the floor and crossed her legs on the bed. She took a long drag and lay back. She could see the piece of sari material he had bought on their trip to the market. It was draped over a line of wire high on the wall in the corner of the room, a repeating yellow over khaki cotton.

'You looking for clues?' he asked. 'You're thinking: a single man, in his early forties, with signs of the onset of male-pattern baldness . . . what does he do when he's alone in his room? Yes? What's his deal? He's a man who lived in a cell for years; what kind of habits has he got? How does he satisfy his urges?'

He made his voice nasal, squashing it into a parody of a wildlife reporter. 'When the ex-prisoner is returned to his original habitat, but without the previous constraints, it takes him some time to realize he is not in a prison at all.'

'You've got a story,' said Ray. 'You've got a story and I need you to tell me what it is.'

'Whoa, there. Has Serena been shooting her mouth off?'

'It doesn't matter,' said Ray. 'You could really help me out here, Nathan. We need something, and you know Nick's making noises back home.'

'OK,' said Nathan. 'What's it worth?'

He stared at her, a challenge in his eyes, blowing the smoke slowly so that it rose in front of his face.

'Come on, man,' said Ray. She scratched at her arm, feeling mosquito bumps rise. 'Just tell me what it is. Is it the governor?'

'Nah,' said Nathan. 'He doesn't even know this.'

'Is it Nandini?'

'Who's she? No, it's Daw-lat. Daw-lat.'

'This is made up,' said Ray, sighing, half from relief, half from frustration. 'That's a made-up name.'

'For fuck's sake! You've bloody interviewed him. Big pink turban? Lives right opposite you?'

'Daulath?' said Ray.

'Right.'

'But he doesn't speak English. How could you –'

'God, you're slow sometimes. He's hardly going to give me the story himself, is he?'

Ray looked around the room.

'Could I have some of that water?' she said. 'I feel a bit sick.'

She noticed his forearms as he got up, thinking how rare it was to see him without his denim jacket. Even when the heat was overwhelming he seemed to keep it on. His arms were delicate; the skin looked soft, a ripple of pale, downy hair on the topside. After fetching the water he picked up an A4 pad, as if it was an afterthought, then returned to sit next to her.

His gaze darted over her as he began to sketch, skittered from her hair down to her nose, her chest, her left hand, which was pressing on one of her feet, crossed in front of her. She put her hand through her hair, bitten by self-consciousness.

'No, no,' he said, leaning forward, holding his right hand up, requesting that she stop. 'That's your thing, isn't it? Your hair is always down covering your right eye. Part of your personality. Put it back how it was, will you?'

She felt absurd, annoyed by the command, but shook her hair back nonetheless, so that it swung loosely over her right eye like a black drape. She could still see through the thick strands, as though she was looking through a fabric weave, some kind of room divider. It was idiotic, mannered, but she did it to dispel the forcefulness of his voice, to stop him from asking her again.

'Better.' He nodded, taking a final drag on the spliff and pressing it into a small steel plate. He exhaled the smoke and began drawing again.

'Beautiful eyes,' he said. 'Or should I say eye? One beautiful eye staring right at me. Always staring, always looking for that which lies beneath. Looking for the horror, your friend, the horror.'

'Please,' said Ray. 'Are you really attempting Brando in *Apocalypse Now*?'

'Worth a shot,' said Nathan.

'Look, I need to know about Daulath,' said Ray. 'What's the thing? Just tell me?'

'He's ill,' said Nathan. 'Doctor told me. He doesn't know it himself yet, poor bastard.'

He pressed the pencil on its side and began to shade in her hair, a scratchy sound.

'Ill?' She leaned over and put her hand on Nathan's arm. 'Stop for a second,' she said.

'Yep. Been a naughty boy. Doctor's noticed the symptoms and is going to test him. Daw-lat hasn't the faintest. Thinks he's unlucky – keeps getting colds, diarrhoea . . .'

Ray took her hand away.

'AIDS,' she said.

'HIV, yep,' said Nathan. 'Doc's pretty sure of it. His wife doesn't know, obviously. Imagine it. He'll have to tell her. I've asked the doctor to hold off. He says he doesn't really need the patient's permission to do the test, so he can find out first and wait for us, then let him know for the first time on camera, out of the blue.'

Ray lay back against the wall. The nausea was with her again.

'Oh God,' she said. 'We can't do that.'

'I thought you'd be pleased! Be careful what you wish for, girl.'

'No,' she said quietly. 'No, we can't go in like this – it's his life, his wife's life . . .'

He put the pad down.

'Look, if I hadn't spoken to the doctor we'd have missed it entirely. Might have caught the tail end of it; the guy would have told us in interview what it was like, finding out. Backstory interview yet again. This way, we can control the whole thing and you can see it all happen in front of you. Isn't that what Serena's always on about: "present tense"?'

'Yes, yes,' said Ray, swaying slightly as she moved to sit up. 'Do me a favour, Nathan, don't tell anyone about this yet.'

He smiled at her.

'Not yet, Sun-ray,' he said. 'Doctor's not due back on site for a while.'

He took a package from underneath the pillow on the charpoy. It was small, and made of leaves bandaged together. He pulled at one end of the thin string that bound it and the leaves fell open, revealing a sticky black globe about the size of an egg.

'Charas,' he said, taking a bite and handing it over to her. 'Solid local hash. Tastes pretty good.'

She took it, absurdly, out of a desire for comfort, the need for a blanket over her tired body.

Exterior: Complete blackness. The characters stagger around the riverbank, struggling to stay upright.

RAY: How did we get here?

NATHAN: You wanted to. You wanted it. 'Get me to the river of black satin,' you said. [*He begins to sing.*]

> Nights in white satin,
> Never reaching the end.
> Letters I've written,
> Never meaning to send.
>
> Beauty I'd always missed
> With these eyes before,
> Just what the truth is
> I can't say any more.

RAY: I feel like I'm going to pass out. [*He grabs her and throws her to the ground. She laughs.*] You're right on top of me.

NATHAN: [*kisses her, then lifts his head. She leans up and kisses him back.*] Feels weird, dunnit?

RAY: Yeah, why is that?

NATHAN: Maybe you should come back with me to the hut and get that sari off the wall, then wrap it round you, and I can lie down on the floor and look up your skirt.

RAY: What?

NATHAN: Yeah.

RAY: I don't think so.

[*They have another go at kissing and Nathan's hands start to move under her clothes. He begins to unzip his jeans.*]

NATHAN: [*in a voice that suggests he is trying to talk up the action, to get things going*] In a minute I'm going to get a condom out of my back pocket and I'm going to put it on my cock and then I'm going to slip it inside your knickers and –

RAY: No, no. [*She attempts to roll to one side but Nathan is holding her fast.*]

NATHAN: What?

RAY: No, I don't want to go that far. [*She pushes against him and he lets go.*]

NATHAN: [*sounds disgusted*] You have got to be fucking kidding me?

RAY: No, Nathan, seriously.

[*pause*]

RAY: [*sounds like an afterthought*] I'm a virgin, anyway.

NATHAN: [*after a stunned silence*] You are fucking joking. Do I look like I'm in the mood for jokes? Twenty-something-year-old virgin? What the fuck you doing getting mashed off your head, if you're some religious nut?

RAY: No, it's not that. I've had boyfriends, messed around. Just not the final act.

NATHAN: Jesus, you're bloody serious! This isn't a joke?

RAY: No, it's to do with love, or something like that.

NATHAN: Love?

RAY: [*exhales loudly*] I decided I wouldn't, you know, have sex unless I fell in love.

NATHAN: How old are you?

RAY: Twenty-seven.

NATHAN: But you must have –

RAY: Fallen in love? No, I haven't. Not yet.

[*He gets up and starts zipping up his fly. He makes sounds of disgust. Ray is lying against the earth. She starts crying as he turns to walk away.*]

RAY: Please, Nathan! Don't leave me here. I feel sick. My mouth tastes of . . . dung. It tastes horrific.

NATHAN: Shut your mouth. You'll wake people.

RAY: But Nathan! Please. [*crying*] I feel like I'm going to pass out. I don't know how to get up. I'm scared.

NATHAN: Scared? Of what? You need to shut up. See this, what you're going through? This is my life, every night back home. This is my fucking life, not some extreme sports holiday. So many nights I lie there in my flat, shaking, wanking, frying my brain to a fucking crisp, sitting there alone, a charred-up, burned piece of flesh. Human flesh. Now you know. Fucking deal with it! [*He walks on, staggers a bit, and looks as if he is going to fall. He turns back and shouts at her.*] Welcome to the gates of hell, love. All I can say is, at least you're going home in the morning.

RAY: Nathan! Seriously. Don't leave me here. Nathan!

NATHAN: Stop squealing like a princess bride on her fucking wedding night. [*He turns his back and walks away.*]

9.

The events played over in her head as the hours jumped, right through to dawn. The lines of dialogue were samples in a mashed-up soundtrack of the night, inserting their words into the cracks of her consciousness as she fell in and out of sleep. The words taunted her through repetition, reflected the urgency of her heart rate, which also stuttered and raced in panic through the night. But they did not change. The words remained the same during every re-run. An accurate transcript of events.

The sky was melting when she woke finally, a thick clot of pink sinking through the clear air to trickle against the pale chocolate of the earth. It made her think of cheap Neapolitan ice cream, the pollution of colour through the borders. Her stomach cramped as she turned, pulled herself up, attempted to start back up the slope of the riverbank. Seeing guards in the outer field of her vision, she looked quickly to the ground and began to walk back to her hut. Sweat patched her kurta heavily under the arms, banding thickly down her back and between her breasts. As she passed the water tap she heard two men whispering.

'Madam!' one of them called.

She looked up instinctively, forgetting to ignore the call.

'Good morning!' he said, smiling, as his friend nudged him. It was the guard who had helped with her bags upon arrival. His moustache bristled in the crisp morning light, his cap slanted and secure on his head.

I still don't know their names, she thought as she walked

on to her hut, nodding at them briefly as she turned the corner, her eyelids drooping in defence against the violence of the brightening sun. Forgot to ask their names over the whole week. How was it possible?

In bed she cried. The tears claimed each cheek in silence, a stream of relief as much as pain. It was something to be inside, alone. Serena was not on her charpoy or in the kitchen even though it was so early in the morning.

She was sensitive to the touch of things, the way the sheet felt against her body. The drug was still in her body, ugly, leaching its taste into the spit on her tongue with authority. Tears mingled with the dirt on her pillowcase, forming a wet, gritty layer on the cotton, abrasive against her face as she turned to lie on her side. She thought of Nandini. She thought of her neighbour opposite, the secret marking his blood. His wife in the kitchen, backing away, pulling her ghoonghat over her face to ward off more questions during filming. She thought of them all: Ram Pyari, her sculpted defiant face, her thin body shrouded in yellow transparency; the girl in purple yanking the water pump for her life; the white-haired woman cradling her dog, squinting her nose in the sun, barking at the humans around, her voice sweetened for her puppy. The images came to Ray with the incendiary force of hallucination, flickering to the rhythm in her chest. She had to do something about them, these people.

She cleaned herself up and made her way out. She did not have the camera, or even a notepad. She walked towards Nandini's hut, head down, hiding under an umbrella even though there was no real need for shade yet. The trucks were already on the road, beeping loudly. She stepped off the path to avoid a ditch, accidentally catching the eye of a boy bathing in a front yard. It was the teenager who had carried her luggage. He lathered his narrow, long torso with a small disc of soap and returned her glance, lingeringly: his eyes constant, indecipherable under the wet black strips of hair plastered on his forehead. She pulled the umbrella down in front of her so that her own gaze on the world was masked until she reached Nandini's porch.

Nandini was dressed in a long, loose kaftan printed in black and white. She stood back to let Ray walk in.

'I do not recall us arranging to meet,' she said. 'My apologies.'

Ray shook her head, aware of the sweat on her face, the layer of wet salt on her body, accumulated during the walk in spite of her shower just fifteen minutes previously. She was shaking lightly. She turned to balance herself carefully against a stack of upturned crates in Nandini's kitchen.

'Ill again?'

Ray nodded, not trusting herself to speak without leaking tears.

'Could I use your toilet?' said Ray.

Nandini's toilet was behind her hut, bordered by a low wall of meshed branches, waist high. Ray crouched over the hole in the ground and used the privacy to cough, retch, cool herself by wiping under her arms with some broad leaves that she ripped from a branch nearby.

When she returned, she was ready to speak.

'Loose motions again,' she said, raising her eyebrows at Nandini. 'I'm such a lightweight. Need to toughen up!'

Nandini took a teaspoon of sugar and mixed it into a small steel cup.

'Drink this,' she said, handing Ray a hot drink that smelled of lemon and cloves. 'Come and sit down.'

They talked around the issues. Ray deflected Nandini's concern by explaining that she was just feeling under the weather.

'You are under pressure?' said Nandini, with politeness in her tone. 'You are on your feet all the time. You have promised a lot to the governor? Or your boss in London?'

'I'll be fine,' said Ray. 'Just missing home a bit, being ill, you know.'

'Who do you live with there? You don't have a husband, I think? Your parents don't mind that you are unmarried?' said Nandini.

Ray laughed.

'No, I don't have a husband.'

'A boyfriend?'

'No boyfriend. But I have had . . . involvements in the past.'

She craved honesty, the shade of confession. And yet, looking at Nandini, observing the modest long plait that reached her hips, the clipped certitude of her manner, Ray couldn't quite trust her. She put her hand to the back of her neck, wiping the sweat with the sleeve of her kurta.

'What about you?' Ray said. 'Don't you ever feel like remarrying? Do you have a boyfriend?'

'Me? We are not so loose here.'

'Not so loose but not so saintly either. Are you in love?'

Nandini laughed.

'You are getting your spirits back,' she said, getting up. 'It's good. Want some paan?'

'Sure,' said Ray. 'But . . . love, *yaar*, seriously – tell me about it.'

'*Arre baba*. OK, OK, wait!' Nandini left and returned with four plump parcels of betel leaf in her open palm. 'Take one, just there. You like sweet paan? As opposed to the savoury ones? These are sweet.'

'Thank you so much,' said Ray, briefly bowing her head and taking one. She had a brief flashback to Nathan, the ritualistic way in which he had unveiled the charas, untying the leaves that bandaged it so that they fell open to reveal the sticky globe.

She took a paan and bit into it, let the juice surge into her left cheek.

'So, you were saying . . .'

Nandini sighed. She was serious now, briefly making eye contact with Ray before looking away and speaking.

'Truth is, you know, with my situation, since what happened to me, I don't feel like I want anything. I have suitors, offers, whatever you want to call them. Someone left me a note just the other day in the pigeonhole at the college where I train once a week. It was very flattering, full of compliments . . .'

'Who was it from?'

'I don't know – a visiting lecturer, or something like that. He saw me from a distance, asked someone my name – I don't know exactly. His note was a bit ridiculous: "I saw you looking so beautiful in your red sari . . ." La la la . . .'

'What!' said Ray. 'Come on, seriously?'

'Oh yes, and he is not the first,' said Nandini, laughing. 'But with my daughter and all, I don't want any men around –'

'Your daughter?'

Nandini smoothed a hand over the back of her head, her fingertips brushing against the start of her plait. Her expression was retreating into formality.

'Yes, my daughter.'

'But, you've never mentioned –'

Ray faltered. The shift in Nandini's demeanour was subtle enough, but it had made her seem vulnerable, as though she was thinning out and ready to snap like dry wood.

'I have a daughter. I didn't think it was relevant before.'

Nandini got up and straightened her kaftan, reverting to the curt manner she had displayed on the first day of meeting.

'Do you want some water? Hot milk? I need to get ready shortly to start work. I don't know about you. Time is very precious in the morning here; there is always a lot to do before leaving the compound.' She began to shuffle the plates in the kitchen.

'But, Nandini, just wait one minute. Come back. Please tell me – I had no idea . . .'

Ray caught a sudden vision of her: large wary eyes in an oval face, the hint of a frown at the centre of a smooth forehead.

'What do you want me to say?' she said. 'She lives with my parents. Because of my situation, being a single parent, no husband, the governor has allowed her to live outside the prison. I see her at weekends. She is my whole life.'

Nandini hunched over. Her face crinkled at the frown point and tears began to accumulate in her eyes, slipping into rivulets down her cheeks. They seemed natural but slightly fantastical to Ray, like the dew in a time-lapse shot of flowers.

Ray was silent. Without realizing it, she mentally zoomed in on Nandini's face and refocused the shot. I am like a camera, with my shutter open. She heard the internal narrator, harsh and unwelcome in her head: Bingo. It's a money shot.

She walked over, anxious to help somehow, opening her arms. Nandini was leaning against the stack of crates in the kitchen, bent in a way that didn't allow a clean embrace.

There was no encouragement to continue but Ray let her arms hang there anyway, not quite encircling Nandini, barely touching her, in the semblance of a hug. The narrator's voice was sticky, pungent as tar: It was under your nose all along, love.

Outside Ray could see the men lining up for their 6.30 a.m. roll call before leaving for work. They stood in line by the entry gate at the other end of the compound: about fifteen of them queuing in two rows, clearly visible through the dry empty space of the field. Rana Pratap dominated the line, a shawl hanging loosely from his tall shoulders, in spite of the heat, his sunglasses blocking any chance for Ray to assess his mood. Two security guards stood with clipboards and pens, making conversation with the inmates as they came up to sign.

She saw a man with wild beard growth sitting on a scooter to the side of the line, identifying him as one of the men who had been on the charpoy listening to Rana's story in the footage Serena had filmed. He was joined by another man, someone Ray did not recognize, someone more non-descript, dressed in brown trousers and a cream shirt. They shook hands, and the new arrival took the passenger seat, lifting his feet, which were in flip-flops, as the engine began to putter up to a loud conclusion. The scooter lurched as it built up speed, the driver beeping the horn loudly as they went through the gate, his passenger waving at a couple of inmates who were waiting for the bus on the road.

Ray watched these men, easy in the familiarity of the morning routine. She wondered about the women – whether they had a parallel registration. How many of them left the compound for work? Other than Nandini she had seen only the stitchers so far, the women who worked within the confines of the prison. Maybe they left to buy vegetables, groceries, that kind of thing.

For a few moments she forgot her sense of shame, the unclean layer she felt over her body, the events of the previous night. She enjoyed the simple inevitability of the line moving forward, each man being ticked off the list, starting his day. She did not have her camera, and she was grateful for that.

She took the long route to Nathan's hut, walking behind the main rows of dwellings, to avoid contact with the residents. She had no choice but to speak to him. They would be working together so there was no way round it, and this knowledge was clotting her thoughts. She passed some goats, a stack of empty crates, a few scattered chickens, the children in their uniforms making their way to the river.

She could see a figure sitting on the verandah as she approached his place. It was a woman, leaning her head back to rest against the rim of a white plastic chair. It was Serena, of course, her boyish crop of blonde hair just visible as she slouched. Below the chair, Ray could see one of her legs dangling, bare, the scuffed heel of her foot kicking lazily against the hardened earth.

Of course, thought Ray, as Nathan pushed open the tin door and stood next to Serena. He was dressed in a pair of boxer shorts, a loose grey T-shirt. He smiled at Serena and tilted his head, indicating that she should come back inside. She stood up, revealing that she was also wearing nothing but a baggy, masculine T-shirt, a white cotton standard that skimmed the tops of her thighs just below her underwear. She bent over and giggled, briefly pulling it down towards her knees, then looked around before disappearing through the doorway.

10.

Slow days, sweat-marked nights. Sleep is banal and slipshod –
permeated with unwelcome heat that causes Ray to wake
fitfully throughout the night, and bed down for siesta in the
scratchy fatigue of the afternoon. In the mornings she films
sequences of daily life – stitching and washing in the prison,
an inmate hammering metal at his employer's stall in the
market, the children flying kites or in their classes at the
local school. This is how the next week lays itself out: a
barely distinguishable pattern of ups and downs in a minor
key, a drone of similar sounds that have little cumulative
meaning.

But there is one major change. She has a story. She is following Nandini, with the agreement of Nick in London,
whom she updates by email every couple of days. But she
has to move slowly. Nandini can take only half an hour or so
of dialogue about her life, before she becomes restless, and
Ray does not want to scare her off.

Ray has managed to avoid bumping into Nathan during
this period. He does not seek her out either, working separately with Serena on pieces to camera. They seem to be
following their own leads, engaging in their own dialogue
with Nick. Nathan does not visit the girls' hut; Serena goes
to him. This means Ray only ever sees him from a distance,
filming with Serena or walking across the compound to get
to Zafar and their car, smoking as he walks, a hand in the
front pocket of his jeans.

Ray doesn't pry too much into their work. It is as though

she and Serena are working on two separate films. At first, after the night by the river, she had expected Nathan to come and find her, imagined that he would need to talk about it, finesse his actions. Seeing him walk past the central peepal, or hovering by the water pump, she feared their inevitable exchange, although she knew it was necessary. He would write off the night, excuse it as a drunken, druggie adventure, maybe. Or he would want to talk about their working relationship, how important it was that it remained unaffected. But the conversation never came. He seemed content to let the night pass without comment.

Serena usually sleeps at Nathan's hut during the after-noon, and for some of the night. She makes sure to wake up in her own bed, though, returning in the early hours and slipping between her sheets with swift economy. It is too hot for the sleeping bag. Still, her return causes Ray to stir, cover herself properly with her own sheets, even alter her breathing subconsciously, so that it becomes more even, mannered.

Ray has mentioned it only once: the new state of affairs.

'Did you stay the night at Nathan's?' she said, when Ser-ena came back to their hut on the first morning after. It was coming up to midday, a few hours after Ray had seen her in the white T-shirt on Nathan's verandah. Serena was wearing her own clothes as she entered the hut, the clothes she had worn to the fort.

Ray was at the desk, making notes on her exchange with Nandini.

'Yes,' said Serena, a smile accompanying her nod, a light shrug of the shoulders – the only indicators that some-thing out of the ordinary was taking place. She looked Ray in the eye, a wordless challenge to continue. The smile continued to play at her lips, hinting at victory or something similar, so it seemed to Ray, who disengaged, returning to her notes.

Sanghvi sat back in his chair and stretched, marking the end of the process. He had put his signature to various pieces of paper brought to him by one of his staff, a man in his thirties, uniformed in a way that was similar to the guards in the prison. Ray sat opposite him in his office, a spacious room at the top of a building with three floors: the Central Prison Department for the state. The papers fluttered in the wind generated by the desk fan, a large book holding them down; two mobile phones lay next to them. His office was generally uncluttered and everything was pretty much as Ray had imagined: the stone walls in the local shade of pale orange, spattered with rising brown lines of discoloration, a flower calendar pinned up with a few framed certificates above the grey filing cabinet, a fountain pen in his hand, the sleek metal of the casing juxtaposed with the varied rings on his fingers. He exuded satisfaction, a sense of leisure; he was a large cat covered in comfortable fur, but with the mild hint of threat. His smile prickled with a kind of static as he nodded at Ray.

'Take, take,' he said, gesturing at a tray of tea, served in small glasses. 'No problem.'

Ray picked up a glass, balancing the heat between her fingertips and drinking cautiously. She burned her tongue straight away.

'Mr Sanghvi,' she said, sucking at her tongue as she put the glass back down.

'Sujay, please,' he said.

'Sujay. Thanks for making the time to see me.'

Ray flicked through her notebook until she found the list of names. She had forced herself to finally identify everyone in the prison by name, so that she would not be reduced to referring to them with vague descriptions during this meeting with the governor. For her own purposes she had written a descriptive list of the main characters in her pad:

Girl in purple jumper from pump – Saira Chokhi
Neighbour opposite, pink turban – Daulath Ramnath
Stitching wife with bangle on foot, wife of neighbour
    opposite – Jyoti Ramnath
White-haired woman with dog – Bharti Patel
Sewing wife often at pump at dawn – Mayawati Kachwaha
Quarry business owner – Rana Pratap
Boy who brings water and tiffins – Raju
Man who plays cards with Rana Pratap – Soumendra
    Banerjee
Woman who buried husband under house – Ram Pyari
Counsellor / Self-defence – Nandini Gupta
Teenager who washes with bucket near Nandini's place –
    Kalloo
Inmate with patchy beard – Jitindra Rathore
Inmate with wild puffed-out beard – Raja Munshi
Guard 1 – short, clipped moustache, mahogany skin –
    Shyam
Guard 2 – taller, white overlying black hair – Ramesh
Guard 3 – paan-chewing – Dularichand

'Things are going very well,' said Ray. 'We just want to set up a formal interview with you.'

'Of course,' said Sanghvi. 'I thought you'd never ask.'

'And I'd like to talk to you about the guards – Shyam, Ramesh, Dularichand.'

'Yes, yes. Go ahead. Is everything to your liking so far?'

'Yes – but how should I put it? Everyone has been very accommodating. Maybe too accommodating.'

'Meaning?'

'I get the sense that . . . that people are on their best behaviour for us.'

He purred with amusement.

'OK. I see. You want some action, is it? Some *dishoom dishoom*?'

He made his hands into fists, shaking them as he used the words for cartoon violence.

Ray smiled. She thought carefully about her next words.

'I just think they are . . . a little inhibited, maybe? Perhaps they think we are making this film for you, rather than with you, if you know what I mean. Sometimes I get this sense that they don't want to rock the boat – which I can understand.'

'It's a subtle distinction, don't you think?' said the governor. 'I mean, after all, no offence, Ms Bhullar, but you are here as my guests. The three of you, that is. The BBC.'

One of the phones on his desk beeped. He picked it up and checked the message.

Ray watched him, searched for something revealing in his facial expression. She could not work out how serious he was being. His smile was contained. He called out to his side, and a teenager in white vest and cotton trousers appeared, took away the tea tray. He turned back to Ray and continued.

'I can help you with the ins and outs of our policy here, my friend. That I can certainly do. But I can't fashion a – what do you call it over there? – "bunfight", is it? I can't cook one up just because people are doing their jobs too harmoniously for you now, eh!'

He laughed, encouraging her to join him, smoothing his sleeves down with the same distinguished, feline quality to his movements that she had noticed before.

'*Arre, Manu!*' he called, turning to the outer office. '*Woh gift, tho le aao. Woh package?*' Hey, Manu! That gift, do bring it. The package?

He nodded enthusiastically as the boy returned with a parcel wrapped in newspaper.

'*De – De!*' he said, gesturing at Ray. Give it.

She opened it cautiously, as though it could be a booby trap, however unplanned, like the tea that had burned her mouth a few minutes previously, or the filter water she had drunk out of misplaced bravado at their first meeting.

It was a red shawl, a fine-knit in heavy maroon wool, the colour of blood in a deep cut, a wound. The embroidery was in white, detailing branches, leaves, tiny birds. It was a beautiful piece.

'I thought you might be getting cold at night,' he said, taking some supari from a silver tureen at the edge of his desk and pushing it over to her side. 'It gets quite chilly when the sun goes down.'

Ray sits at the table and waits for the boy to approach her. Eleven thirty in the morning should be a busy time of day but the dhaba is not full. In front of her is an A4-sized menu encased in vinyl, a steel cup full of tap water, a small china plate filled with onions and sliced lemon. Around her there are mostly empty tables, but two men sit alone at opposite corners of the room. One is counting money and making notes in a large ledger; the other is eating a plate of chole-bhattura, the steaming chick peas presented in a steel dipping bowl next to large oval pieces of deep-fried bread, each torn to reveal a fluffy steaming centre.

This is a place not usually graced by females. Ray is aware that she is a curiosity, sitting in the corner, alone. Even the book she has open on the table serves to attract attention rather than deflect it away, as it would in London if she was in a similar situation. She had known before asking that Zafar would clearly be surprised at her request to stop here after the usual cybercafe visit, but, with no break in his habitual discretion, he unloaded her without question, disappearing for half an hour at her recommendation.

She flicks a page and attempts to look casual. At the edge of her vision she can see that some of the staff are now looking at her intermittently: the small boy in navy shorts who is rubbing a rag over the tables on the opposite side, the sleepy owner in oversized white kurta and Nehru cap, cross-legged and prodding the spit-roasting chickens on the open grill with his tongs, his teenage sidekick in the paisley shirt and drainpipe trousers who is standing against the door to the kitchen.

Ray looks at the plate in front of her and registers the dryness in her throat. She thinks about dipping an onion in chutney, and washing it down with a large draught of water from the steel glass. Tap water is, of course, off limits, similarly salad and chutneys, for their high water content. Anyway, she has come here to eat chicken. The smell, through the passenger window, as they hovered in traffic, was too much for her. She is satisfying a craving.

'It is all about how you place yourself and how you name yourself.' A line from Nathan.

'You are veg, yes?' Words from the governor.

Ray is officially classified as 'veg'. Or, more bluntly, this is her default way of classifying herself. On flights, when invited to a dinner party, or when she eats out in a group, she places herself in that category. And yet she does not conform to the accompanying categories expected of someone here who is veg. She smokes cigarettes and marijuana occasionally; has drunk alcohol of late; has, of course, had different types of liaisons with people of the opposite sex, several times; and sometimes eats dead animals when no one is looking. However, she cannot but think of herself as veg.

Nick's latest email is weighing on her mind. She takes the printout from her pocket and looks at it again.

OK, we've done enough prep with Nandini and it's time to get her full story on camera. Remember, this is only going to broadcast in the UK so it won't be seen by the victim's family. What we need is full-scale honesty and emotion on camera – tears, etc. That's how we'll empathize with her. Great that she speaks English, which will make it more direct. But we need a blow-by-blow account now, if you'll excuse the pun, as much detail as you can uncover in her own retelling. We may end up doing a small drama recon to go with it visually. Main thing is, viewer needs to really feel her pain if we are going to care.

Thanks,
Nick

The chicken tikka arrives. Ray glances around. She knows no one is going to come into this tiny alleyway curling off Ramini Bazaar, such a small tendril in the undergrowth of passageways. There is no way that one of the others can know she is here, and yet it is habit for her to check, privately, that she isn't being watched whenever she performs this particular transgression. The process itself is a secret, a small bubble that forms around her as she observes the required rituals.

Serena and Nathan were at work when she returned to the compound. They were filming Rana Pratap in his front yard, with a small entourage of guards, children and some animals – a goat tied to the outdoor charpoy, a handful of hens and chicks scurrying around their feet. Nathan was talking in an animated fashion to Rana, who stood in front of him, straight-backed, tall, wrapped in a thin khaki shawl, his usual gold ear hoops prominent in the dappled light from the peepal tree above. Freshly washed sheets were hanging on the tangled branches of the fence in the foreground; three children aged between four and six years crouched in the corner of the yard near a large steel tureen on a wire tripod, throwing stones into the dust beneath it. There was a woman standing next to Rana, near the multicoloured backdrop of his truck, who was also part of the dialogue. As she drew closer, Ray saw that the woman was Nandini. She seemed to be acting as an interpreter for the crew.

'What he is saying,' said Nandini, 'is that there is no problem in our society. You repent for your wrongdoing, and you do this as part of your religious customs, and people accept that you have moved on. This is part of the cycle of life. It is not considered a kindness, it is part of reform.' She paused and looked at Nathan, gesturing at Rana with one hand as if to dispel any confusion that she might be voicing her own thoughts. 'He believes this, that is.'

Serena, standing to the side so that Nathan and Rana were together in the shot, in profile, was holding the camera firmly against her chest and peering down at the viewfinder.

'Right,' said Nathan, addressing Nandini and Rana alternately. 'When I came out of prison, because I'd been locked in a cell so long, I couldn't cross the road. I was like a child. I couldn't use the phone. I had forgotten so many things that you need to know. Little, everyday things. So I'm not talking about my inner self being released and coping. I'm not talking about my inner spirit. I'm not talking about society. I'm talking about me, having a problem negotiating my way across a road. Because I'd spent so long being told, "Do this, do that, do this, do that." And I'm just wondering if the prisoners here have those sorts of problems. Not spiritual problems, yes? Not economic problems. Not those sorts of problems. Not problems with their neighbours, society. But practical problems.'

He grimaced, laughing, his face suddenly youthful, wide-eyed, as if astonished by the thought he was about to reveal.

'If you don't cross a road for ten years in India,' he said, pointing over at the bustling highway, 'how do you cope? It's so fast!' He threw his hands around to simulate chaos, smiling, raising his eyebrows to indicate that Nandini should commence translating.

Nandini waited for a moment, looking at the ground. Ray felt for her. It was a lot to translate accurately.

'*He's saying that he was alone when he was in prison,*' Nandini began. Then she continued brusquely, a note of intimacy with Rana in her tone. '*He's on about control. You're in prison for years, you don't have a phone, and don't you feel confused when you come out? That kind of thing.*'

Rana Pratap began to reply, pushing his sunglasses to the ridge of his nose whilst giving rise to an authoritative river of words. Nathan gave Serena a concerned look, surprised that his lengthy question had been reduced to just two lines. Serena shook her head from behind the camera, dismissing his worry.

Ray watched, unseen, from the main drag of the settlement. She could hear everything so clearly, even register their expressions.

'You see, if you are on good behaviour,' said Nandini, translating, 'there is a lot of contact with the outside world. You can have visits from your relatives every week, even whilst in the traditional jail. He himself enjoyed fourteen paroles over his sentence of seven and a half years before coming here.'

There was a look of astonishment on Nathan's face, held in a gradual smile of understanding. He nodded as Nandini spoke.

'That's it,' he said to Rana. 'Fourteen times, eh? That's why you're so together. Back home –' he put his finger to the side of his head and started whirling it around – 'they come out and they're all gone, they've lost it. Lost their minds.' He made his hands into the shape of a machine gun. 'Then they're, like, bam-bam, yes? It's over. They've lost it.' He turned to Nandini. 'Tell him prison isn't the best of places anywhere in the world, but never do prison in England!'

Nandini smiled and proceeded to translate.

'Imagine the Home Office, if a prison governor had an idea for a place like this back in Britain?' said Nathan to Serena, while Nandini was translating. 'They'd never be able to get it through.'

Ray was surprised when they came back to the hut together, an hour later. It was the first time she'd encountered Nathan face to face since the night by the river.

'All right?' he said to Ray as he bent to come through the door. 'How's tricks?'

He sank onto Serena's charpoy and began to roll a cigarette. He seemed tiny to her, crumpled, diminutive. He stared at Ray blankly, like a man waiting for a traffic light to change colour.

'Yeah, fine,' said Ray. It seemed impossible that anything had happened between them.

She was sitting on her own charpoy, drinking some water from a two-litre plastic bottle. Her stomach had begun to churn again. 'How are you guys doing?'

Serena was connecting up the camera to the laptop.

'We're good,' she said, 'aren't we, Nathan?'

Ray looked at the laptop screen, squinting against the lines of sunlight coming through the holes in the stone wall. The nausea was rising in her stomach, a reminder of her weakness, her foreign sensitivity to local food and drink. It taunted her at the back of her throat, an unresolved threat.

'I saw you filming on my way back,' said Ray. 'You're using Nandini to translate?'

Nathan took a drag from his cigarette and lay back on Serena's pillow.

'Your idea, wasn't it?' he said to Ray. 'But I'm not sure she's doing a great job.'

'She's fine,' said Serena. 'She gets the gist across. So long as I get your questions on camera, Nathan, it's fine. She's getting good responses from the inmates, as you can tell from how animated they get.'

'She's my main character, though,' said Ray. 'I'm following her for Nick.'

'I don't think there's a conflict of interest,' said Serena. 'Don't worry. I've spoken to Nick about it. He wants us to all work together on Nandini once you've got more out of her – a present-tense narrative we can follow together. So it's only going to be beneficial if we spend time with her, get to know her a bit.'

Ray paused, pressed her hands on her stomach to still a momentary contraction. She retched and bent over.

'Jesus,' said Nathan. 'You're not ill again, are you?'

Serena laughed.

'You're one delicate petal, aren't you?' he continued, making a show of his astonishment. 'What've you been ingesting this time? Didn't you learn your lesson with the water?'

Ray drank from the bottle, breathing deeply at intervals. That this should be her interaction with them, now that they were finally together after a week . . . It was humiliating. Inwardly, she cursed the chicken, her need to go to the dhaba.

'Well, you can see the doctor tomorrow,' said Nathan. 'We've called him in to talk about Dawlat.'

Ray flinched at the mention of the man's name. She looked from Nathan to Serena.

'Don't look so shocked,' said Serena. 'Nathan told me he's filled you in on the Dawlat story. It's good stuff, isn't it? Nick is really pleased. This is what we need to talk about. We've just got to work out the details: prep the doctor tomorrow, arrange a day with him when he can do the HIV test on camera, work out how to break the results. He's pretty sure it's going to be positive, though.'

Ray stood up and walked to the door.

'Non-violent protest?' said Nathan, grinning, sucking deeply at the wet filter of his cigarette.

'Not funny,' said Ray.

'We're going to need to work together on this, Ray,' said Serena. 'One of us on sound, one on camera. It's too important a scene to screw up. We're only going to get one chance to break the news to him –'

Ray retched violently and pushed her way through the tin door. She vomited before she could shut the door behind her, hampered by the awkward curvature of the corrugated metal, the weight of it, unable to prevent them from seeing the fluid spatter over the dry earth, or avoid the quick-rising smell of rot and damp.

In front of her she saw Daulath's wife, Jyoti. She was feeding the chickens, scattering some seed in the front yard. She looked up and Ray smiled automatically, in spite of the situation she was in, holding up her hand, palm facing outwards, fingers outstretched in a frozen wave. It was the universal sign of friendship, the sign that everything was OK.

Jyoti nodded back in acknowledgement. Her eyes were curious, a light frown marking her forehead as if she was trying to work out what was happening. She threw another couple of handfuls of grain to the ground and the chickens fluttered at her feet. Ray had a sudden, absurd image of herself retching on the verandah of her hut, then understood the possible meaning in Jyoti's eyes. In several Hindi films that she had seen, especially the grand family sagas, vomiting was a common motif: the new bride in the joint family's household would always run somewhere out of sight at some point early on in the movie, clutching her stomach underneath the folds of her pallu as celebratory bells rang in the soundtrack, the in-laws and husband giving each other looks of quiet congratulation, in anticipation of the forthcoming child.

It was a ridiculous idea that Jyoti might think she was pregnant. And yet she couldn't shift the thought that this possibility was in Jyoti's mind. Ray smiled again, bringing her hands together in namaste rather than using them to wipe away the saliva at the sides of her mouth, then she retreated back into the hut to find some tissue paper.

II.

Ray lay on her side, holding a sheet to her body, slowly waking. Serena had not returned from her trip to Nathan's that night, and now it was morning; the light pressing through the window holes and long cracks in the walls was violent and hot on Ray's face. The little tap on the door was more like a click, repetitive and forceful. She sat up and pulled the sheet towards her neck.

'*Aap kaun?*' she said. Who are you?

'Dularichand, *guard*.'

Her mind worked through the sleep and nausea. Dularichand, guard: the middle one.

'One minute, I'm coming,' she said.

She looked around for her trousers, shouting the words out again, loudly, worried that he might look through the holes in the wall to check whether she was ready.

She dressed and opened the door. He was the guard who had looked at her, leered maybe, while he was chewing the paan, the night she had gone to Nathan's hut. The same guard who had snickered as she walked back from the riverbank at dawn, dishevelled.

'*Water, madam,*' he said, handing her a bottle of mineral water.

She took the water and stared at him, hoping to divine something from his expression. She couldn't be sure whether she had interpreted it correctly that night: the snide quality, the twist of his betel-stained mouth. It could have been the drug warping her brain, the requisite paranoia that accompanied any drug-taking experience. It could just be an example of her own petty, embarrassing prejudices coming out. She wasn't confident in her perceptions now, especially the accuracy of her memory.

'*Thank you,*' she said.

He did not leave, but stood and watched her for a few seconds.

'*Everything is OK?*' she said.

He still did not speak. He adjusted his cap slightly, and waited, looking her directly in the eye.

'*Tell me,*' she said.

His smile was a flicker, barely there before it was gone.

'*Tip, madam,*' he said.

She frowned, uneasy. It occurred to her that water was never handed over like this; it was delivered daily by one of the teenagers, often Raju, and usually left in the shade outside the front door. Why was he here to give her this bottle so ceremoniously? And why was he asking for a tip, something that had never once been requested of the crew, to her knowledge. They had planned to tip for the catering in a lump sum at the end, after agreeing on the amount with the production manager back in London.

She stepped backwards into the hut and got her purse. She opened it, nervous at exposing the money inside, a large wad of notes of different denominations – ten, twenty, one hundred, five hundred rupees, a couple of red thousand-rupee notes dwarfing the rest.

She took a ten-rupee note and gave it to him, unsure that it was the right thing to do. His eyes were wide; she could feel the round force of them. He shook his head.

'A big tip, madam,' he said in English, nodding at her purse. 'You will be giving me a very big tip.'

He gestured at the thousand-rupee notes. She stepped back, sickened by the intensity of his eyes.

'A big tip, madam,' he said. It was underlined. There was nothing covert about it.

'But . . .' she faltered, then continued in Hindi: '*Does the governor know you're asking for this?*'

'*Governor?*' The smile flickered over his face again. The glimmer of a flame's light on a person's face at a bonfire. '*You want me to talk to Thakur Sahib?*'

She stared at him, comprehending slowly. She had forced him to verbalize the threat. He was asking if she wanted him to tell the governor about her sordid experiment with Nathan. She had no doubt that he knew everything. He'd seen them stagger down to the river together, and witnessed her coming back alone at dawn. Nathan's room would have reeked of the freshly burned charas when the boy went to collect his dinner tiffin for washing that evening, while they were both at the river. Maybe Dularichand had even watched her and Nathan tussling on the riverbank. He could have easily found a discreet vantage point with his colleague, the white-haired guard who had been on night patrol with him.

She gave him both notes, watching him fold the outsized papers into small rectangles, the pink print smooth under his fingertips, then put them in the front pocket of his khaki shirt before bowing lightly and turning to go.

Why not, she thought, looking at the notes remaining in her purse. Who could blame him for trying to get some of this cash? There was so much of it here, compared to his probable monthly salary. She watched him walk away down the dirt track towards the water pump, stopping by a gathering of kids in uniform, collecting together for the walk to school near a few stacks of wooden food crates, empty, piled in a tower that came up to his head. He ruffled his hand through the youngest child's hair, teasing the others.

She was repelled by her own actions, not his. She imagined the governor's reaction to their deeds thus far – the respected BBC crew – to their swollen, perverse presence here in this village.

It was the big interview, the culmination of the week's reconnaissance: the interview in which Nandini explained everything.

Ray took the footage back to the hut straight after filming her, and began the process of logging and transcribing immediately. The hut was damp, the air a little fetid from unwashed clothes that lay in heaps by both of their beds.

She worked with the practical drive of a robot, stopping and starting the machine to write down the details of the build-up, each word used in the line of questioning that led to the key moment. Everything went into the transcript – Nandini's movements and expressions; audio interruptions by birds or traffic; the full details of each question asked by Ray.

When the pivotal moment came, and Nandini began to cry on screen, Ray felt her own eyes fill up.

TAPE 14 LOG
Interview, Nandini Gupta and Ray Bhullar (Out Of Vision)

OOV: Tell me what happened, what led up to it. How is it possible to explain what you were going through? I can't imagine it.

NANDINI: Seven days they starved me. Locked me up, no food, no water. Seven days, and I was seven months pregnant.

OOV: How did they do it? Who did this to you? Please tell

me in full sentences, if you can. Sorry, Nandini, but my questions are going to be edited out of this.

NANDINI: My husband and his mother locked me up in the box room of our house. It was because they wanted more dowry; they said my parents hadn't delivered the agreed goods. It was an arranged marriage, you know, and my parents had no idea that they were sending me to this kind of family. They gave so much when we were married: fifty thousand rupees cash, a gold chain, a scooter – furniture for the house, a fridge, a washing machine; my mother gave me pure-gold sets of jewellery that became the property of the household.

OOV: This kind of marriage means you naturally went to live in your in-laws' house – was it a joint family set-up?

NANDINI: Yes, it was a joint family household. They were traditional. And arrogant that they were the son's parents, although who knows why. He wasn't even educated as much as me. [*Horn beeps loudly. She breaks and begins again.*] He told me he was B.Com. pass, and I was M.Com., so I thought OK, fine; then after marriage I found out he had only studied as far as tenth class in school.

OOV: What age is the tenth class? What job did he do? Can you explain in a full sentence? Sorry again, Nandini. Thanks for bearing with me.

NANDINI: My husband was just tenth pass, which means that he left school aged sixteen. He was a loan financier for a bank. I was educated until I was twenty-two years old, through to master's degree level.

OOV: The discovery must have been very hard. There must have been a sense of betrayal? [*Birdsong interruption. Repeats question.*] The discovery must have been very hard. There must have been a sense of betrayal? How did it make you feel when you found out?

NANDINI: How do you think I felt? Ray, can you imagine? I was so educated, I had my master's. I thought I would work – my father had always made sure that we valued education very highly . . . Then I was suddenly in this family, and they began to treat me like that, with the demands for money, not letting me even leave the house, expecting me to work day and night in the kitchen. It was a horrible shock but I did not want to reveal things to my parents because I did not want to upset them.

OOV: It must have been so difficult.

[*pause*]

NANDINI: [*Nods. Quivers slightly. Is starting to get upset.*]

OOV: What happened next?

NANDINI: I got pregnant within weeks, like I was supposed to. No contraception, of course. And then – I'm pregnant and he is having an affair with an old girlfriend. I find out. It's too much. I tell him to stop seeing her, but he laughs at me and says she is the number-one woman in his life. [*Stops and gulps.*]

OOV: That sounds terrible. Did you feel like leaving? It sounds unbearable.

NANDINI: I was pregnant. He used to hit me if I argued with him.

OOV: But you didn't leave?

NANDINI: I didn't leave because I didn't want to shame my parents, to sadden them. They are good people.

OOV: And then they locked you up? Why did they do that? Why did they do something so terrible?

NANDINI: [*Face creases. Mouth wobbles. Tears appear in eyes.*]

OOV: You were seven months pregnant and they starved you, locked you up in the box room? What happened to your baby?

NANDINI: [*Face contorts. Slow breakdown. Begins to heave. Crying and gasping.*]

OOV: What happened, Nandini? I can't imagine how painful this must be for you to remember. What happened?

NANDINI: [*Gulping back tears, holds head in hands, shakes her head.*]

[*pause*]

NANDINI: [*Looks up into camera.*] She was born early. She was born without fingers and toes. They are all stuck together like this. [*Holds up her hand. Creates webbed effect by pushing fingers together closely, and looks at hand.*]

[*pause*]

NANDINI: [*Looks back into camera. Ragged breathing, like hiccups. Face is streaked with lines of tears.*]

OOV: How did you cope? What did you do when you came out of hospital after the birth? You must have been so weak. So angry. It's so sad to think of it.

NANDINI: I left. I had dignity, finally. I went to my parents after the birth. It is not so easy for a woman who leaves her marriage to survive here. You can't just go and rent a room somewhere, earn a living. You need money, you need acceptance, you need respect. Women don't live alone here; we are trapped within these boundaries of society. But my parents took me back.

OOV: You went back to your parents. Then what happened? How did you see your husband and his family again?

NANDINI: I went back to get my things. That was when it happened. I phoned them to arrange it.

OOV: Tell me what happened. Did you take your child?

NANDINI: No, I didn't take her. They knew about her. They wanted nothing to do with her. They were worried that I would expect something from them, for her upkeep.

[*pause*]

OOV: [*Nods off camera.*]

NANDINI: I walked into that house. He was sitting and watching the television. My husband. He ignored me when I walked in. It seemed that the house was quite empty. I couldn't see anyone. But I could hear my mother-in-law. Afterwards I thought they had planned it that way. I looked for my jewellery. It had all gone. My cupboard was locked. I went into the kitchen. He came from behind and hugged me, put his arms around me. I was shocked. I started to push him away. I did not want him to touch me. Then I smelled it. My pallu was burning – the pallu of my sari. I started screaming and he hit me. Then I realized he had set fire to me. He held my arms down and I could see the fire. I was screaming and screaming. I pushed him away and his mother came in the kitchen. I tried to run out through the back and she blocked the door. She was quite a heavy woman. I pushed her. I was burning. I was next to the sink. I took a knife and I stabbed her with it before he could come. I stabbed her and I ran out screaming. This neighbour came and helped me. I threw myself down on the mud, and she used a blanket . . . She saved my life. His mother died. He took her to hospital but she died. [*Looks into camera. Waits for a response.*]

[*pause*]

NANDINI: Is that enough? You want to know anything else?

[*cut*]

Watching the tape reminded Ray of a moment from her first job in television, working as a development researcher on a current affairs strand for an independent production company in London. A producer had come back from interviewing a woman about a child she had lost over a decade previously, and he played the rushes back on a small television on their shared desk in the open-plan office.

'Getting someone to cry,' he'd said to Ray, 'takes just one simple thing. Someone told me how to do it when I worked in news. You just sympathize with them every time they speak. So you say something like, "That must have been so difficult," after one response. Or, "That must have been really, really hard," after the next. Simple stuff. "How terrible for you. It must have been so difficult." That kind of thing. You find different ways in which to keep on saying it, and eventually they break down. Look, you can see from this –'

He pressed the fast-forward button and paused it right at the moment when the woman's face creased into tears, slowing down the action and rewinding it so that her face became a gloopy horror mask of slurred activity. He found the audio of the question preceding the tears and proudly played it back for Ray, turning up the volume at his interjection of sympathy: 'That must have been really difficult.' When the tears began, he made a right angle with his thumb and forefinger and pointed his hand, like a gun, at the screen. 'And . . . bang!' he said with a smile.

Ray had found this despicable at the time. And yet, writing down the transcript of the build-up to Nandini's tears, she realized she had followed this lesson exactly.

Ray felt a soreness, a blister on her conscience as she watched Nandini. Like the woman on the screen all those years ago, Nandini had the contorted face of a gargoyle: mouth gagging, forehead creased. The tears on her cheeks were not apparent until Ray hit the play button and let the shot play.

I2.

The doctor was a temperate man, determinedly unflus-
tered. This was Ray's main assessment of him as he pored
over her face, taking her temperature at the charpoy.

'You have been including non-veg in your diet?' he asked,
after noting down a list of symptoms.

Ray flushed. She hadn't expected the question, let alone
that it would arise so quickly and directly. She shook her
head.

He was a short man, his broad body busting out of a small
frame, black rectangular glasses bringing a sense of order
and command to an otherwise nondescript face, a head of
tight black curls. His skin was on the darker side; his accent
also suggested he was from the south. His age was indeterminate to Ray, anywhere from mid-thirties to mid-forties.

'Water? Chutney? Salad? Yoghurt?'

He listed the offending items without any particular intonation, as though calling out names from a register at school.

Ray nodded at each one.

He gave her a brief look over the top of his spectacles.

'Risky behaviour. But no non-veg?' he asked again.

She frowned momentarily, wondering why he would
repeat the question, whether there was something particular about her demeanour that suggested this label.

'No,' she said irritably. 'I am veg, as I said. Why do you
ask?'

He scribbled in his pad then gave her a cursory glance
before continuing to write.

'Food poisoning from meat, chicken, fish can be particularly nasty and, of course, needs particular medication. Water-based goods have their own problems – typhoid, dysentery, that kind of thing. I am merely trying to ascertain what may have stimulated your illness in this instance. Do not take offence.'

His tone was admonitory, certain of the need to put things straight. She felt duly corrected, instantly wondering at her own righteousness. It was easy enough to forget your own actions, it seemed – her recent escapade at the dhaba was not something that had caused confusion or conflict in her mind when he'd asked the question.

He clicked open a briefcase on the charpoy and the heavy lid of thick moulded plastic sprang back onto the mattress, just below her feet. Inside, he began to feel his way through an array of small glass bottles and papers.

The door of the hut was open suddenly, pulled expertly in one large clean motion to allow Serena and Nathan into the room. Ray pulled her knees up to her chest.

'Dr Sahib!' said Serena warmly, moving to her side of the room to offload the camera kit. She took some tissues from the front pocket of the camera bag, patted the sweat on her forehead and at her neck.

'Raj! How are you doing?' said Nathan.

The doctor stood up and shook Nathan's hand. His facial expression was unrecognizable, invigorated by the smile that split the whole of his face. Ray marvelled at it, wondering how he had kept such a smile from her during the whole consultation.

'Just seeing to this colleague of yours. She needs to take more care with her food and drink.'

'Oh yeah,' said Nathan. 'She's a thrill-seeker, that one. Goes wild if you leave her to her own devices. All kinds of illegal stuff – salad vegetables, I've seen her eat, even drinks filter water, would you believe? Crazy, eh?'

The two men laughed. Ray forced out a smile, unwilling to allow them to exclude her from the joke. The doctor found a bottle of small white capsules and handed it to her.

'Amoebic dysentery,' he said. 'Three times a day, one tablet. It goes without saying that you need to cut out any water-based products, and stick to bottled mineral water only.'

Ray looked at the bottle. She needed to get better, so it was important to get the correct medicine. Now was the time to confess that she'd recently eaten chicken, just in case. But it didn't seem possible. How could she do it in front of Serena and Nathan? She would seem so absurd for having lied about something this trivial in their eyes. Maybe there was no need. There was a fifty–fifty chance that this had come about from water, anyway.

'Listen, Raj,' said Nathan. 'We're ready to move on the Dawlat story. How do you think we should play it on the day?'

'Yes,' said Serena. 'How long does the test take, and, most importantly, do you think you could have an outcome for us then and there? Presumably you will be duty-bound to tell him what you are testing for, when you first take his blood and urine? Or do those rules not apply here?'

The doctor clicked the briefcase back together and sat on the chair by the desk.

'See, it's like this,' he said. 'Daulath is exhibiting all of the signs of being HIV positive and my main concern is that he needs to know this as soon as possible. The reasons for this are very obvious, right? First, he could be having intercourse with his wife. That is very likely, and thereby he could be passing it on that way. Secondly, he could be having intercourse outside the home, and this is how the virus is spreading generally – through sex-workers, drug use and the like. We do not know how he has contracted it. Thirdly, there are his children. The older one is unlikely to have it, but the younger one is a possibility, depending on how long it has taken for the disease to manifest itself. All in all, this is an urgent matter and I would like to test him as soon as possible.'

'How's tomorrow?' said Serena.

'Soon enough for you?' said Nathan.

The doctor nodded. 'It will work like this. The finger-prick test can give results within just five minutes. It uses the whole blood composition, and is a pretty accurate test now – it has been in usage for about two years. I need to pick up a kit and . . .'

He took out his phone and pressed a few buttons, searching for something.

'OK. I will be back at Ashwer in a few days. We can do it then.'

'The sooner the better,' said Serena.

'Will you be able to offer him some counselling before the test?' said Ray. 'And after the results?'

'Yes, great idea,' said Serena. 'If you could also translate for Nathan we'd be very grateful, Raj.'

'I mean for him,' said Ray. 'For Daulath. Will you be able to help him through this so it isn't too much of a shock?'

The doctor looked at her abstractedly, nodding, checking his mobile for messages.

'I will explain it to him fully, don't worry,' he said, buckling up his briefcase. 'It is something very serious. Meanwhile, you need to apply some more care in looking after yourself with regard to food and water consumption.'

He shook Nathan's hand as he left. Nathan pulled him in and slapped him loudly on the back.

'Let's have a drink soon, eh?' said Nathan. He made a motion with his hand as though tipping a glass up to his mouth. 'I'll bet you've got a nice selection of local whiskey round your gaffe.'

The doctor laughed. 'Local and *imported*,' he said as he pulled the door open. 'You are welcome to visit any time.'

Nandini was sitting by the river when Ray found her. She was talking with the older woman, the white-haired one, who was without her dog today. They sat close to the edge, watching a few women squatting in the water, their saris hitched up over their knees, cardigans over their blouses, beating and wringing clothes. The air was muggy, the sky overcast.

'*Namaste*,' said Ray as she joined them, bowing deferentially to the woman with Nandini.

The woman nodded at her, giving a grin that was cluttered with browning teeth.

'Hi,' said Ray to Nandini.

Nandini smiled.

'We were just finishing,' she said. 'I was talking to Bharti-ji here about her illness. She has heart problems.'

'Oh,' said Ray. 'I'm sorry to hear that.'

'We're just talking about whether she can be transferred to a hospital for some long-term care. But her son is not able to pay for her. He can't afford it, he says.'

'*Ask her*,' said the woman in Hindi, gesturing at Ray. '*Ask her how much she earns. What's her salary, out of interest?*'

Nandini translated, her eyes crinkling with humour.

'Yes, I understood her,' said Ray, laughing. 'Wow, that's direct.'

'What's your answer?' said Nandini.

'Well, it's difficult to work out the equivalent salary here,' said Ray. 'I suppose you'd have to take into account the cost of living . . .'

'Don't get nervous,' said Nandini. 'It's a standard question here.'

'Do you get asked it?' said Ray.

'Sometimes.'

'But I doubt the governor gets asked it?'

Nandini laughed.

'Yes, that is unlikely.'

'So I should take it as a compliment, maybe,' said Ray. 'That Bharti-ji feels she can ask it of me.'

Bharti nudged Nandini, clearly bored by the exchange. She spoke in an animated mutter, the words at times inaudible, but with gusto, interest. *'Has she been to a hospital here? Ask her something else. I heard this from my brother-in-law's son. He went abroad for his business. He said that he went to hospital there, and he was lying in the bed for many days. One thing he saw – tell me if this is true. He said next to him in the bed there was an old woman, my age, and every morning she used to wake up and look in a hand mirror, like this – and then she would put make-up on. Lipstick, colour on her cheeks, even her eyes. The whole lot, she bedecked herself with, like some newly-wed. And she was as old as me, he said. Can it be true?'*

Ray put up a hand to stop Nandini translating. She replied in Hindi.

'Yes, it is probably true, Bharti-ji,' she said. *'People wear make-up there at all ages. Or not, as the fancy takes them. Do you ever feel like wearing make-up?'*

Bharti gurgled with laughter, leaning over and slapping her knees. It was infectious. Ray chuckled spontaneously, joined by Nandini.

'That old woman,' said Bharti, pausing and gasping for breath. *'I just keep thinking about it. So funny! She's getting*

herself all dolled up and she's – what? Just an oldie, in the end! When she takes the hand mirror away, what's left? Just an oldie.'

'But you're not that old, Auntie-ji,' said Ray, herself unable to stop the giggles. 'How old are you – sixty-something?'

'What's she saying?' said Bharti to Nandini, pushing herself up and putting her hands together to signify that she was leaving.

'Don't worry,' said Nandini. 'Nothing in particular.'

Ray watched her leave: her crooked body swaddled in the white sari; the striking flash of her oiled hair, even whiter; her staggering steps up the slope, chappals slipping against the dry earth; periodic stops to catch her breath.

'Do you think she needs help?' said Ray. 'Even I find it difficult getting up that hill without losing my grip.'

'No, she's very proud,' said Nandini. 'She's determined to do everything by herself. This heart thing . . . it's an established route out of this place after being here a few years. But it requires a lot of money, unfortunately. In order to get the kind of medical report that she'd need.'

'Bribery?' said Ray. 'Surely the governor is on top of that stuff?'

'Come on,' said Nandini. 'Rich people don't stay in prison long. You must have noticed that.'

Ray cast her mind about, trying to think through the list of inmates.

'What about Rana Pratap?' she said, thinking of his silhouette in the hazy atmosphere of quarry dust as he stood shouting orders to his labourers.

'He's an entrepreneur,' said Nandini. 'He's got a good thing going here. He didn't come with that much, but got a loan from the bank to start his business. He's very commanding, so they invested in him. He's not going anywhere, even when his term is up. He'll settle locally and keep his business going.'

Ray stretched her legs out and looked at the scene before her. One of the women was walking out of the river; her dark green sari was pressed against her body, drenched, clinging to her hips. She was carrying an armful of under-clothes, welding them fiercely to her chest so that they were unable to straggle free, to slip back into the water.

'I wanted to talk to you about something,' said Ray.

She paused. It was a difficult thing to bring up.

'I was thinking about . . .' Like Nandini, she found it diffi-cult to name the man. 'Your ex-husband,' said Ray.

A wavering line insinuated itself into the blank width of Nandini's forehead. She nodded.

'I was thinking about your daughter too,' said Ray. 'And what an incredible job you've done in raising her.'

Nandini brightened momentarily.

'She's begun dancing, would you believe,' she said to Ray. 'No fingers, no toes, and she dances so naturally, like a leaf in the wind. So strange that she has chosen this particular activ-ity at school. But it is hard to explain what it is like when she dances. Very bubbly, she is. Expressive. It comes instinctively. I say to her, you just work hard and become something. You are so special; you don't need to get married when you are older. Not that she's going to get any proposals, with her disability. I know that now, even though she is only six years old. But then I am hardly a great fan of marriage myself.' She laughed.

Ray smiled.

'She could fall in love, though,' she said. 'She sounds incredible. Someone is bound to fall in love with her when she gets older. She might well get married, you never know. It's a long way off. '

'You think so?' said Nandini. 'Really, Ray? You think someone would be interested in actually marrying her?'

There was melancholy in her voice, at odds with her earlier defiance.

Ray paused again before speaking.

'Just think of the matrimonial ad!' said Nandini, forcing out a half-laugh.

'This is the thing, Nandini . . .' said Ray, looking back over the river.

The sun was beginning to splinter through the clouds, causing pinpricks of light to appear on the surface of the water. The women were starting to leave the river one by one, ready to spread their clothes and catch the sun. She continued, her voice swelling with gravity, with the suggestion that she wanted to talk about something important.

'These things that have happened to you,' said Ray, 'the events that you have overcome – your husband trying to kill you, setting fire to your sari whilst giving you a hug – you managed to survive these by defending yourself, but you're the one who's ended up in jail. He walks free because he has good relations with the police, or, more to the point, he has money for the police, and you never see him again. It makes me so angry. It's still hard for me to conceive of your strength, your ability to move on and build so much after all this. It seems incredible to me. I admire you so much.'

Nandini shrugged, smiling.

'You talk as if there is a choice,' she said.

'But you do choose certain things,' said Ray. 'You've chosen to offer counselling to women who need you in the prison; you've chosen to train as a lawyer on the side to offer them advocacy. All this whilst bringing up your daughter, making a good life for her, making choices for her every day, every week.'

Nandini laughed. 'Ha! I am not training as a lawyer just to help the women here,' she said. 'Make no mistake about it, I don't care how long it takes for me to qualify, but one day I am going to take my own case to court and try that man, bring him to account. Five years, ten years, whatever it takes. Call it revenge. I do not have money but I have my will. I will get him. He starved me when I was pregnant, damaged my child when she was powerless, before she was born. And he will get what he deserves. I remember what happened very clearly. I will have no trouble making a case, however many years pass by.'

There was a new heat in her face, a vigour to her language. Ray was surprised at how overt it was. She was excited by it. She had not seen this side to Nandini before.

'That makes a lot of sense,' she said, widening her eyes. 'Now we're getting somewhere. Nandini, I feel like you've been carrying so much, with regard to your husband, for so many years – don't you ever feel like the events have become almost fantastical in your mind? Do you think it would help to do something, to make them more real, in a way, so that you're not just dealing with the memories from years ago? Don't you think it would help to meet him, talk to him in some way, confront him? There must be a part of you that wants to do that? Show him you haven't just conveniently disappeared out of sight? I mean, he doesn't even contribute to the support of his daughter . . . Don't you feel he owes you something after all this?'

It was finally out. Ray had been carrying this question around for days now, wondering how to put it to Nandini. It had begun as a phone conversation with Nick, and it was his suggestion, but over time Ray had absorbed it into her own reasoning. She would film this meeting if it ever took place, of course, and it would be incredibly dramatic. But, aside from that, didn't this man need to be confronted? It angered Ray, inflamed her thoughts at times, the arrogance with which he had apparently just begun again – with a new wife, a new child. She thought back to the phone call in which Nick had first put the idea across.

'We'll need to cover ourselves,' he had said, 'but that's fine. Compliance, legal, etc., will need to clear the final programme. Especially as her charges against him were dropped due to lack of evidence. But if we do it all through Nandini's point of view, we should be fine. You know the type of thing: voice-over intro with "Nandini claims" and "Nandini believes", etc. That should do the job. Plus, it goes without saying, it has to look like it was her idea to see him, and that we just tagged along.'

Nandini did not respond to the question. Instead, the frown deepened in her forehead. She leaned forward, supporting herself lightly on her knees, her back still straight, her kurta pulled forward over her calves.

'It's just a thought I've had, Nandini,' Ray continued. 'It just seems to make sense. What do you think?' Out of the corner of her eye, she could see two security guards walking over the hill, behind Nandini's head. One of them was Dularichand. He smiled at Ray, bent his head in greeting. She nodded back, uneasy at the arrangement between them, the worrying link it had formed.

'You really think so?' Nandini said finally. It was an echo of her earlier question, the question about her daughter getting married. *You really think so?* It made Ray stumble for a moment, the honesty of the question. It was not coded in any way; there was no subtext of mockery or sarcasm to sheathe the arrow. It was so direct. *You really think so?*

'Er . . . what do you think, Nandini?' said Ray, unable to trust herself to give a response of equal sincerity. 'I want to hear what you think. Do you want to meet him? I can come with you, of course.'

Nandini shrugged again.

'I think . . .' she said, faltering. 'I think that if you think it is a good idea, then . . . But it seems so impossible. He's never going to agree.'

'You could write him a letter, and suggest the meeting,' said Ray. 'And then see what happens. If he wants to meet, fine.'

'He won't meet,' said Nandini. 'Why would he?' She smiled sadly. 'Obviously I have fantasized about confronting him a thousand times. You really think it is possible? What purpose can it serve? He will just deny it.'

'Don't think about that right now,' said Ray. 'The purpose is to be yourself – show him how strong you have become. Let's just write to him and see if it is possible. We'll work out what to do if he agrees.'

Nandini leaned her head to one side, closing her eyes.

'No, I don't think so,' she said.

She was aware of his mood, even though there were about twenty yards between them. It hung from him without effort, a thin anorak of mischief that could also shield him from adverse reactions. He was sitting on the low wall watching her work, his back against the traffic, leaning forward, a cigarette in his mouth. She couldn't see his face. The sun was behind him so to look over would involve looking directly into the most intense part of the vortex of light. But out of the corner of her eye she could see his posture: relaxed and content. He seemed pleased with himself, somehow. It made her angry.

Nathan was watching Ray film the children after school. They were gathered at the centre of the land, using the giant peepal tree as their main location. There were around fifteen of them and they played here every day in the early-evening cool: cricket, tag, and when there was a breeze they brought kites. The older ones looked after their younger siblings – a ten-year-old girl sat under the tree feeding a one-year-old baby, his cheeks swelling as he crushed a piece of fruit, his forehead framed by a mushroom-hued knitted woollen hat that pointed upwards in a soft peak. Ray had been trying to build up a relationship with these children over the weeks, whereby she hoped to get them to talk to her, rather than giggling together in group huddles and falling about in front of the camera in sudden chaos and hysteria. They were fascinated with the camera, taking it in turns to watch themselves back in the viewfinder, asking Ray to film kite fights, in which they would fly their kites against each other, expertly harnessing the force of the wind to swoop and cut up each other's strings, until there was only one winner left in the sky.

Ray did everything they asked. It was all part of gaining their confidence, inching closer to the point of trust where they would start talking to her openly. She had tried with the teenagers, asking them about the difficulties they faced here, the feelings they had towards their parents or other children at school, but so far there seemed to be a tacit agreement between them that they wouldn't reveal anything. The younger ones were shy or feigned lack of understanding when she tried to get down to their level, both physically and verbally. She knew that it was time, stamina, persistence that led to trust when it came to children. But they didn't have endless months here, and they were already well into the allocated time.

At this moment she had grouped four of the younger lot – those under seven or eight – to sing into the camera, purely because she found it cute. They found it amusing themselves, whispering and conferring about the song choice. There were two girls, their hair still ribboned in tight plaits to go with their school tunics, and two boys, fidgeting in short-sleeved shirts and shorts. In the end they stepped forward, organizing themselves into an unsteady curve that swayed back and forth, and sang a song clearly selected for her benefit, from the film *Raja Hindustani*, which was more than a decade old.

> *Pardesi, Pardesi, jaana nahin,*
> *Mujhe chodke, Mujhe chodke.*
> *Pardesi, Pardesi, jaana nahin*
> *Munh mod ke, dil tod ke.*
>
> Foreigner, foreigner, don't go,
> Don't leave me, don't leave me.
> Foreigner, foreigner, don't go
> Don't turn away from me,
> Don't break my heart.

Ray laughed outright when she heard the reference, letting the surprise in her voice rip through the air with pleasure. She was flattered, and something instantly softened inside her. She sang the next verse back to them, and the children grabbed each other around the shoulders and laughed, pleased with her knowledge, the giggles hiccuping out of their bodies as though they were being tickled.

> *Pardesi, mere yaara!*
> *Vaada nibhana –*

Mujhe yaad rakhna
Kahin bhuul na jaana.

Foreigner, my friend!
Keep your promise –
Remember me,
Make sure you don't forget me.

They joined in when she sang the chorus: *Pardesi, Pardesi, jaana nahin*. It was almost romantic, the goofy way in which they found the intimation so amusing.

She turned to wave at Nathan, gesturing at him to join in. It was a good time to try to get him amongst them, on camera. He took a deep draw on his cigarette and waved back at her. The light of the sun had diffused, and was radiating out in a fan shape behind him, the outer border fringed with clouds. She turned and filmed him for five seconds, his crouched shape sitting inside this suddenly epic backdrop, then moved her arm in a big circle through the air to get him to come over. He came slowly, with exaggerated reluctance.

'What's this in aid of?' he said. 'I had a good view where I was.'

Ray put her hand on his shoulder. She was determined to stay unruffled with him. She would begin again; it had to be possible.

'They're being so adorable,' she said. 'Can't I just get you playing with them?'

He grimaced, stubbing his cigarette out under his shoe.

'I thought you were self-sufficient these days,' he said. 'Miss me, do you? Doesn't Serena have the exclusive rights? To me, I mean: the Nathan rights.'

'We both need to get you on camera since you're the presenter of the whole programme,' said Ray, turning the camera to film the girl and the one-year-old, who were just getting up from the tree to walk back, the baby's peaked hat bobbing as his sister clutched him with one arm, lifting a cloth bag containing the fruit and snack remnants with her other hand. Ray steadied the camera, letting the girl's retreating back get smaller, then she moved the camera to the left so that some of the weighty tree trunk came into the foreground, allowing them to exit the frame in a natural-seeming fashion.

'You've come on,' said Nathan. 'Pretty long shot, that, to hold right up, hand-held. Ambitious. This time apart, it's doing you good. Are you sure I won't put you off your game?'

He ran amongst them, playing the clown, weaving and joshing so that their squeals and shouts dispersed around him wherever he was, proportional to his efforts, like the dust kicked up by the football. When he tried for a goal, it was expertly negotiated, and she couldn't be quite sure if he'd missed on purpose – the way he interrupted the game to career in joyfully, as if in victory, hugging the goalie, raising the boy's hand up to punch the sky. Ray ran in close and filmed their two faces laughing. The boy was Anup, the elder son of Daulath and Jyoti. Ray was surprised to see how relaxed and happy he seemed with Nathan. She was used to a more hunched, silent boy with a general air of dismissal, which she attributed to the awkwardness of being thirteen, and to an understandable lack of interest in being filmed all the time, especially by two women – herself and Nandini. Anup being with Nathan so informally like this was a great set-up, a real opportunity to get him to talk.

'Stay'n'there,' she called to Nathan, rolling the words together so that they wouldn't be immediately understandable to Anup. The children spoke mostly Hindi in the compound but understood a lot more English than their parents, due to the local school.

'What?' asked Nathan, looking over at Ray whilst putting his arm around the boy's neck in a mock wrestling position.

She shook her head, moving it diagonally to nod at the boy, not wanting to speak now the others were quietening down. Nathan frowned as if to say: I don't know what you mean.

Ray came up close to them.

'You don't make it easy, Nathan,' she muttered, bringing the camera to her chest, adjusting the focus and smiling at Anup.

'What!' Nathan laughed and hugged Anup closer, rubbing his fist on the boy's head. 'What's she on about, eh?'

'Help me out here,' said Ray, speaking quickly whilst gesturing at Anup to move his head slightly to the left so that it didn't bob out of frame, giving him a thumbs up as he acquiesced. She continued, speaking in a fast patter.

'Quick interview about football, what it means, relaxation, escapism, compared to the stresses at home, get on to problems – parents, school, acceptance, change, his dad, yes? His dad is the same person we were discussing this morning with Raj, OK? Lives opposite me. We need to sympathize with this family, what they are going through.'

Nathan nodded, straightening himself up slightly, as if to indicate that he was ready to be professional.

'It's great,' said Ray, looking into the viewfinder. 'Casual, kind of . . . fluid. He's much more relaxed than normal. I'll come in with the first question and you just take it from the translation.'

'OK,' said Nathan, raising his eyebrows and rolling his eyes in an exaggerated fashion to make Anup laugh. The boy smiled uncertainly. He seemed anxious about what might be expected of him. They began the three-way of question, translation, boy's answer and the return translation. Nathan asked a series of football-related questions: which position did the boy like playing, how long and what kind of practice did he get at school? Ray knew he was doing it to bond with the boy, but she began to glaze over at the lack of emotion in the answers. The boy was perfunctory, straightforward, slightly admiring of Nathan, still shy. She translated quickly, hoping to move onto something more interesting.

'*I have a lot of studies to do as well,*' he said in Hindi. '*I have my eighth-class exams coming up next year.*'

'Is it hard here?' asked Nathan. 'Miss your old school, your old home?'

The boy shook his head, a response that Ray had seen many times to the very same question.

'Is it nice living with both your mum and dad?' said Nathan. 'What was it like when he was away?'

The boy shrugged.

'*It was OK,*' he said.

Ray was reminded of the boy's father, in the initial interview with the family. '*I just don't like it with them,*' he had said. '*I don't like it. What else is there to say?*'

The gaping pauses, these odd pieces of speech, exchanged without momentum or interest, were beginning to frustrate her. She felt, with urgency, that something had to happen.

'What do you want to do when you leave school? Got any ideas about jobs? What did you want to be when you were little?' asked Nathan.

On impulse, Ray decided not to translate the question. Instead, she found herself substituting her own.

'*Would you say you love your father?*' she said to him. '*Do you still believe in love? Didn't he screw up your life, in a way? Don't you wonder why he didn't think of you before he killed someone?*'

The boy looked shocked. He glanced surreptitiously at Nathan and back at Ray. She raised her eyebrows briefly to empathize, as if to say that she was also surprised that these words were coming out of Nathan's mouth. And yet the question seemed to galvanize him in some way. He answered with vehemence, a strained form of outrage.

'*Well, what do you think? How do you think it feels? But I have to live here now. I am a child so it's not my choice. People talk about prisoners' rights, but what about children? They have no rights, do they? The prison said I had to come and live with my father, come with my mother, so I did that. We did it for him. We came here to the open camp so that he didn't have to live in a normal prison cell any more. But what about you?*' he said, looking directly at Nathan. '*You went to jail, they say. Do you have a child? Do you feel sorry for that? For what you did? You tell me!*'

Ray allowed herself a few seconds to think about how to trim the answer. He had spoken quickly, colloquially, and yet she was surprised by how much of it she had understood. She was getting used to the local dialect. Nathan was looking at her with hope, now that it was clear the boy was stirred up. She translated in detail, just substituting 'I can't think about the future, I'm thinking about now' for the first two questions in his answer, so that it would seem more like a sudden decision to turn the conversation towards this area. She also trimmed the end of his answer, removing 'You tell me!' – concerned that it might seem too aggressive.

Nathan was taken aback, and yet he also seemed excited by the intrusion.

'Fair play . . .' he said, nodding. 'Yes, I get you. Of course I get you. Yes – I do have a child, and I don't see him much.

And that's my regret, my scar, my – how to say it? – black hole . . . you know? That's my loss. And that's why I envy your dad, because he gets to live with you here like this, like a family. He can watch you and your brother grow up. When we were in prison – I was in and out of normal prison for years and years, from when I was your age, although I didn't kill anyone, I was a robber – but I was in and out of prison, and we used to think this kind of thing was science fiction. We'd sit around and say, "Wow, imagine a prison where you can live a normal life with your family and other people, imagine that!" And here it is. It's a chance for him, isn't it? Your dad. A chance to make up for it, to start again. Most of us don't get that chance.'

Ray translated pretty much accurately, just removing the reference to Nathan not killing anyone, for fear of upsetting the boy by the differentiation.

'*But what if I don't want to live with him?*' said the boy. '*What if I want to go somewhere else but I'm not allowed to? What if I want to be far away from him? Far away. Anyway, I can't leave my mother. And my father is ill, so she can't . . .*'

He trailed off.

'Ill?' said Nathan. 'How is he ill?'

'*Who knows what it is? I don't even care. Partly he vomits, partly he has diarrhoea. And other things. I don't care. I don't care what happens to him. I have no interest in him.*'

'How long has it been going on?'

'*I don't know. I told you, I don't care.*'

'What does the doctor say?'

'*He won't see the doctor because he is such a big man. Why would he show that he's weak? He's just weak when he's behind closed doors with us but he likes to throw his weight around in public. That's the kind of thing he likes doing. I see him even if no one else does – shaking and sweating in the middle of the night*' *and waiting for my mother to make it go away, throwing up her food that she cooked all afternoon for him. I see it even if the doctor doesn't see it; the guards don't see it. He has a big stitching business he wants me to take over; this and that he says sometimes, all these big ideas. But I don't care, like I said. I just want to live with my mother and look after her, and make a life for my brother. I want to get out of here when I am old enough to take them with me.'*

Nathan nodded, speaking to Ray whilst keeping his eyes fixed on the boy. 'Got what we need?' he said quietly.

Ray cleared her throat in a sound that indicated yes: 'Uh-huh.'

'Thank you for talking to me,' said Nathan to the boy, patting him on the side of his shoulder. 'It's hard for you. I know it is. I really feel it.'

The boy waited while Ray translated, uncertain as to how he should respond.

'You can go play with your friends, if you like,' said Ray finally, taking the camera down. *'Thanks, Anup – you spoke to us honestly and we appreciate that very much.'*

He looked at them both, eyes shuffling from one face to the other, surprised at the abrupt ending. It was as if it was taking him some time to realize that he had been in an interview, not a genuine conversation, and that it was now over.

13.

Dank, full, sticky: her mouth sent her the dominant sensations on waking. It was another of the series of recent dreams in which she was unable to empty her mouth. Sometimes it was chewing gum, stale and rotten, which she pulled out in long strands that would not separate from the roof of the cavity, swelling with the effort, increasing in volume. Sometimes it was regurgitated food, foul and recalcitrant, right up against her tonsils. Sometimes it was even excrement that came into her mouth, leading to the most horrific of the night-time sweats, so that she woke shuddering, the taste bitter and real on her tongue.

The dreams suggested a translation that was so literal it embarrassed her. She thought she couldn't stop talking shit these days, was that it? But the bitterness of the medication she was taking also had to have something to do with it. She had been instructed by the doctor to take the last pill of each day on a full stomach, just before sleep, and she didn't really have anything around with which to blunt the taste. The tiffins were gone by then, and they weren't in the habit of keeping snacks in the hut, due to the heat.

She sat up in bed, moving her lower jaw up and down to try to rid herself of the feeling. She was awake, and yet the texture was still with her, the image coming to her vividly, in moments of increasing disgust: today it was faeces, thick and sodden. She widened her mouth, shaking her head to try to dispel the image, leaning to the side of her bed in search of a bottle of water.

★

'Where's the rest of your gang?' said Sanghvi. 'Out with their cameras looking for *dishoom dishoom?*'

He accompanied the phrase with a slapstick action, zigzagging his fists in a way that was deliberately haphazard. He was drinking a cup of tea as he sat in a cane chair on the raised verandah of the 'office hut' located at the back of the compound. The guards were standing behind him at a respectful distance. She could see the lower half of their torsos, the faded khaki uniforms, bronze belts and buckles. She prevented herself from looking up. One of them would be Dularichand.

Ray smiled at Sanghvi, but a response did not come naturally to her. There was something harder about his humour today, something stony hidden beneath his usual mischief. She felt queasy suddenly, and looked up involuntarily at the trio of guards. Dularichand caught her eye immediately. He was in the middle of the three men, rubbing the side of his face with the tip of his index finger. He twitched with a brief smile, undulated his head, reassuring her with his eyes. She looked away.

'They've gone into town,' she said. 'Following one of the prisoners who works in the market, I think. I forget which one.' In reality, she had no idea where they were. She was glad of her ignorance; it was likely that they were pursuing something that would need to be kept from the governor. She only hoped that they were not still in Nathan's hut, which was just a few yards away from where they were sitting.

'Well, I wish them luck but I'm not sure they'll find their action-movie scene there,' said Sanghvi, dispensing of his cup of tea to Raju. Ray gave the young boy a furtive look, unable to control her anxiety at what he might know. He was always with Dularichand and reported directly to him for much of the fetching and carrying needed by the crew. But he left without a glance.

'Most of the prisoners are so pleased to be earning again that they keep things harmonious with their employers,' Sanghvi said, pushing himself up and brushing a few motes of dust from his jacket. 'Or their employees, for that matter, if you count someone like Rana Pratap and his quarry business. Anyway. Come, let's go.'

He was down at Ashwer for a standard inspection. Ray had arranged to film him doing his rounds, and also to do a general interview. To this end he was dressed less flamboyantly than usual, in a sober black suit with white shirt, a saffron tie patterned with small red boxes. Only the clear aviator glasses hinted at his earlier style.

'Did you get some use out of that shawl, by the way?' he asked, as they walked together.

'The shawl is great,' said Ray. 'So warm. And a beautiful colour. I'm very touched to have it. Thank you so much.'

She gave him a radio mic and indicated that he should put the wires through his shirt then attach them to the battery pack, which he could carry in his jacket pocket. They made their way to the riverbank, led by the guards. Four men, dressed in white jackets and turbans bordered in red and gold, waited to greet the governor. As he approached they began to play a variety of brass instruments.

'Ah yes,' said Sanghvi. 'This is the wedding band I was telling you about when you first arrived.'

Ray got the camera going as quickly as possible and began to film them. She recognized one of the inmates – Raja Munshi – the man with the expansive beard who had proudly declared to Nathan that he was in for homicide, on that early tour of the camp. Like the others, he blew into his instrument with confidence and skill, but also a jovial vitality. The united sound was cheeky, tuneful, immensely energetic. They punched their tune into the air with the flashy bombast of local wedding bands.

Ray raised her thumb whilst filming.

'They're brilliant!' she said to Sanghvi.

She panned across the four faces, surprised to note that she did not know the other three men. They had been on site for a while now, and still there were so many unknown prisoners.

'Very good, very good,' said Sanghvi when they had finished. He shook each man's hand. 'Keep up the good work!'

'Do you mind if I ask you some questions here?' said Ray. 'It's a lovely backdrop and less stuffy than if we do a sit-down interview.'

They made their way slowly along the hillock at the top of the riverbank, Ray tracking backwards with the camera opposite him, and talked about the ethos of the prison and his own personal vision. He must have come up against some resentment initially, suggested Ray, from his own officers, from the government. Did no one use the punishment versus rehabilitation argument to shoot his idea down?

'Well, it's not always easy to sell an idea,' said Sanghvi. 'To sell an idea you've got to convince people. Many apprehensions were sounded on the part of the government: will it work, will it not invite some escapes? It is fraught with some dangers, they said. I said, "No. To my mind it is a basic question of trust. You trust them and they will return the trust. You provide humane conditions, living which is humane, and I am sure they will come up to my expectations." And the proof is visible. We have had hardly any escapes since we began.'

He coughed and adjusted his tie before continuing.

'Ultimately, a prisoner has to revert back to society one

day. He will not be with us for an indefinite period. Now, since he has to revert back to society, why not prepare him? Why not make him eligible? Create conditions in which he can go back with his head high, self-confident, self-reliant, and a useful citizen to society.'

They paused for a moment, having come to a natural break. Ray used the opportunity to rest her arm briefly. Some water instantly appeared for Sanghvi; he produced a handkerchief from his jacket pocket and mopped his face.

'It's OK?' he said.

'It's great,' said Ray. 'It's going really well. Very interesting answers. Thank you for doing this.'

They began again, walking together in the same chain: Ray stepping cautiously backwards with the camera in her hand, and Sanghvi walking towards her, the guards further back, out of vision.

'What would you say is the most revolutionary aspect of Ashwer?' said Ray.

Sanghvi waited a beat before replying.

'Probably the concept of family,' he said. 'Earlier on, in a conventional prison, for a prisoner to even see his family he would have to take permission from the governor, naturally. Now, you see, I reversed the process. I ensured that a prisoner will not be allowed to live in the prison unless he is with his family. And this means that he has to provide for his family; he has a motivation to earn, to care. Family is a great moderator. It is of big benefit to the mental make-up of the human being in the wall-less prison. And we have no system of surveillance, because we do not need it. We have proved that trust is enough.'

'That's great,' said Ray. 'But what about having a deterrent?'

'Focusing on only the punitive is a very old-fashioned

idea; it goes back to the nineteenth century. You know –
protect society from the evils of mankind by using detention.
To my mind, detention impairs a prisoner's values. If a man
has spent some years of his sentence demonstrating exem-
plary conduct in a normal jail, why shouldn't he come here,
be with his family, look after them?'

Ray felt a sadness come over her as she put the camera
away after the interview. She thought of Nandini and
Daulath, and the real storylines of her film. Sanghvi could
be a little pompous at times but you had to admire his ideal-
ism.

'I thought it was very interesting what you said about
family being key to mental stability,' she said, taking the battery out of its slot. 'Responsibility. A moderator. I wonder
what that says about all of us, myself included.'

He laughed, brushing himself down and indicating to the
guards that he was ready to move on.

'Well, I'm divorced,' he said. 'It was some time back.
Things didn't work out. It happens like that sometimes. One
of those things.'

They sat on their respective charpoys, notes in hand. It was
a planning meeting. Serena was fresh, her short crop of light
hair still wet from the shower, sleek against her pale skin.
She seemed energized, her legs folded to one side on her
bed as she studied her sheaf of papers, a weightless, gamine
quality to her physicality. Ray watched her, wondering at
her relationship with Nathan. What did they do when they
weren't in bed? Talk about ideas for the film? Share secrets
from childhood?

'She doesn't want to do it,' said Ray, opening the discussion by referring to Nandini. 'And it isn't that easy, justifying
it to her.'

'You're only at the first stage,' said Serena. 'She'll come round.'

Serena wanted more details. It was time for her to come in on the Nandini story, she said; Ray needed to bring her up to speed. Nick wanted them to combine forces now that they had two strong storylines, and work together strategically.

'She doesn't think that her ex-husband will want to do it,' said Ray. 'And you can see her point. What's in it for him? I was struggling with that a little, as well.'

'She doesn't need to worry about that,' said Serena. 'Things are looking promising on that front.'

'What do you mean?'

'We've already found him, and he hasn't refused communication.'

'What?'

'Why do you always act like some innocent at these moments? It's really tiring.'

'What do you mean? You've already approached him?'

'We haven't spoken to him directly. We just sent someone to test the water. Raju, the kid who brings Nathan his drink and fags. He stopped by the guy's office, asked him if he was willing to talk to us. He's amenable. Next step, Nathan can have a conversation with him, man to man. Easier than a woman trying to talk to him, I reckon.'

'Right,' said Ray. 'You paid Raju to do this, I suppose.'

'This is my job, Ray. This is the point of a planning meeting. So we can update each other on progress. You've got to give up being so bloody possessive over things; it means nothing ever gets done. It's time to break a story on screen. This is not about whether I am treading on your toes –'

'No,' said Ray. 'This is about Nandini. How would she feel if she knew we had already approached him? Here I am, trying to show her that I understand how painful it must be for her, and meanwhile we're going behind her back.'

Serena sighed, rolling her eyes.

'Next,' she said. 'Can we be done with Nandini? Convincing her shouldn't be that difficult. Have you tried the whole "It's important to get your story out there, to educate, prevent the same thing from happening to other people" line? It usually works, in my experience. Really powerful motivator. And a true one – nothing is more effective than seeing someone's story on screen.'

'But this programme won't be shown here. So that argument requires her to invest in people in the UK.'

'Your problem. You solve it. I'm just giving you ideas.'

'The thing is,' said Ray, suddenly pensive, 'that is a good point you've just made, actually. Domestic abuse happens all over the world. Nandini's story is an archetypal one, in terms of violence within marriage.'

Serena laughed.

'Yeah and men in Romford are setting their wives on fire because they didn't get the Ford Mondeo they were promised when they signed on the dotted line at the registry office? I don't think so. It's one thing convincing her, but you need to keep your head screwed on, mate, or we're all doomed.'

Ray flushed with anger. She spoke haltingly, stuttering with rage.

'Dowry is economic,' she said. 'I'd have thought you'd have understood that? It's a bartering system that surrounds gross inequality, poverty. People have such little control over their lives that they gamble on some way of making existence better, based on the roulette of whether they give birth to sons or daughters. Do you think men don't beat or kill their wives in Romford? Come to that, do you think they don't kill for money in Romford? Or commit crimes of passion? Are you mad? Do you ever read the fucking paper when you're back home?'

Her voice was trembling.

'Right,' said Serena, glaring back, affronted, her eyes wide open. 'And I suppose that's why they drown their girls at birth, like kittens, in this country. Or – sorry – haven't you been reading the paper while you've been here?'

'You –' Ray caught herself before the expletives tumbled out. 'How dare you!'

'God!' said Serena. 'This is completely off topic. How do you do this? You have a knack, don't you? Come on, we need to get back on track. I don't have all day.'

'I'm trying to understand,' said Ray, 'how you can talk about female infanticide like that. How do you come off being so self-righteous? I repeat: do you think people in Romford don't abandon or abort children they don't want? I'm astounded at the way you come at this with a "them" and "us" mentality, it . . . it *sickens* me. I feel physically sick to hear you speak.'

Serena laughed.

'Bloody hell,' she said, pushing herself off the charpoy. 'You are one draining piece of work, you know that? Dealing with you is like walking through cement. I just want to be able to do my bloody job.' She began packing her rucksack with notes, the laptop, grabbing her pyjamas from the foot of the bed. Ray watched her, confused, the anger burning quietly through the fabric of her thoughts.

'If you start living with Nathan full-time,' she said finally, 'it is not going to look good. We have to uphold our reputation here, and they keep a close eye on us.'

Serena turned round and stared at Ray, her hand against the door.

'I'm just saying . . .' said Ray. 'Seriously, Serena, you don't realize –'

'Do you ever just stop and listen to the things coming out of your mouth?' said Serena. 'I've been working in television for fifteen years. Successfully. Where I choose to sleep is none of your fucking business.'

He was a little younger than Ray: early- to mid-twenties, tall, strong-limbed, comfortable in his body. His hair was cut in an offhand style, thick at the top, slightly asymmetric at the sides, gently fashionable, like the cut of his jeans, which were hanging neatly from beneath a striped linen shirt tailored to fit a lean torso. He was talking to Ram Pyari in a voice that Ray envied: respectful, contemplative and, above all, useful, somehow. This sense of utility was something he seemed to emanate without effort, so that it had an almost cooling effect in the close quarters of Nandini's hut, where he was sitting cross-legged on the floor, with the rest of them.

Ray watched him. It is as though he is unlikely to waste words, she thought; any information he imparts is likely to have some value to the recipient; any questions he asks can be only for their benefit.

She had knocked on Nandini's door and been invited in on the tail end of one of her counselling sessions, this time orientated around a young man from an NGO based in Delhi. He was visiting Ashwer to talk to inmates about micro-finance.

'It is a way in which you can borrow money for very little interest,' he was saying to Ram Pyari, 'without going to costly moneylenders. I know that a bank won't talk to you when you *need money, so it's very difficult for you, Didi. But right now you're paying back more than ten times what you've borrowed from the mahajan in the market. This means you can never build up any savings, or be finished with what you owe him.'*

His Hindi was not much better than Ray's own, and yet it was delivered in an Indian accent. He was from the city, Indian born and bred, or so she imagined from his voice. Ram Pyari was open and engaged, responding to him without inhibition, even though he was a man.

'I didn't know it was ten times the amount,' she said, shaking her head, clutching part of the pallu of her sari so that it came over her cheek on one side of her face, the brash outlay of colour in the yellow material standing out against her skin, accentuating the lighter tones.

'I was just so grateful he gave me the money. I couldn't have got started with my ironing business otherwise, and he gave me what I needed when the bank wouldn't even let me in the door. But now, when I pay him back every month, I have so little left. I have enough for food for the next few days, and that is it. It's like I'm always carrying a heavy rock on my back that I can't put down. Even when I sleep it is with this jagged rock stuck on my back. Sometimes I worry about what will happen when I get ill. My father died of tuberculosis back in my village; he was thirty-seven years old, they said. We all get ill in the end, but it happens quickly if you're poor. How will I pay for hospital, medicine, when it happens to me?'

The young man listened to her very closely, nodding and shaking his head at key points, looking at the floor while she spoke, his gaze resting on his feet, which were large and bare, housed in canvas chappals, a few tufts of fine hair marking his toes. He began to talk through some of the options available to her, and in this patient rhythm of call and response, confession and understanding, they continued their dialogue. Ray made eye contact with Nandini, who was sitting further back, positioned against some cushions in the corner. She smiled at Ray, nodding her head to suggest enthusiastic endorsement of the approach in front of them.

Ray had a brief conversation with the man when it was time for him to leave. She explained that they were filming in the village for the BBC.

'I think it is so interesting, what you are doing,' she said. 'Thank you for letting me sit in on it.'

'Here is my card,' he said, picking one out of his back pocket, from a battered plastic wallet in neon orange. 'Definitely stay in touch. We do a lot of work in rural areas like these. Not just lending, but a whole range of things you might find interesting: low-cost sanitation, clean water, insurance against crop failure for farmers, solar-powered lanterns . . .' He laughed, throaty and convivial, bringing his hands together in namaste. 'I'd better go, Nandini-ji,' he said, lightly bowing his head towards Nandini. 'Before I send you to sleep. You've heard it all before!'

Nandini shook her head.

'You're always welcome here, Jai,' she said, pushing the door open for him.

He bent to walk through the canopy at the porch, his head just touching the new material that was tied to the posts, a thin cream muslin with a border of gold block print, floral cones and sprays in a dancing pattern around the sides.

'We're very grateful to you,' said Nandini, returning the namaste. 'I hope that you'll continue to visit and help in this way. It is so valuable, but you know that . . . there is no way to express it.'

Ram Pyari left at the same time, issuing a hurried nod to Ray in goodbye as she got up from the floor, her hands pressed together and a shy smile appearing on her face for Nandini as she made her way through the door.

Nandini went into the kitchen and picked up a long steel ladle. She removed the lid of the earthenware mutka in the corner of the room and scooped out some water, moving back her head and holding the ladle a few inches above her open mouth, tilting it with comfortable aim so that a stream of water fell against the back of her throat.

'That's better!' she said after a few seconds of continuous swallowing, taking a deep breath. 'I'm so dehydrated today. Do you want some?'

Ray shook her head.

'I'd better not,' she said.

'Shall I boil you some?' said Nandini. 'I don't keep any mineral water, I'm sorry.'

'No, don't worry,' said Ray, sinking back against one of Nandini's cushions. She was reminded momentarily of the taste she had experienced upon waking, the putrid horror in her mouth. The idea of a cold rush of water was intensely appealing, but she needed to abide by the doctor's instructions.

There were a few moments of silence as they looked at each other.

'You have come to talk about the filming, presumably, is that right?' said Nandini.

She set herself down opposite Ray in the cross-legged position, and passed over the usual steel bowl. She was smiling. Ray was suffused with relief.

They chewed supari together. Ray watched Nandini's small mouth moving quickly over the assortment of sweet, woody textures, the tiny shudder in her cheeks, the pronounced ridge of her cheekbones in the long, narrow face.

'I've been thinking about it,' said Nandini. 'In terms of . . . well, I have to trust you on this. You really think that it is a good idea? For me to meet him?'

Ray nodded.

'Nandini, it is something that will really help people who are in a similar situation.'

'Yes, I have thought about that too. I don't want to be selfish. You are trying to make something that will educate people, much like my counselling. That's a good thing.'

'Yes, but I'm aware that this meeting will require you to really put yourself on the line, Nandini. I'll be there with you, though, you know that. On a personal level, I'm hoping this will mean that he can't manipulate you emotionally. Maybe we'll be able to overcome any remaining power he has over you.'

Nandini was quiet. She poured some seeds into her hand and passed the bowl over to Ray, who noticed the brief, minimal streak of a frown appear in her forehead.

'I don't mean that he has any control over you,' said Ray hastily. 'I'm full of awe and astonishment at how strong you are, raising your daughter and working to liberate other people here, emancipate other women –'

'Yes, yes, I know that,' said Nandini, waving away the rest of Ray's sentence. 'I'm not looking for compliments.'

'I just meant that . . .' Ray paused, searching for the right words. 'You experienced severe abuse. You've transcended it admirably, but it must have left its mark. You know, with domestic abuse, it's very intimidating to face the abuser in the first instance, naturally, but it can be so empowering in the long run – to have a witness there who is in agreement with you, in spite of the man's denial or recriminations, to establish that it really happened, to rearrange the grid, the hierarchies of power, to get it across to him that you are sure and secure in the facts, that they aren't open to interpretation.'

Nandini looked doubtful.

'I don't know about that,' she said. 'But I'll do it, don't worry.'

They discussed how best to approach it. Nandini said he was lazy, self-involved, which only spelled trouble. She was willing to meet, but she didn't understand what his incentive would be.

'I think you should write him a letter,' said Ray, taking the camera out of her bag. 'We could get one down now, if you like.'

Her handwriting was surprisingly florid, not how Ray had imagined it. It contained the curls and flourishes of a young girl, like a long crawling strand of honeysuckle. She trailed the words through the lens in close-up, almost feeling the scent come off the page, the prettiness at odds with the formality of the words.

For the attention of Mr Sanjit.
   I would like to request a meeting to discuss his daughter.
   I am available from 12 p.m. to 5 p.m. on most weekdays.

Long after the day was over, Ray still floated in the images it left behind. She washed her bra and knickers in a bucket under the tap at the hut, barely concentrating as she squatted over them, her mind glancing over the task at hand. Serena and Nathan were sequestered together somewhere in Nathan's shuttered hut, hidden in the black exclusion of the night. She did not mind. She only wanted things to work between them all, somehow. She lay in bed like a puppet, a marionette that has come off stage, limbs collapsed, misshapen. The matrix of small holes in the wall was before her, siphoning in rations of breeze, piping through the rustle of trees outside. She lay on her back with her palms facing upwards, as if she was waiting for something holy.

14.

Zafar was in the driving seat, phone pressed against the steering wheel in one hand, a shaft of sunlight hitting the left side of his face and superimposing a small, perfect rectangle of illumination on his cheek. Ray watched him from the back, in the rear-view mirror, taking in different features depending upon his angle of movement. His face remained generally invincible. It announced indifference to all elements of the world; but, to her shame, she still had not been able to work out whether this was part of his job – a careful construction for the benefit of his employers – or just his natural way. Their interaction remained rudimentary, confined to directions and timings. His phone rang.

'*Hanh hanh*,' he said, twisting the wheel and pressing the horn loudly at the same time. Yes, yes. '*Bilkul*.' Absolutely.

She wanted to ask him the impossible. Who are you talking to? What do they want? His tone was familiar, but abrupt. It was a no-frills form of intimacy, the kind you might share with a close colleague, or even a long-established lover. She had no idea.

'*No, no,*' he said. '*It's nothing like that.*'

He put his right arm out of the window and whipped his hand in a slapping motion, urging an auto-rickshaw to move more quickly at the crossing before them.

'*Eh?*' he said. '*I said already, didn't I? It's not like that.*'

They entered a nexus of traffic whorling around a central tree in the road, the unofficial roundabout of the village marketplace, and became part of the usual hurl of trucks, cycle rickshaws, pedestrians and scooters. The combined volume of horns and engines increased. Ray looked out at the rows of huts and shops. A man sitting next to a sewing machine in one small shack was nailing some leather shoes, pressing pins into the back of a pair of chappals. The neighbouring shop was a small jeweller's, built into a sunken valley in the pavement, clear panes protecting the two owners, who sat in front of opposing glass cabinets and tables with weighing scales, showcasing their wares against velvet boards of deep midnight blue. On the pavement a large poster of a bride with heavy gold necklace, regal nose adornment and chandelier earrings filled a sandwich board.

'OK,' Zafar said into the phone, which was now cradled at his neck, his left hand on the wheel. 'OK. OK. OK, bye.'

He drove on for a few more minutes until they were out of the hustle, and pulled over on the right near a long red-brick wall, the outer perimeter of the college grounds where Nandini studied. There was a placard next to the entrance gate with the name of the institute printed on it in English and Hindi. Nandini was already standing next to it.

It had been two days since she had written the letter to her ex-husband. Raju had taken it into town for them and delivered it by hand the morning after it was written. The response had been verbal, then and there.

'He says yes,' Raju had said when he brought Ray her water that afternoon. 'He says to come to Rosa restaurant at 1 p.m. on Thursday.'

Nathan was talking to the man when they arrived, a mixture of mischief and conspiracy in his manner as he directed a continuous stream of words at the sleepy-eyed, bloated face opposite him. They were drinking from small glasses and the alcohol was the colour of dark honey – whiskey, rum or brandy. Nathan nodded, spoke a few words. The man's hands toyed with his glass, which was a quarter full, his fingertips moving against it in a wave-like motion. He slouched against the wall and his face was under strain, as though he was being prevented from falling asleep by the enforced conversation with Nathan.

He did not acknowledge Nandini when she walked in with Ray. Instead, he downed the dregs in his glass, his sloth-like eyes passing through her to follow one of the waiters. The restaurant was mostly empty. It had no windows and was lit instead by the long tubes in the ceiling, which sent out a clinical, bluish half-light to the enclosed space. Ray took a deep breath as they walked further into the room. She felt a fatalism, a mundane sense of anticlimax. She put her hand on Nandini's shoulder.

Serena was at the camera in the corner, a couple of yards behind the men, twisting the tripod base to set the spirit-level.

'Are you OK?' Ray whispered to Nandini, whose eyes revealed nothing. She seemed to have glazed over with a soporific expression, not dissimilar to that of her ex-husband. Ray wondered if it was a defence mechanism. She felt uneasy and put her hand on Nandini's arm. 'Come with me. Let's get you set up with a mic.'

They walked over to Serena.

'How's it looking?' Ray asked.

Serena nodded. She was brusque but detailed as they discussed the practical aspects of the shoot: Serena was to be at the camera, Ray with the boom mic. They were to film the conversation without intervention, as naturally as possible, just observing the dialogue between Nandini and her ex-husband. Serena had slept the night at Nathan's but her manner with Ray was utterly professional – just friendly enough, no visible remnants of resentment or anger from their argument.

'Nice to see you, Nandini,' she said. 'Can we just get this contraption on you? You're used to it by now, I know!' She handed over the radio-mic pack, the wires wrapped around the central metallic pouch.

Nandini began to assemble it, putting the wires through the neck of her kameez and pulling them down. She turned around and began to clip the battery pack to her hip.

Serena spoke in a low voice, so that only Ray could hear.

'We've already filmed him reading the letter,' she said. 'So that's done.'

Ray nodded, uncomfortable.

'And we've paid him up front,' said Serena.

Ray flinched.

'Do you want to talk through the questions again?' she said, walking over to Nandini. 'The ones we discussed might work?'

Nandini shook her head.

'Let's just go and do it now,' she replied.

Nathan shook the man's hand and got up from the cushioned seat, leaving it free for Nandini to take his place. The waiter had brought a new glass of the brown liquor and was hovering for the other order.

'*Paani laa dijiye,*' said Nandini to the waiter. Please bring me water.

Serena filmed the silence between ex-husband and wife. Ray watched them, holding the large furry boom mic at a distance. They did not make eye contact, looking mostly at the table or at articles on it. Finally, Nandini spoke.

'Moushami is six years old now,' she said to him in English.

He looked up at her, frowning, as if he was struggling to hear her, or understand her words.

'She is a dancer,' said Nandini, speaking slowly so that the words would have impact.

He took a drink from his glass.

'Her hands are still like this,' she said, putting forward her palm, the fingers stuck together. 'Her feet also. But she is doing well.'

There was no response. He stayed as he was, slouched slightly against the side wall, one elbow on the table.

'You remember that?' said Nandini. 'When she was born?'

He shrugged, his eyes half closed.

Ray watched him, infuriated. But there was no way she could intervene.

'Do you remember anything?' said Nandini. 'Do you think about it?'

Her words seemed to evaporate seconds after she spoke them, dissolving into the surroundings like cigarette smoke.

Ray watched him breathe, the buttons on his shirt moving with each heavy flow of air, in and out. Why had he agreed to meet? Was it just the money? They couldn't have offered him much – a normal contributor's fee was what? Fifty pounds maximum? On a programme like this it had to be even less. She did a quick calculation in her head: fifty pounds was over three and a half thousand rupees. In truth, it was a lot of money; even half that, a quarter of it, would be worth turning up for.

'That day with the fire?' said Nandini. 'Do you ever think about it?'

He finished his drink and looked around for the waiter.

They shovelled through the air, insignificant against the force of the traffic, propelled forward like insects in the tunnel of wind. Nandini had refused to travel back in the car with the crew, hailing an auto-rickshaw and giving her

instructions to the driver within minutes of leaving the restaurant. Ray sat next to her in silence, absorbing the heave
of air from outside, the hot turbulence that tussled and
fanned against her face like a passionate, conflicted embrace.
They were moving so fast that she had felt nervous of getting the camera out, fearful that it would fall from her hand
and over the side bar of the vehicle. It was already in her
rucksack when she jumped in with Nandini, without checking that she was welcome.

'It must feel strange,' Ray said finally, raising the camera
in her right hand and pressing the record button as it came
up to her chest. 'That it worked out like this.' The vehicle
jolted, so that her whole body swayed back against the seat.
'It's disappointing, Nandini, I know,' she continued, increasing the volume of her voice, twisting the focus quickly and
turning the lens on Nandini. They were close enough for
speech to be picked up by the camera mic, but it required
Nandini to speak up.

Nandini looked away, leaning against the bar on her side
of the auto.

Ray spoke loudly over the wind.

'Nandini, please,' she said. 'I'm really sorry. But we have
to talk about it.'

Nandini leaned further away, so that her head was outside
the auto, thrust fully into the atmosphere of charging traffic, smoke, roadside living.

'Nandini!' said Ray, shouting at Nandini's back, despair-
ing of being heard over the noise. 'I KNOW IT WAS
PAINFUL, BUT WE HAVE TO GET YOUR REAC-
TION NOW WHILE YOU ARE STILL FEELING IT
STRONGLY.'

Nandini turned round, her jittery eyes searching through
Ray's face.

'Nandini,' said Ray, 'I only mean that otherwise it won't be a natural reaction. We'll just overanalyse it later and this way we can still –'

'NO.' Nandini put her hand on the lens and pushed the camera so that it turned on its side. 'NO,' she said again, her voice deliberately deep and firm, a directional punch in the face, the voice a woman might be told to use with an attacker so that there is no doubt about her reaction. 'NO,' she said once more, the word booming around them as she stared – constant and thorough – until Ray had to look away.

'Waste of fifty quid,' said Nathan, taking a long drag from the damp rollie at his lips.

'Come on, we weren't to know,' said Serena.

'Waste of fifty quid, waste of time,' said Nathan. 'I could have told you it would pan out like that.'

'Well, I disagree,' said Serena. 'I think Nick is going to be pleased with it. There's something in the drama of his lack of response. She asked him all the questions – so we've got all that. We get a sense of her disappointment, everything that she is carrying around with her. It's still a powerful scene. You really feel for Nandini when you see it.'

Nathan exhaled the smoke in rings, leaning his head against the wall, rolling his eyes. He was slumped on Serena's charpoy, his legs hanging over the edge, while she scrolled through the footage of the meeting on her laptop.

'Too fucking right,' he said. 'Poor girl. What the hell was she going to get out of that? He did right to keep his mouth shut and just take the money. I'd have done the same. Fuck, I felt sorry for her.' He shook his head. 'Does not feel good.'

'Come on,' said Serena. 'We've got Dawlat to film tomorrow.'

Ray sat on her own charpoy with a ring binder of notes.

She could hear them speak but did not join in. She looked up at the pattern of holes through which the sunlight was burning, flushed and strong, from a high point in the sky.

She walked out of the hut.

Slowly, with infinite care. This is how she walked, parallel to the prison, on the other side of the great road, looking over at the low wall through the vehicles, the fumes and metal bodies of cars and scooters. She had walked out without hailing a vehicle or asking for Zafar, to the surprise of the guards at the gate. She had bumped eyes with Dularichand by accident, but even this did not register, or provoke the usual twinge of shame.

She had crossed the highway without fear, taking the spaces as they came, faltering only when confronted by a tonga, the two horses carrying a cart full of men and boxes. On the other side, she made her way along the footpath with a constructed dignity, aware that the guards were probably still watching her, wary of stumbling against the shacks or ditches on her way.

'No one uses the pavement to walk on here,' she had said to Nathan on their first trip into town. 'The footpath is a dwelling place; people make their homes there.'

And it was true, even here, on the border of such a huge carriageway. Now that she was on foot, not watching from the car, she was close to the roadside population. She walked past tents made of blue plastic sheeting. A woman was crouched inside one at the kerb, brewing something on a small stove. Ray side-stepped past an old man rolled in a blanket on the ground, a couple of little girls sitting and talking by a large metal drum of oil, their hair in plaits. They all stared as she made her way through their world.

She absorbed the gazes without embarrassment. It was appropriate that they should look, be curious.

She found herself walking past a kiosk, a place selling incense sticks, hundreds of boxes stacked on narrow shelves along with diyas, sindhoor, cotton wool, some small artefacts for prayer arranged in a cabinet in the corner. Outside, a man was beating out a long sheet of metal on the ground, an acute, reflective streak of sunlight running through the column of grey. She noticed the proprietor dealing with a man over the counter. He was familiar, with his rough woollen jumper, the wide black bandana tied in a knot on one side of his head. She caught a glimpse of his eyes – there was something insistent about them – and then suddenly she remembered him.

They had interviewed him on one of the early days of filming. He was the employer of a young inmate from Ashwer, a prisoner who had been too shy to speak on camera.

'*He's a prisoner from the open camp,*' the man had said, standing at the entrance to his shop, patting the shoulder of his employee with a munificent sense of bounty. '*And he also happens to work for me. Now, if I was to be thinking "He's a prisoner" all the time, there would be a fear in me. Should I keep him on or shouldn't I?*' His eyes had widened as he explained his thoughts, giving him a messianic air, and it was difficult not to listen. '*But if I'm to watch him work instead, and judge it that way, over time I can see that his spirit is so pure, and that he absolutely isn't like that, you see?*'

'Enthralling,' Ray had described him later, trying to conjure up his energy, the inspirational quality of the man's certainty. That was the word she had used to portray him to Serena, even to Nick in an email about possible characters. 'In just a few moments he shows us everything we are trying to say in this film,' she had written. But, without the participation of the inmate himself, who remained mute despite several attempts to interview him, they had not been able to use the material.

She crossed back over the road and stood at the corner of the prison boundary.

The sky was changing as the clouds dissipated, the light forming a diffuse apricot stain that spread over the dusty field, skimming the tops of the peepal trees, emphasizing their differing heights, their huge shapes of dull green. The colour hovered in the sky over the row of patchy white huts, their straw-piled roofs, the water well, the tiny white bordering wall, just a few bricks high.

A man with a bicycle and wheelbarrow was selling something to a couple in the central empty wasteland of the camp; it looked like food of some kind – she could see him spread a knife both ways over the item in his hand. He gave it to a skinny woman in a fuchsia lahenga. Her skirt, chunni and choli were all dyed in the same startling pink, the colour overwhelming against the pale backdrop. They were too far away for Ray to be able to recognize them. Near them, under the central tree, a two-year-old child stood with a yo-yo, turning his whole body round and round in clockwise circles, his arm extended so that the string whirled at full length, outstretched, carried by the speed. A couple of older kids watched him. They were also distant, unlikely to see her.

She did not want to walk back to the gate and return through the sieve of the guards, their questioning looks, their silent judgement.

She put a leg over the wall. Her foot touched the ground easily. She walked swiftly to Nandini's hut, which was close, nestled right in the corner of the land. She crouched as she neared the unit, moving to hide herself at the back of the property so that Nandini would not hear her approach. She sat on her haunches behind the toilet area. In front of her was a low fence made from thick branches. It was the only divider. She put her hand on it, felt it prickle against the flesh of her palm.

Nandini, Nandini, Nandini. The name repeated itself in Ray's head.

What would she say to her?

Her temples throbbing, she lifted herself over the fence, staying low, then moved over to the side of the hut. She raised her body a little and looked through one of the small window holes in the wall.

Nandini was inside. Ray could see her pressing a papad on the tava hot plate, so that the round of dried gram flour blistered up in the heat, hardening into a brittle disc. There was a large spider in the corner of the kitchen, on the floor behind the stove. Nandini took the jhadoo, a long-handled broom with stiff, spiky bristles, and chased it in the direction of the door. Some dust rose around her, tinting the air momentarily.

Ray stayed where she was, watching. She did not go to the door; instead she remained with her eye against the hole for a while, a minute, maybe two, before returning to her own hut.

15.

The doctor was in a buoyant mood, holding his squat frame with purpose, a sense of expectation. He offered Nathan a cigarette, pulling back the top of the carton and silver foil to reveal two pristine rows, tightly packed. Ray expected him to lift the pack to his nose and make a show of smelling the tobacco, then offer the scent to Nathan. Instead, he tipped the carton and tapped the bottom, so that a cigarette emerged, halfway. The white paper in which it was rolled was like satin in the sunlight, a thin circle of gold at the filter. Nathan took it, joking with him about how it was mandatory for those in the medical profession to drink and smoke, abuse their bodies over time to deal with treating others.

'Smoking these is not an abuse,' said the doctor, releasing his fulsome smile suddenly, his cheeks swelling around the severe dark lines of his spectacles. He gave a brief, jaunty nod, his dense head of curls glistening. 'They are amongst the smoothest you'll find anywhere. India's own luxury brand. Beautiful smoke, I must say.'

'Right,' said Nathan, winking, taking a leisurely pull. He held it in for a few seconds before releasing the smoke. 'Smoking, drinking, it's all about moderation. Isn't that the other thing doctors always say?'

The two men were standing on the verandah of Ray and Serena's hut. Ray was watching them through the doorway. She was crouched on the floor assembling the sound equipment and untangling the wires on the radio mics. She struggled with the task, was slow and constricted, thinking constantly of the events of the preceding day. Serena was already at Daulath's house with the camera.

She gave Nathan a mic for the doctor, and walked over towards the yard of the facing hut, not wanting to engage in any awkward jokes or innuendoes that might ensue from arranging the wires by pulling them through the front of his shirt. She looked up at the sky, which was blank, an endless frame of space. It was maddeningly bright, scorched through with white light. Mid-morning, and already the air felt toxic with heat, smothering her within seconds of emerging from the shade of the hut. She thought of the men on their scooters in the local traffic, driving with a handkerchief wrapped over the nose and mouth to block out the fumes.

There were no chemicals here, though, no pollutants – they were in the middle of farmland, more than distant enough from the main highway. Still, the humidity felt like it was blocking her ability to breathe; it was threatening, had the power to hold her hostage. Somehow, she was still not used to it.

She could hardly face another day of filming. The idea repelled her, and yet she walked on.

The chicks fluttered in Daulath and Jyoti's front yard as she entered, chipping their beaks at the pale dust on the dry ground, scratching for grain. She noticed them in close-up for the first time. They were a little peaky: the feathers on them were sparse, their eyes swollen and prominent.

She thought of Anup, the couple's older son, and what he had said when she and Nathan had interviewed him: 'People talk about prisoners' rights, but what about children? They have no rights, do they? The prison said I had to come and live with my father, come with my mother, so I did that.'

He was at school now, like the other kids. They had

chosen this specific time of day for filming, to make sure the children would be absent, and she was glad of it.

The doctor spoke to Daulath in an avuncular tone, staying gentle as he forced the line of questioning about his patient's recent health.

'You have diarrhoea still?' he said in Hindi. *'Vomiting and tiredness? Loss of appetite? How is your sleep?'*

He sat with Daulath on the rug, drinking tea that had been brought for them by Jyoti. She was now in the background of the shot, squatting in the kitchen area on a low wooden stool as she scrubbed quietly at some steel dishes. She worked with a small amount of cloudy water, swirling it in two large thalis, using the same fluid over and over again for scouring or rinsing. Her sari was purple, patterned in large orange diamonds, the pallu pulled right over her head to form an overarching hood. The hem was pulled up, away from the water, revealing her lower calves, the thick silver bangle around her ankle visible to Ray.

Serena crouched in front of the two men in order to film them at their natural eye line rather than from above. Ray stood behind her, holding the boom so that the furry mic pointed at a central point above their heads. Nathan was sitting on the floor to the side, his back against the wall. He was due to go on camera after the test was done – to interview Daulath and the doctor separately about the outcome.

'It's been getting worse?' continued the doctor. *'Or would you say things were changing for the better?'*

Daulath shook his head. His eyes were sunken in shadow. He looked at the floor as though he was being weighed down by the turban on his head, which was wound tightly, accurately, creating the usual flamboyant tower of striking pink. A series of tiny nicks and pocked scars formed an intermittent pattern on his skin. He looked up momentarily at the camera, shifting his gaze back to the floor in seconds, clearly uncomfortable with the situation.

'*I want you to do a blood test today, Daulath,*' said the doctor, pressing the two aluminium buttons on his briefcase so that the lid sprang open with a loud click.

Serena spoke from behind the camera.

'Sorry, Raj, but could you explain the test for us as you do it? We'll subtitle this bit so continue in Hindi.'

The doctor nodded. Serena gave him a thumbs up with her right hand as her eye pressed into the vertical viewfinder.

'*This is a test in which I will prick your finger with this tiny needle,*' said the doctor. '*Don't worry, it won't hurt very much, and it will take only a few seconds.*'

'*What's it for?*' said Daulath. His voice was weedy with nerves and sounded especially high-pitched and feeble when juxtaposed with the confidence of the doctor's bedside manner.

Ray watched him and felt her own chest contract, reflecting the anxiety she could see in Daulath's face.

'*We are going to test you for many things,*' said the doctor. '*But this test is for the HIV virus.*'

Daulath recoiled suddenly, his eyes darting from side to side. He looked over the doctor's shoulder in the direction of his wife.

'*AIDS,*' said the doctor. '*You probably know it as AIDS, do you? You have heard of AIDS?*'

Daulath frowned, hunching his shoulders at the mention of the disease, nodding quickly, his head bobbing fractionally, but at great speed, as though he hoped the motion would make the doctor stop speaking.

The kitchen sounds of sloshing water and clattering utensils were curtailed suddenly. Jyoti stood up. She walked over to the charpoy in the corner of the room and sat on it.

'What is it?' said Daulath, turning and squinting at her. There was some sweat forming on his forehead; it slipped into the groove of his frown, the wet trail continuing down to the tip of his nose. 'What have you come to watch?' His voice was dressed up in mockery, the hurried delivery betraying his anxiety. 'Go back to your work. What are you waiting for?'

She shook her head. The movement was minimal, her face impassive, immobile, as if hewn from rock. I am not moving, it said. And I am not changing my mind, whatever you say.

'You find it nice to come and sit and display yourself in front of these male folk?' said Daulath. 'Whatever pleases you.' He turned back.

Serena stayed locked in position, her eye pressed against the viewfinder. Ray looked at Nathan, feeling the responsibility of the tension. She was the only one in the crew who could understand the language. Should she do something? Offer support to Jyoti in some way? Nathan's eyes connected with Ray's for a second, acknowledging that he could tell something was happening.

'This hand, we'll use,' said the doctor, taking Daulath's left hand. 'You use the right hand for stitching, yes?'

He took a shiny white plastic packet from his briefcase and ripped open the seal, pulling out some thin latex gloves. He wore these and tore open another, slightly bulkier pack, pouring out the contents onto the opposing side of the case, where they rattled against the black-plastic shell. He lifted each piece and named it clearly in English, looking over in the direction of the camera.

'Sterile pad. Lancet. Test card. Pipette. Dilutant.'

He opened up the test card and swab, putting the packaging to one side then rubbing the swab on the side of Daulath's ring finger and index fingers.

'*You can use one or two fingers for this,*' he said in Hindi, taking the lancet, which was housed inside a turquoise rectangle of plastic. He pushed a small clover-shaped key at one end so that it clicked into position, twisted the key twice more before pulling it out, and pressed the central button of the turquoise piece against Daulath's index finger.

'OK,' he said, taking it away after hearing another click. There was a tiny red dot visible on Daulath's flesh.

Ray saw Serena pressing on the zoom button, her hand turning the lens, refocusing as she went in for a close-up. She looked at Daulath's face, searched it, but the sunken eyes showed no reaction.

The doctor pressed on either side of the dot so that it grew larger, simultaneously drawing up the blood into the pipette. He repeated the action a couple of times.

'OK,' he said, releasing a few droplets into the well of the test card. '*This can take one to five minutes. It is a recent development, being able to test so quickly like this, find out here and now.*'

He held the card in both hands and studied it.

Ray looked around the room and over at Jyoti, who was still frozen, a monolith on the bed. Her body did not betray even the smallest of movements. Serena stayed in position, using the time to shift from one knee to the other. Nathan was staring at the two men with severe concentration; he did not meet Ray's gaze this time.

Ray felt a tiny piercing of fear, a small, vulnerable hole in her consciousness, like the prick of blood she had just witnessed. What were they going to do now, run this in real time? Just keep filming while they waited? It was excruciating. She could hear noises outside, reminders of the continuum of domestic life: the moan of a bullock or goat, the rustle of vegetation, something bulky scraping against the earth, human footsteps. There was the smell of cooking nearby, the steamy rise of mid-morning baking, accompanying shouts and instructions, even the water pump clanking at a distance – either in her imagination or in reality.

'*We are watching this line*,' said the doctor, lifting the card so that it would be visible on camera. '*This is the line which tells us whether it is positive or negative.*'

Daulath did not look at the card. He looked at the floor, frowning, closing and opening his hooded eyes.

'*And you can see here, already,*' said the doctor. '*It is a positive test.*' He pointed at the dark line which had spread halfway along the length of the test card.

Ray watched him, shocked at the speed of the outcome. It seemed impossibly quick.

'*I'm sorry, Daulath Sahib,*' he said, looking deeply into the man's face. '*Do you understand this result? It means you're HIV positive. It means you have the virus that you may know as AIDS. We will need more tests to know which stage you are at. I'm sorry to have to give you this news. You'll need special medication. We don't know if it's full-blown AIDS yet, but –*'

There was a loud wail from the corner of the hut. Everyone turned to look at Jyoti, except for Daulath. She was shivering, biting her lip. She pulled the pallu of her sari over her mouth, the loud orange diamond pattern covering the lower half of her face. She released another wail, her eyes swelling up so that they looked wild, terrified. Serena refocused the camera on her.

'*No!*' she said, staring at her husband. '*We are shamed. We are in shame.*'

She shook violently and bent forward, releasing a tangled scream from her gut.

'*After all this . . .*' she said. '*And now we will just die. Like pigs in a ditch.*'

Ray dropped the mic and began to make her way over to the woman.

'What the hell are you doing?' said Serena in a loud whisper. 'Ray! Get out of the frame!'

Ray continued walking over and tried to put her arm around the woman.

'For fuck's sake,' muttered Nathan from the corner. 'Ray, don't be an idiot.'

'Didi . . .' Ray began.

Jyoti shook her off and began to scream again. Her voice clawed at the air, teetered in pain.

'*Bhen-ji, please listen!*' said the doctor, entreating her loudly. '*There is no guarantee that you or your children have it . . .*' He trailed off. '*But still, yes, we must test you all, especially the little one. In case –*'

Jyoti screamed, one long terrifying note. She stood up, hitting her head repeatedly with one hand, banging it heavily so that the slaps rang out, vibrating. '*Our life is over. Over. My children. There is nothing left.*' She cried in huge, hulking gasps.

Ray struggled with her, trying to get the woman's hand to stop hitting her skull. Jyoti pushed Ray away, so that she fell against the charpoy.

'*Bhen-ji . . .*' said the doctor, standing up, a series of raised lines forming on his brow. '*Please, you should calm down . . .*'

The screams got louder and she stuttered for breath, hyperventilating, her hand whacking her skull harder and harder.

Daulath pushed himself up from the floor and began to walk over, his expression null, void of all emotion.

'*NO!*' she screamed. '*I will kill myself first. My life is already ended. There is nothing left now. We have nothing left.*'

Jyoti looked around the room, her eyes skittering from side to side, searching for something to use. Two steps and she was back at the dishes on the floor, picking up a carving knife and holding it to her stomach, her eyes threatening anyone who dared come close.

'Hang on a second,' said Nathan, getting up. 'Listen . . .'

Her husband went to her, struggled with her, pressed her wrist so that she dropped the knife.

He knelt down to pick it up and she took another, holding the blade flat against her chest, then she pushed past him and all of them so that she was running out of the door into the searing light, dragging herself as though she was limping, her screams rebounding through the atmosphere with increasing violence. It was the sound of a person being beaten repeatedly, over and over again.

Nandini was at the riverbank by the time they caught up, holding Jyoti in her arms at the edge of the water. She held her hand in the air, palm facing the crew and doctor, indicating that they should step back, walk away. She flicked her hand dismissively at them as they faltered, unsure, at the crest of the hillock. Ahead of them, further down the bank, two security guards stood in the same arrested position.

'I've got her,' she said. 'Please leave us alone now.' She projected her voice like an official during an emergency, giving instructions to a crowd through a megaphone. 'Things are under control. Please move away. Now, please. Do not come further. Any fuss could endanger the situation. We are fine here.'

Ray was the only one to continue down the slope, disregarding her request. The crew and doctor turned back. Daulath was not with them. The security guards stayed where they were.

'No,' said Nandini. 'I mean it, Ray. Do not come near us.'

Ray continued to walk, her chappals slipping in the powdered earth.

'You arrogant, selfish . . . Can you not see that it is time to stop?'

'Nandini . . .' said Ray. 'Let me explain.'

'No,' said Nandini. 'I know enough. I don't need an explanation. You people are degenerate.'

She had one arm around Jyoti, whose face was turned away. The knife lay on the ground next to them. It was the meat knife, lengthy and flat, the one Ray had filmed Jyoti using to prepare chicken. The dull steel caught the sun's light.

'Nandini . . . it's natural to be angry, but we have to talk –'

'I know all about you,' said Nandini. 'The guards have told me about your leisure activities. Degenerate. Sick people, you are. All these drugs you smoke together. They say you all sleep in each other's beds, roll around with each other on these riverbanks at night after getting intoxicated. It disgusts me how I listened to you, how you portrayed yourself as an "Indian girl".'

She said the last two words with distaste, her top lip curling.

Ray stopped walking.

'They even say the driver took you to eat meat secretly, alone. What, you had to hide even that? As if people don't eat meat here? Who do you think you are? How dare you treat us with such superiority? Who are you people?'

Ray stared at her, devoid of words. She could not speak.

'We let you all film us because you are supposed to be good people. The BBC. So civilized. And this is what you do?' Nandini nodded at Jyoti. 'We willingly let you do it. We are the idiots. How you must have laughed at us, doing your bidding, whatever you asked. And all the while you are just visiting your own degenerate ideas upon us, taking what you can, looting us. For some TV programme?'

Ray shook her head.

'Nandini, please . . .'

'Get out of here,' said Nandini. 'Get out. At least acknowledge what you have done, the dirt, the filth of it, and have the decency to leave now. '

She began to talk to Jyoti, murmuring quietly in Hindi, inaudible to Ray.

The sun was on them both as Ray stared, the light defining their shapes in silhouette on the shore of the river, their bright clothing standing out in utter lurid clarity. Jyoti was shuddering, the words coming out of her mouth half expressed, fighting each other. She clutched at Nandini's arm, bowed her head, turned it from side to side in a tortuous movement, so that Ray could see her face, the rattling horror of it.

16.

She is in a second-class compartment, on a train. The night devours the space: there is black air rushing through the bars, submerging her; it is persistent, like the waves of an ocean seeking out high tide. She abandons herself to the cold volume of the breeze, drinks it in, closes her eyes, presses her cheek against the metal tubes that slice through the window area. When she opens them she can see a fire burning in the distance, some huts in the foreground, shapes and light that disappear into outlines, become memory within seconds, against huge plains of dark land and sky. The train is fast.

There is another woman in Ray's carriage. She is wrapped in a voluminous grey shawl that makes several passages around her body, falling in drapes over her salwar kameez. Her hair is cut short, leaving brash loose curls of dark brown. She is in her fifties, plump-faced, skin the colour of wheat in the sun. She wears a red stone in her nose, some gold studs carved as flowers at her ears. There is a sensuality about her, something modern . . . the sense that she has lived freely, without care for convention. She watches Ray with great curiosity, makes no show of hiding her interest.

The train begins to slow as it enters a station, the lights flickering in the ceiling near the fans. Noise is filtering in. Ray can see people resting, sleeping on the platform near their luggage. Young men run alongside the train, making their offerings through the window: paper cones of peanuts, deep-fried kachoris in cellophane, rice and dal packaged in banana leaves, masala crisps, bottled drinks, hot tea that smells of cardamom and malai. Ray shakes her head each time, simultaneously putting her hand up in a wave.

Suddenly, there are boys in their cabin, four of them, with shaved heads, another waiting at the doorway to the corridor. They are young, ranging from about six to ten in age, and they move quietly, confidently nocturnal, jumping onto the cushioned seats so that they are on all fours, crawling underneath the benches.

'*Abhe!*' says the woman, raising her hand and making a dismissive clicking sound. '*Abhe chal haat!*' Move on!

The boys are not affected by her reprimand; their eyes stay wide, filled with pools of light, watchful and precise. They are searching for something. Finally, one gets hold of Ray's empty bottle of mineral water, which is lying on its side underneath her feet, and they begin to leave the carriage. She stares at them, totally disorientated. One turns back and sits next to her, holding his hand out for money, his body curved, patient, waiting in position. His manner bewilders her; he is so small, feral but dignified, like the monkeys she remembers from the fort she visited with Nathan and Serena.

She is shaken, right at her core. She wants to howl out at the desolation of it. There is something about them as they spring out together, the expertise of their dusty, soundless feet and hands as two of them climb up the ladders to check the top bunks as an afterthought. They are all grey-shirted, grey-trousered, almost in uniform, their features stunning, prominent without the hair on their heads to frame them. She can't work it out, why they seem so haunted, yet self-possessed. They are methodical; they do not seem to fear anything or anyone.

She looks for money in her purse. The boy can't be more than seven years old. There is a white crust around the base of his nostrils, thin red striations mark the whites of his eyes, which are huge, gripping her, as he stares.

The woman tuts as Ray hands over twenty rupees.

'You shouldn't do that,' she says, in English, clicking her tongue and shaking her head. 'These kids are addicted to glue.'

The whistle blows. It provokes scampering and loud thuds as the boys crowd towards the exit. The train begins to move; a man starts to shout, barking commands, harsh and fluent. Ray can hear the sound of plastic bottles, more than one, banging or being crushed as the boys leave the train.

'That money will go straight to their ringleader,' says the woman. 'He is the one who has given them their clothes.'

She has striking olive eyes. They show concern. The skin around them is lined heavily now as she frowns.

'See, these kids live on the station,' she continues. 'They pick through the trash in the morning, use what they can find, refill water bottles, that kind of thing. But they all take this –' she lifts her hand in a fist to her nose and sniffs, to demonstrate '– this glue thing. Or you see them with rags; they dip them in this –' she rubs her fingertips together '– this thinner for ink. I don't know what they call it in English. They inhale that too.' She shakes her head. 'Very sad.'

Ray watches the woman's hand, which she shakes in a kind of parallel sorrow. It seems so genuine that she wants to reach over, hold the hand, stare into the woman's eyes, and say, 'Yes, lady, it is bitterly sad, my heart is brittle, cracking up with this sadness. I can't bear it.' She wants to ask, 'How do you bear it?'

'At least they don't get taken off to the sex trade, like the girls who are homeless,' continues the woman. 'You don't see those little girls living in the station community. And some of these guys work as porters, you know, lifting luggage and all when they are older, which is a decent enough job. They play together too, like normal kids – you see them with their bats and balls if you go through a station at dawn; they support each other, wash together, eat together. There is love there, of course, and they make a life somehow. But these drugs they use . . .'

She shakes her head again, lifting her legs up onto the bench, slotting her bare feet to the side. She pulls her shawl around her body like a blanket.

'This is the sad thing. When they get hooked on this glue . . . They think it is the only way to make life better or something, I don't know.' She shivers suddenly, as the wind begins to collapse into the carriage. The train accelerates, as does the sound of its machinery pushing through the night. 'It must be hard,' she says. 'Difficult not to do it.'

It is midnight now, and neither of them has shown any sign of bedding in. In fact, the woman is snacking, running a piece of chapatti around the top compartment of a steel tiffin to wipe up the remaining droplets of yoghurt. The TTE, the travelling ticket examiner, has been and gone. Ray has successfully bought a ticket from him for her sleeper, in spite of boarding without one. It is a relief after the risk of her entry – she had just got herself on the train to Delhi, found a compartment with a woman in it, and hoped for the best.

The woman twists the lid of her tiffin and slots the compartments back together. She regards Ray quite seriously before speaking.

'I have something to show you that may be of interest,' she says, dabbing her mouth with a handkerchief.

She stands and locks the door to the compartment, wobbling due to the movement of the train, holding onto the top bunk on her side, to steady herself. She unwinds the shawl and then lifts her whole kameez over her head. Underneath she is wearing a large, crossover, flesh-coloured brassiere and salwar trousers tied at the waist with rope, but her stomach area and much of her chest are covered by a lengthy cloth bandage that is also wound around her body. The material is about six inches wide and divided into packets that bulge with lumps and hidden shapes, some more than others.

'If you could avert your eyes for a second, please,' she says, smiling.

Ray nods, but keeps staring at the cloth contraption, without realizing it. The woman is bathed in the weak light coming from the bulbs behind the mesh of iron in the ceiling. Her body is fierce, mesmeric, without shame. She is in utter control of her life, thinks Ray. Who knows what she is about to do?

'Just for one moment,' says the woman. 'If you don't mind.'

'Sorry,' says Ray, blurting the word out and turning her face towards the window. She presses her face to the bars again, feeling the heat of her cheeks calmed by the chilly breeze once more.

The woman rustles and zips, makes some louder sounds of rearrangement.

'OK,' she says, after a few minutes. 'Thank you for your patience.'

The roll of material has been laid along the bench when Ray turns round; it is formed of a series of identical rectangular pouches.

'Now,' says the woman, who is fully dressed again, snug in her shawl. 'Tell me what you like and need. Do you prefer necklaces or rings, earrings or bangles? I have them all.'

She unzips a pouch and pulls out a gold chain. The metal is plaited as three strands; it is a deep, bright yellow.

'Twenty-two or twenty-four carat only in purity,' she says, handing it over to Ray. 'That is obvious, I know. You don't tend to get eighteen carat or below here, like you do in Europe. You probably know that by now. Anyway, go on, try it.'

Ray takes the chain. She does not try it on, but she does look at it, examines the tiny linking scales of each thick strand of precious metal in the plait.

In this way, they journey through the multifarious wares that emerge from the woman's stores. There are winking emeralds set in drop earrings with succulent white stones: cubic zirconia.

'I don't carry diamonds on me in transit,' says the woman. 'Too dangerous.'

There are heavy pendants in woven gold, shaped as teardrops, flowers, stars, elaborate geometrics: interlocking circles or triangles. There are rubies studding 'antique look' bangles, carved with serpents' tails that curl at the joint; fat wrist clutches imprinted with the outline of intertwined doves; delicate hammered-gold bracelets with heart and key charms. Rings are produced, anklets and toe clips.

Ray asks about the prices. She only has enough money to buy something small, she says.

'Don't worry,' says the woman. 'I won't cheat you. I work by weight. I will charge you very little for labour. Just choose what you like and we can talk money later. Don't worry about that right now.'

Ray settles on some studs, in the end, simple pressed-gold latticework forming two flowers, the central calyx painted over in red and white. She can sense the woman's disappointment – they are very small – but Ray knows that even these will be too expensive for her.

The woman does the calculations based on weight (the grammes are written as decimals on a tiny white slip that is attached to the pole at the back of the earrings), plus a discounted five-per-cent charge for labour. They come to the equivalent of two hundred and sixty-five pounds.

Ray thinks about it for a moment. She has enough cash in the programme kitty, which she is carrying with her in a separate bag. She will have to replenish it from her bank account when she returns to the UK. She feels a sudden vertigo, a pressure on her brain. It isn't the only thing she will have to sort out when she returns.

She looks at the two studs, delicate and appealing against the flesh of the woman's palm, then moves her gaze up from the lined, luxuriant mound underneath the woman's thumb to her face. She has to buy them. They have spent more than half an hour going through everything, with the increasing sense that a purchase is going to be made.

'You seem troubled,' says the woman, laughing. 'Don't worry. I am not going to cheat you! On the contrary, when you take these to any jeweller's they will remark on what a good deal you have got for yourself. In two years' time, these will be worth one and a half times the amount, I tell you. And so on.'

She smiles at Ray, her eyes beautifully complicated by greens and brown, bordered with fine lines.

'Gold worn next to the skin brings good luck,' she says. 'Again, it is obvious, I know. It always requires a measure of trust to buy gold. You have to be ready to lose something, and not mind that possibility – of an empty exchange, I mean – in order to be able to gain something. You have to get over the fear that you will be cheated. So you are cheated, so what? Never mind! That type of thing. That is the attitude it requires.'

She laughs again, her face the picture of merriment, lustrous and full. Ray watches her, envious of her abandon. It is as though the flesh of her face is also tinted with trace elements of gold; it glows with such conviction.

Ray wears the earrings immediately after handing over the money. She feels them in her ear lobes as she lies down to sleep, soon after. It soothes her greatly to rub the ridged metal with the tips of her fingers.

'You are married?' says the woman.

They have turned the lights out and are lying on sleepers opposite each other.

'No,' says Ray. The darkness is not heavy around them; grey shades reveal the woman's body in silhouette. She lies on her back, seemingly at ease, wearing a local razai quilt, a patterned silk coverlet stuffed with cotton wool. Ray shivers. She has only a chunni to cover her body – there had been no chance to pack her sleeping bag on leaving the prison.

'You are from the US? Or UK? Here on holiday?'

'UK,' says Ray. 'I came here to make a film . . . a television programme.'

'I see,' says the woman. 'Showing people the real India, eh!'

Ray is quiet. After a few moments there is a tacit acceptance that it is time to sleep. The woman turns onto her side.

Ray stares at the underside of the top bunk. She thinks about the moments before leaving Ashwer, the dry asphyxiation of the hut. Even standing in the same space as Serena had become unbearable.

'It's tricky,' Serena had said, when Ray returned from the riverbank after her attempt to speak to Nandini and Jyoti. 'But I think there's a good scene hidden in there.'

She did not look up at Ray. She was scrolling through the rushes on the laptop, her face determined, the nostrils flared with effort. She dominated the room: her muscled, boyish frame radiated power, conviction.

'I mean, obviously it's not ideal,' said Serena. 'You're in the shot at the key moment . . . You walk into vision, and there's no way of explaining who you are. But I definitely think there's a way round it if we get some exterior shots of their hut to use as cutaways for that moment –'

Ray laughed. It was a forced sound. She quivered as she made it.

'Ha! You are fucking joking,' she said. 'Ha!'

Serena looked up from the laptop. She stared, as if taking some time to realize that Ray was talking to her. Her skin was raw from the heat, her cheeks dry. The understanding spread through her expression like a rash.

'Why did you come? What did you think when you started on all this?' She was tight with distaste; her face was an apple from which the moisture has drained. 'This is a TV pro-gramme, not a bloody charity. What did you think we were all doing here? You think you're special? Why? You need to stop being so fucking holier than thou.'

Her voice escalated, so that she was almost shouting.

'There's some good stuff here and I'm going to make it into a PROPER fucking film. You can do what you like.'

Ray stood in front of her, seething. She was scalded with the image of Nandini's face; it would not leave her. Nandini glaring at her on the riverbank, the centre parting of her hair filled with a mirage: a glutinous streak of blood. It glis-tened in the sun, a wet, scarlet line, taking the place of sindhoor, the red powder usually worn by married women.

They were both silent, breathing heavily.

'Seriously,' said Serena. 'Just tell me. What did you think?

237

When you came up with the idea? What did you want? I just need to know that.'

She stood up, her eyebrows raised, entreating Ray for an answer.

'Please,' said Serena. 'Just tell me.'

They surveyed each other. Ray did not speak. She looked up from Serena's face to the matrix of holes in the stonework behind her head, the naked bulb suspended from the mesh of wires against the turquoise wall. She thought of her first day in the hut, the sweat encasing her body, the moment of nakedness when changing her clothes; how she had feared people looking in at her, through this circular and hexagonal latticework. What had she expected? She had wanted to live like them, be part of their community, empathize with their lives. It seemed absurd now. She looked at the stack of tapes on the steel cabinet in the corner of the room, labelled with contents and dates. A shiver passed through her, the awareness prickling over her body. They had both filmed these people. Ray's handwriting was on more than half of the tapes.

Serena had left the hut after it became clear that Ray was not going to answer her. She did not take anything with her, just walked out, leaving the laptop open on the table, the image paused, cursor hovering mid-screen. It was a shot of the interior of Jyoti and Daulath's hut, blurred by the movement of people in the frame, the barely discernible figure of the doctor in the foreground.

Breath enters and leaves her body: an indolent, parched labour of movement. She can hear it in her eardrums, this heavy trajectory of air. She cannot sleep and the sound marks out her time. It is meaningless. Each inhalation takes merely seconds, leaving her with the rest of the night ahead. Her eyes are closed, her throat arid, nose clogged with the dust.

Ray shifts on the cushion of the sleeper, pulls the chunni so that the scant material is tight over her body, trembles slightly beneath it. She remembers the shawl from the governor, the way the wool looked like it had soaked up the blood from a heavy wound. She had left it at the hut along with so many things, slipped out with her travel bag, walked quickly to the perimeter and climbed over the compound wall. She had managed to hail an auto within seconds, taken it to the railway station.

It was so different from her arrival. All her tiny anxieties then, the luxury of them as they had competed in her mind. Raju balancing the luggage on his head, the perspiration on his back slipping between his shoulder blades as he ricocheted across the dry field, too fast for her to keep up. The fear that he would drop the precious film kit.

She sits up, looks ahead at the caliginous space between the bars of the window, registering the absolute opacity of the darkness outside. It reminds her of the words of a female inmate: 'I cry every day when the sun is going down.' A formless woman, a shadow on the retina. She cannot remember who said these words. 'I don't know why but it wrings itself out of me like a wet cloth. I heave and I cry and then I am spent. Every day I do it. I noticed only over a long time that it was at the same hour every day.'

She leans over and feels around for the travel bag under her seat. The woman on the adjacent bunk is not snoring any more. Ray lifts the bag and pulls the zip slowly, so that it squeaks with a flatulent, tortuous sound. Inside, her passport sits on top of the multitude of tapes.

She picks a tape at random. It is one of her own. Her

handwriting is squashed, barely fitting on the label: KALLOO. TEENAGER. SON OF JITINDRA RATHORE.

'*What do you want?*' Ray had asked him, in an impromptu interview by the central peepal tree one evening. '*Is there anything you want that you don't have?*'

'*I want a tie,*' he had said. '*Can you get me a tie? People listen to you if you wear a tie.*'

She picks another tape. Jyoti Ramnath. At the sewing machine in her front yard.

And another, labelled by Serena: SAIRA CHOKHI IV. CHOPPING VEGETABLES.

'*Take me to your country,*' she had said to Serena as she chopped the mooli on the first day of filming. And then, after Serena's non-comprehension, '*I would have looked after you well.*'

She has the whole film in her bag. Every single tape. She could make an entirely different film: one that they deserve, the people of Ashwer.

The laptop in the hut has been taken care of, the video files deleted before her exit. Serena's film would not do these people justice. Ray looks out through the bars and on into the darkness. Justice suddenly seems like a very odd word to use in this situation. The village was the last place that needed her own or anybody else's ideas about justice. In fact, if she was going to be honest, they didn't need her at all. The film wasn't for them.

She looks down into her bag and pulls out DAULATH AND JYOTI RAMNATH. IV ON CHARPOY. Wedging her fingers between the bars at the window, she pushes the tape out onto the track. NANDINI GUPTA. ESTABLISHING IV is next, followed by another.

They fall in different ways. Some hit the side of the train on the way down, others soar into the air, careening like frisbees in a park. She imagines them crushed on the tracks, the oblivion.

The woman stirs.

'What are you doing?' she says. Her voice is not sleepy. It is crisp enough to suggest that she has been watching Ray for some time.

Ray does not answer. She continues to post the tapes through, one by one, then puts her face against the bars, tucking her hair behind her right ear so that the wind assails her exposed earlobe, scouring the new gold flower that sits in the piercing.

Acknowledgements

My gratitude to Vik Sharma for his love and acute, bounteous vision. My mother and father for the heartening shade of their support and belief. My brother Nishant for his insight, the largesse.

For unique, generous discourse around this novel I must thank Ian Breckon. I am indebted to my agents, Andrew Wylie and Tracy Bohan, for their conviction and sincerity, to my editor, Mary Mount, for the ambition and clarity she has shown regarding this book, to Clare Parkinson, Kendra Harpster, Chiki Sarkar and Vaishali Mathur.

My respect to Gerard Woodward and Tessa Hadley, who read the manuscript with such valuable honesty. Also, the tertulia writers, I salute you: Harry Man, Simon Johns, Ros Wynne-Jones. I am grateful to the Katherine Blundell Trust, whose help was much appreciated, the AHRC and the team at Bath Spa University, particularly Tracy Brain.

For important dialogue: Shloka Nath, Nirad Pragasam, Bucy McDonald, Krish Majumdar, Julia Miranda, Stephen Merchant, Adam Shatz, Yasmin Hai, Susanna Howard, Paul Berczeller, Joanna Perry. Also Rani Shankardass, Neelam Vishnoi, Arun Dugar and Negar Akhavi.

For solidarity and hope: Camille Thoman, Kamila, Aysha, Sam Harvey, Sonia F., Ben M., Avni, Hale, Pascale, Brij, Caroline, Sunanda, Mahender, Kavi, Bidi, Gabriella, Christel, Johanna and Bellos.

My thanks to Ama, whom I continue to admire deeply. And to my sweet, inspirational Papa, who was there when I finished, and blew me a kiss.